Night of the Hawk

D1606403

Also by Vonna Harper:

Surrender

Roped Heat

"Wild Ride" in *The Cowboy*

"Restraint" in *Bound to Ecstasy*

Night Fire

"Breeding Season" in *Only With a Cowboy*

"Night Scream" in *Sexy Beast V*

Going Down

Night of the Hawk

VONNA HARPER

APHRODISIA
KENSINGTON BOOKS
http://www.kensingtonbooks.com

APHRODISIA BOOKS are published by

Kensington Publishing Corp.
850 Third Avenue
New York, NY 10022

Copyright © 2009 by Vonna Harper

All rights reserved. No part of this book may be reproduced in any form or by any means without the prior written consent of the Publisher, excepting brief quotes used in reviews.

All Kensington Titles, Imprints, and Distributed Lines are available at special quantity discounts for bulk purchases for sales promotions, premiums, fund-raising, and educational or institutional use.

Special book excerpts or customized printings can also be created to fit specific needs. For details, write or phone the office of the Kensington special sales manager: Kensington Publishing Corp., 850 Third Avenue, New York, NY 10022, attn: Special Sales Department, Phone: 1-800-221-2647.

Aphrodisia and the A logo Reg. U.S. Pat & TM Off.

ISBN-13: 978-0-7582-2945-8
ISBN-10: 0-7582-2945-3

First Kensington Trade Paperback Printing: February 2009

10 9 8 7 6 5 4 3 2 1

Printed in the United States of America

Night of the Hawk

1

Captured in flight, the hawk commanded most of the photograph. Its wings were spread as if embracing its world, talons stretched, haunting yellow eyes seemingly trained not on the world below but at whoever had taken the picture. The rest of the picture was a blur of greens and browns, undoubtedly an image of the forest it lived in, but the hawk's image was so sharply defined Smokey could make out the individual tail feathers.

Stepping closer, Smokey continued her study of the 11-by-14-inch picture that had been placed at eye level on a wall of the art gallery. Except for the faint drum and flute notes from the Native American instrumental playing in the background, the gallery was silent. She could hear her heart beating, feel the pull and release in her lungs as she breathed.

What could be so incredible, mesmerizing, captivating, eerie? Eerie?

Yes, she acknowledged, there was something otherworldly about both the hawk and the way the photographer had frozen the predator in time and space. It wasn't that large a bird, certainly not as imposing as an eagle or osprey, and yet there was no doubt of its confidence and power. What would it be like to have such faith in one's physical ability, to be utterly at home in the wilderness?

"Pretty amazing, isn't it?"

Startled, Smokey turned around. Behind her stood the young woman who'd greeted her when she'd first come in the door. As they were the only two people in the building, she shouldn't have been surprised that the woman—whose name tag identified her as Halona—had joined her, but the hawk had captured her attention.

"*Amazing* is the right word, all right," Smokey acknowledged as she returned to her study of the photograph. Her fingers tingled, and she longed to be holding a paintbrush. "I wonder, do you know who took that shot? I'd love to paint the bird."

"That's one of Mato's creations. In fact, he's responsible for every wildlife and wilderness photograph in here."

"Mato?" The name seemed to settle on her tongue. "He's local?"

"As local as they get. I don't know how many generations his family goes back. Certainly long before white men arrived."

Halona was dark skinned with high cheekbones, most likely Native American herself. "No wonder he knew where to find this magnificent creature." Smokey indicated the hawk, who now seemed to be watching her. "But that doesn't account for the quality. What does he do, work for *National Geographic*?"

"Hardly, although I think he's good enough. He contracts some with BLM—Bureau of Land Management—in addition to managing his own timber acreage."

Although Smokey wanted to say something, for some reason she couldn't concentrate enough to put the words together. In her mind's eye she clearly saw Mato slipping silently through the forest, a shadow among shadows, camera at the ready, senses acutely tuned to his surroundings. He saw the forest not as a great unknown but as home, *his*. Maybe the creatures who lived in the forest sensed this about him and shared their wilderness knowledge with him.

A man like that would be physically hard, primal, alive, real. If he saw a woman he desired, there'd be no game playing, no dance of attraction, no slow getting to know her. Like the animals who shared the forest with him, he'd claim his mate, take her down, and fuck with her.

Struggling to ignore the heat chasing up the sides of her neck at the decidedly uncivilized thought, Smokey concentrated on swallowing. "What do you think?" she tried. "Any chance he'd sell me that picture? I notice it's not for sale."

"None of his work is, because he wants visitors to see and appreciate what exists around here."

Around here meant the Oregon coast, specifically the vast forest that extended to the seashore and that was in danger of swallowing the little town of Storm Bay, where she would be spending the next few days.

"I'll tell you what," Halona continued, "I can give you directions to where he lives. Hopefully your vehicle's made for off-road travel because the road into his place can get pretty hairy, depending on the weather."

"Mine's four-wheel drive," she supplied. Her gaze strayed to the one window and beyond it, the gray clouds and wind-whipped trees signaling an approaching storm. As though she didn't feel isolated enough. "He wouldn't be there this time of day, would he?"

"I doubt it. I don't know how pressed you are for time, but I'm sure of where he'll be tonight."

A small alarm went off in her mind, but she kept her expression neutral. "Oh?"

"The meeting." Halona made it sound as if nothing else mattered. "The whole town's going to be there. There're even re-

porters hanging around, although maybe they're still here because that man's been missing since a week ago."

Not breathing, Smokey waited to see if Halona would ask if
she was one of those reporters. Instead, Halona shrugged as
though dismissing the whole thing.

Lying could come back to haunt her, and damn it, she wanted
to be open and honest with this engaging young woman, but
she had a job to do, one that wouldn't be easy and maybe would
be impossible if she didn't keep certain things to herself, starting with her full name, Smokey Powers. Reconciling herself to
deception—although she already knew the answer—she asked
where the meeting was going to be held and when it would start.

"The school auditorium, seven o'clock. The school's the
only place large enough to hold everyone."

"It sounds important."

"It is to us. What's at stake is whether the land our people
have lived on in harmony for generations will remain unspoiled
or if greed . . . I'm sorry, I'm sure you don't care. You're on vacation. You are, aren't you?"

Shrugging, Smokey divided her attention between Halona
and the piercing yellow eyes that wouldn't leave her alone and
that seemed to have seen beneath her deception and omission.
"How will I know who Mato is?"

"He'll be speaking, I'm sure of that. And even if he
doesn't—" pressing her hand to her chest, Halona sighed,
"—he's the sexiest man alive. Early thirties and in his sexual
prime. Unless you're dead from the neck down, you'll know."

"Oh."

"Okay." Halona grinned. "Maybe not the sexiest man alive
but definitely the finest representative of his sex I've ever seen,
not that I've observed that many in this one-horse town."

She hadn't come here to lust after a man. She'd driven south
and west from Portland because what had happened in Storm

Bay—not just recently but over a long period of time—had gotten her reporter's juices flowing—more than just flow: she'd been both fascinated and horrified by what her digging had turned up. When she'd told her editor at *Northwest News* about the story she wanted to do, his reaction had been exactly what she'd wanted.

"Hot damn, that's unbelievable. Fucking unbelievable! Go for it! Your instincts have yet to fail you, which is what makes you so damn good at what you do. Just be careful. There's something seriously weird going on there."

Well, *careful* didn't get the story researched and written. Probing, listening, watching, questioning, and sometimes taking chances did. And because she was who and what she was, she was willing to take those chances.

"I don't know about trying to approach him," she said, pretending a hesitation she didn't feel or at least wasn't willing to admit. "If he's all involved in this meeting, he's not going to want to talk about selling a picture or giving me permission to paint it." Taking a deep breath, she looked at the photograph again. Yes, no denying it, the hawk was staring at her. How could she not paint something that intense? "But if I go, I'll at least get some idea of how my request will be received, don't you think?"

"When it comes to Mato, I don't make predictions. You know that saying about what you see is what you get? Well, there's a lot more to him than what shows on the surface, not that I have any objections to the physical package."

"He sounds interesting."

"Interesting?" Halona winked. "Let's talk after you've laid eyes on him. See if you still say the same thing. If I was ten years older—"

"Is he married?"

"No. Not sure why. Maybe because he's so restless."

Like me. "Mato? Is that his first or last name?"

"First. Full name, Mato Hawk."

Against her better judgment, she again glanced at the photograph. "Same as the bird."

"There's nothing woo-woo about the connection. At least I don't think so. After all, he's taken thousands of wildlife pictures; you just happen to have zeroed in on this one of the red tail."

Halona explained that the rich, russet red coloring of the predator's broad, rounded tail identified it as the largest hawk species, this one weighing close to four pounds. What fascinated Smokey was that the wingspan could be as much at fifty-six inches, and its cry resembled a hoarse, rasping scream—two pieces of information Mato had told Halona.

"I'm sure he believes I'm nothing more than a curious kid." Halona sighed. "Little does he know that when I'm asking him about his photographs, it's so I can stand close to him. What is it about some men? They give off this electrical charge, this heat. Shit. Mato's heat is enough to start the woods on fire."

You have to be exaggerating. "Sounds fas—ah, about the meeting. Will there be fireworks? I'm thinking it must be about something important if so many people are going to be there."

The youthful eyes sobered. "Yes," she said slowly. "That's something everyone here feels passionately about. It might not matter to outsiders, but there's no reason for greed and money to jeopardize this precious land, none at all! Whatever it takes to protect it, we will do, and no one is more committed than Mato."

Committed enough to kill?

Before she could come up with something to say, the gallery phone rang. Rolling her eyes, Halona headed toward the front counter. Alone again, Smokey deliberately avoided looking at the endlessly gliding hawk. Though the art gallery was small, the pieces on display were first class. Mato's photography was the star of the show, but among Storm Bay's residents were also a master wood-carver, an oil painter specializing in ocean scenes, two spectacular free-form metal pieces reflecting the overhead lighting, and excellent pottery in a subtle rainbow of colors.

This wasn't what she had expected when she'd decided to come to Storm Bay to dig into a number of mysterious deaths going back more than a hundred years. Small and isolated, the town had apparently come into existence as a fishing village, although Indians had lived here since before recorded history.

She'd learned that with fishing in decline and timber harvesting controlled by complex regulations, the town was losing its economic base. It had lost some population but not as much as she'd expected—proof maybe that something beyond economics kept people here. Whatever that something was, it obviously fed some residents' creativity.

What fed Mato Hawk's creativity, his photographer's eye, his patience, his ability to find and capture what lived among the massive, rain-fed trees? One picture was of a great bull elk nearly hidden among dense ferns, a thin ray of sunlight highlighting its antlers. Another, obviously taken with a powerful zoom lens, showed three young foxes—kits, she thought they were called—wrestling while their exasperated-looking mother watched. A third shot zeroed in on a white butterfly about to land on dead pine needles sprinkled with either rain or dew. A close look revealed a spider clinging to one of the pine needles.

A man of contrasts? One willing to stand up for what he believed in and speak passionately, one capable of becoming part of his surroundings so he could identify and share its life force?

A sexy man.

She didn't know about the sexy part. After all, Halona might not yet be twenty-one and could be filled with the romantic notions that came with youth and ignorance. Once she'd put a few more years behind her, Halona would learn there was more to a man than what lay between his legs. Broad shoulders and narrow hips might still get Smokey to occasionally, very occasionally, spread her legs, but it would take a hell of a lot more than that before she'd even consider hooking her life with some man.

And until or if she found the man with that nebulous something, she'd concentrate on a career she loved. And do a little painting on the side.

Glad she'd left her cell phone in her car, because she didn't want anyone guessing the real reason for her being here if a work-related call came in, she continued her aimless wandering. She'd come into the art studio because she had time to kill until the meeting started. Oh, she could have stayed in the cabin she'd rented, but doing nothing always made her a little crazy. She didn't want to go into the one bar in town at which she figured the other reporters would be killing time, because she didn't want anything they said to influence her—or for them to know she was here before absolutely necessary. All too soon word would get around that the driving force behind the *Northwest News* award-winning column "Just the Facts" was hot on a story.

Some fifteen minutes later, Smokey pushed open the gallery door and stepped into a swirling wind. Lowering her head against flying pine needles and other debris, she made her way to her SUV and closed herself in. When she picked up her cell phone, she saw she had two messages, both from her editor. True to his nature, he had kept his messages brief: "Call me."

"You were supposed to check in," he snapped when she got through to him.

"I did. Called this morning to let you know I was almost there, remember?"

"What have you been doing since then? This assignment you gave yourself's making me uneasy. If you're right about a series of deaths passing as accidents when they're really murders, that's serious shit. It's bad enough that no one's seen hide nor hair of what's-his-name in over a week—now you're there alone in enemy territory."

"His name was . . . is Flann Castetter, and so far I don't have proof that this is enemy territory." *Feels a bit like it.*

"The official search for Flann's been called off. Did you know that?"

"Yes," she said without revealing that a state-police source had told her yesterday. "There's no sign of foul play, nothing to justify expending more man hours looking for someone who may have decided he'd taken enough heat for a while and was getting out of Dodge."

"He brought the heat on himself," he pointed out unnecessarily. "Him and the rest of that NewDirections bunch. I can't say I blame the locals for not taking kindly to that resort proposal of theirs."

She muttered something to the effect that she agreed, but she didn't bother adding that Castetter's disappearance might have been the latest in a number of strange things to have happened around Storm Bay. She'd already laid out what she'd uncovered and didn't need him to keep warning her to be careful. Hell, she wouldn't be the successful newshound she was if she'd taken the safe route, if she didn't question and probe. Let other reporters chase after celebrities. She thrived on real stories, gut churning sagas about real people.

People like Mato Hawk?

Trying not to own up to the shiver down her back and a certain increase of heat on her breasts and in her crotch, she told her editor she'd call him after tonight's public hearing. Then she hung up before he could get another word in. However, instead of starting her vehicle and going to one of the five cabins that passed for a motel in Storm Bay, she stared out at the world around her. The art gallery was set back several hundred feet from coastal Highway 101 at the end of a narrow gravel road that snaked through the dense vegetation. Though there were signs that someone had recently cut growth back from the road, what remained made her think of a living green wall.

Isolation. In a word, isolation.

And that makes you vulnerable; never forget that.

Where had that thought come from, damn it! She thrived on her fast-paced life, the thrill of chasing down rumors and getting to the truth. Pouring the truth out through her fingers and onto the keyboard made her feel strong and in control, not vulnerable.

Mato Hawk.

Startled because she hadn't known the name had been about to burst free from her mind, she leaned forward and rubbed condensation off the windshield with her sleeve. As her surroundings cleared, she looked up but could barely make out the clouds for the trees. That's why she was feeling a bit spooked. Who wouldn't when it felt as if everything were closing in on her?

Mato Hawk.

"Knock it off!" she snapped. Just the same, the heat and energy between her legs increased. Damn it, how long had it been since she'd gotten laid? That's all this was, a little pent-up sexual frustration on a miserable day in the middle of nowhere while trying to run down some information about a man who might have met with foul play but more likely was off getting some R & R.

She'd see this Hawk character tonight, put him in his place somewhere far from her mind.

Either that or learn he had something to do with Flann Castetter's disappearance.

A whoosh of movement killed the thought. Gripping the steering wheel, she shivered.

No, she hadn't just seen a hawk!

Or had she?

2

Sweat.

Sweat from too many bodies crammed into too little space. From where she sat in the second row, the stench filled Smokey's senses and made her crave fresh air. Outside the storm threw its strength against the building's west wall, and rain hit the windows with a staccato sound so sharp she thought the old glass would shatter.

Still, this was the Oregon coast, an area accustomed to powerful winds and urgent rain. Most of those in the packed school auditorium seemed unconcerned that the old structure might not survive, and except for Smokey, the hearing officer and his assistant, and the other reporters, everyone in the room all appeared to be locals. Those locals would know if the little town was in danger of being pummeled out of existence.

The question was, would they tell her?

The middle-aged hearing officer, Mr. Jacobs, looking remote and authoritative in his navy-blue suit with the red power tie, hadn't moved in the past five minutes as he led the meeting, but she sensed that underneath he boiled.

Pondering the whys of his mood distracted her from trying to identify Mato Hawk among the audience. She also hadn't spotted Halona, but that wasn't surprising, because the young woman was only a little over a five feet tall and could have been sitting in the middle of the crowd.

Mr. Jacobs's assistant, a slight man with thinning hair who'd been standing near the hearing officer's desk, held up a watch. "That's your time, Clyde," he said, his eyes on the man who'd just spoken his peace among the nearly two hundred people hunched on folding metal chairs. "You want to leave your map with Mr. Jacobs?"

"Don't bother." Mr. Jacob's mouth barely moved. "The thing's not drawn to scale and doesn't show any topographic features. It's all but useless."

"The hell it is," Clyde sputtered from the audience. He jabbed a thick finger at what he'd sketched on a piece of typing paper. "That's my place. Right there not more 'n half a mile from the river. I'm affected. I don't want you forgettin' that. I'm affected."

"I'm aware of that." The hearing officer sounded both weary and angry. "You said so, at least three times. How many more are set to speak? It's getting late."

He was right. It would soon be ten P.M. Thanks to the insufficient lights, she could barely make out those in the back rows. Still, she wished Mr. Jacobs had kept the irritation and impatience out of his voice. After all, he was being paid to conduct this public meeting about reaction to a resort a group of investors known as NewDirections wanted to build along the Spruce River, an issue vitally important to these people. They'd trooped into the elementary school hours ago, voices hard with determination, eyes cold and distrusting of the officer from the Northwest Fisheries Council.

If NewDirections's vice president, Flann Castetter, had grown weary of butting his head against this collective opposition to his proposal, she couldn't blame him for taking off—unless some of what she'd dug up about the past was responsible for his disappearance.

Something Mato Hawk was part of?

If only she could stop thinking about painting the damnable hawk, stop aching to challenge her artistic skill by trying to bring the predator to life on her canvas.

"Just one more speaker," the balding assistant said. "Mato? You want to get yourself on up here?"

As a broad-shouldered, black-haired, dark-eyed man clad in work-worn jeans and an unironed flannel shirt emerged from the back of the room and took his place at the speaker's podium, her mind stumbled. *Male! One hundred and fifty percent male.*

Just like that, she was no longer in this stuffy building but somewhere deep in the forest, walking alone down what might be a deer trail, her nerves on alert, ears tuned for any sound, eyes constantly scanning. She was being watched; she knew it! By a man, a primal and possessive man.

Whether she walked or ran through the forest made no difference because when he was ready, he'd reveal himself to her. More than just reveal—he'd touch. Rub his body against hers, press his strength against hers, pull her into his space. And change her.

No, damn it! What are you thinking!

Most of those who'd preceded him had brought along notes to which they'd frequently referred. By their body language and the way their voices either turned shrill or fell away revealed that they obviously were unaccustomed to public speaking. Mato was as casually dressed as the others, his thick black hair long and unkempt and begging to have her fingers in them, his feet locked into sturdy boots that said he didn't earn his living sitting behind a desk.

The resemblance between him and the others ended there.

He was the first to fasten his unwavering gaze on the hearing officer, the first to use his own silence to quiet the room. The only to rattle her. She didn't feel anger in him so much as determination, but that might have been deceptive.

At least he was unaware of her existence.

So far.

"When my ancestors fished the Snake River," he began, "nearly twenty thousand sockeyes returned each year to spawn in Redfish Lake. Now there are only a handful. Once the Columbia River watershed was one of the richest salmon-producing areas in the world. Now those salmon are in danger of extinction." He took a deep breath that expanded his chest and sent her fingertips tingling from the need to touch him. "Governmental agencies study and research, argue and assess blame, while the clock ticks. A few more years, and there won't be a need for you people because there won't be any fish left to mismanage."

He paused, and she wondered if he was waiting for his words to settle in; it worked, at least on her. Heat pressed on her temples and crawled over her thighs. "That's what the NewDirections corporation will accomplish," he continued. "Tens of thousands of years of existence snuffed out because of man's greed."

To her shock, his gaze slid to her and held for a few seconds. There was a message, something, in the contact that turned her hot and cold at the same time. A warning maybe? A promise? A challenge? Just like that, her skin from the top of her head to her toes burned. *Oh, my god. Turned on with a look.*

Black hair, midnight eyes, body honed from physical labor, passion and power rolled together, hands . . . those incredibly sexy and dangerous hands.

"I'm a fact finder," Mr. Jacobs said, his voice even. "I didn't build the dams or canneries that put your salmon in jeopardy in the first place."

"Forget the past; we're trying to salvage the future." Mato

folded his arms across his chest and tilted his head to the side, the gesture putting his features into shadow except for eyes, which had the power to dig deep into her. "It doesn't matter whether we're talking about a dam that prevents salmon from spawning or logging near a river until the banks erode. Impact is impact. There's no such thing as a salmon being a little bit dead."

A number of people grunted agreement, but, against all reason, she believed he was speaking to her alone. More than speaking. Touching. Igniting. He didn't even have to look at her again for her to feel that way. "So far the Spruce has escaped the caging that's taken place along the Columbia and Snake only because the Spruce is smaller, wilder, less easily reached and contained. Anyone who believes that all it takes to protect something is to draw up regulations is an idiot."

A shaft of lightning outside the window closest to Mato painted his features blue-gold. He paused while thunder rumbled, and she pondered whether the environment were trying to swallow him. "Developers such as those who destroyed Lake Owyhee in eastern Oregon went through your organization and got your so-called stamp of approval. Either the council looked the other way, or you're incompetent. Only one thing works. Leaving everything the hell alone."

"Leave it alone? Then I'm assuming I can put you down as another vote against, Mr.—"

"Mato. Mato Hawk. You're damn right you can. I read NewDirections's proposal. Read every word of that piece of garbage. It gave lip service to EPA, DEQ, LCDC, even BLM, but what it all boils down to is that the land around the Spruce, and the river itself, is going to be impacted the way Owyhee was. I love that word, *impacted*. Why don't they come out and say it? Raped. Destroyed."

Unfolding his arms, Mato gripped the speaker's podium with fingers that looked capable of any physical task. His eyes were fierce and angry and more alive than any eyes she'd ever seen. She would die for eyes like that—fight and die. "My ancestors walked this land. They didn't own it, because that isn't the Indian way. For tens of thousands of years they lived in harmony with the environment; they understood its balance. Today people have gotten too far from the land. They don't know its song. The only way that song is going to continue is by keeping the Spruce free."

Mr. Jacobs grunted. "This isn't ten thousand years ago. That's what the Fisheries Council is for, to accommodate change."

"To accommodate greed." The flesh around Mato's knuckles bleached white in contrast to his dark flesh. He seemed too large for the packed room. Too *everything* for her senses, and yet she prayed the sensation wouldn't end. "There's nothing necessary about rich people building five-thousand-square-foot homes in the middle of a forest with a river in their backyard. This so-called planned community doesn't have to be. It *can't* be."

"Because you want to live the way your ancestors did." Sarcasm coated Mr. Jacobs's words. "Spare me. This is not about ideology or tradition, Mr. Hawk. This is about whether you want Storm Bay to continue to have close to thirty percent unemployment and a stagnant population because residents can't make a living fishing anymore. Wake up! Adaptation's the name of the game."

"Adaptation, yes. Destruction, no!"

"Enough! Damn it, I've got only one thing to say. If you and the rest of your people refuse to embrace and exploit change, you'll wind up as endangered as the sockeye."

Shocked, she dismissed Mato's eyes, the storm, the dark room, and the foul-smelling air and for a heartbeat hated the man who'd just spoken. He was a fact finder. His job was to conduct public hearings and report back to the rest of the Northwest Fisheries Council. Their decision to approve or reject NewDirections's development would be based on his objective findings and recommendations.

Instead, he was arguing.

"I'd rather be extinct than insensitive to what's been on this earth for generations." Mato let his arms drop to his side, but they remained rigid, like the rest of him ready for action. "Most of us in this room refuse to see the remaining salmon and the river they thrive in sacrificed to greed. We won't allow another Owyhee disaster. If you can't see what's being risked here—"

"That's enough!"

"No, it isn't. It won't *ever* be enough. There's nothing I won't do to protect the river that fed my ancestors and that deserves to be here for my grandchildren. Laws, regulations—" he tapped his chest, "—have nothing to do with what happens inside a man when he looks at wild water."

Powerful words. Words with the strength to tear at her soul—and to drop her to her knees at his feet?

"Laws and regulations are what keep us a step above animals, don't you get that?" Mr. Jacobs heaved himself to his feet. "You said you'd studied NewDirections's concept. If you really had, you'd see they've addressed all environmental considerations."

"The hell they have."

"The hell they haven't! This hearing is concluded, done and over. Wake up, people. Progress is the only thing that's going to keep you from rotting in this backwater town."

Hawk wasn't rotting. He was alive, maybe the most rawly alive man she had ever seen. Looking at him took her back to youthful emotions when not a moment passed that she didn't think about the differences between the sexes. Before life had taught her its lessons, she'd dreamed of falling hopelessly in love with a perfect male body and a quick, inquisitive mind. They'd never argue, make nightly passionate love, and ride into the sunset together.

Mostly they'd have sex because she couldn't get enough of that perfect body, and he was tireless in bed—or wherever they fucked.

3

In Smokey's mind, rain was a step up from mist, a dripping, quieting condition leading to long evenings with a good book or a lingering fuck—not that she'd had the latter opportunity in too long. In contrast, this was a deluge, an angry sky demonstrating how much power it contained. Maybe, she pondered, the storm gods were angry. If so, she knew at whom the anger was aimed: the closed-minded hearing officer.

Instead of making a run for her vehicle and risk falling on her ass in the mud, she paused under the pitiful metal overhang outside the front door. The pounding drops made so much noise she had to strain to hear the nearby reporters and couldn't begin to pick up what the hunkered-over men and women who stood in tight, wet groups on the ground three steps below were saying.

Cursing the rain not for what it was but because she'd lost sight of Hawk—why had she stopped thinking of him by his first name?—she searched in vain for him. Something seriously strange had happened during the meeting. Bottom line: for a few seconds there'd been only the two of them. At least in her mind.

His body had spoken to hers. More than spoken—it had called out, demanded. The aftermath had left her weak and hungry in a way that both frightened and strengthened the woman in her. After a hibernation of months, her sexuality had awakened. In spades.

But why was Hawk the trigger? Yes, he epitomized everything rugged about the male sex that had always appealed to her, but she didn't know a thing about what went on inside the man's head. For all she knew, he was gay or over-his-head in love.

Please not that.

"Smokey? Smokey Powers, right?" one of the reporters called out, his voice tearing her from her thoughts. "I recognize you from the picture in your column. What are you doing in this hellhole? You don't cover this kind of news."

"Maybe I'm taking a busman's holiday," she countered. "On a fishing trip but not knowing enough to stay away from the only piece of news in this town."

"The hell you are," the twentysomething reporter said, his gaze trailing from her face down her body but not touching her as Hawk's look had. "No one would willingly take a vacation here, especially this time of year. What are you sniffing around? Hell, I bet I know. That developer guy who up and poofed. What do you think happened to him?"

"Give it up, Brad. She's not going to tell you." The reporter who'd spoken this appeared to be much older than the first, though with his jacket collar up around his neck and a rain hat pulled low, it was hard to be sure. "But I'm guessing Brad's right. You're looking to see if there's a story behind what's-his-name's disappearance. From what we've seen and heard tonight, I'm thinking the man's met with an '*accident*' at the hands of these people. It's no secret they aren't crazy about what he stands—or maybe I should say stood for."

"The police aren't sure what's happened to him," she said in what she hoped was a casual tone. "There are strong indications Castetter was under a lot of pressure from the rest of the NewDirections partners. He might have decided 'To hell with the whole thing.' After what I just saw, I don't blame him. Maybe he concluded everyone in town hated him, said screw that, and rode off into the sunset."

"With that kind of money at stake?" the older reporter countered. "Not likely. Men like this Castetter character thrive on a challenge. Besides, from what we saw tonight, it's obvious the hearing officer is on NewDirections's side."

Stifling the urge to agree with him, she shrugged. "If it's been raining like this very long, I vote for Castetter getting fed up with this whole part of the coast. How many inches a year does it get around here?"

"He isn't the only one who's had it with this joint," Brad grumbled. "I don't care what time it is, I'm heading inland. What about you?" He directed his question at her.

Shrugging again, she explained that she'd rented a place to stay. If anyone asked how long she intended to remain in town, she'd change the subject. Fortunately her fellow newshounds didn't show any inclination to stand around talking. Trying to work up the courage to step out into the rain, she looked down.

As she did, the largest group shuffled, changed configuration. As they put their backs to the wind, one form stood out. Mato Hawk. Though most had on yellow slickers, he stood bareheaded and straight-backed as if oblivious to the wind. Suddenly he looked her way, a long, strong stare.

Your flesh scraping mine. Peeling off the layers.

Everything about Hawk held her attention. She hadn't realized the solidity of his chest before because the flannel shirt, when dry, had hidden more than it revealed. The sodden fabric was now plastered to him and highlighted too much muscle. A man like that wouldn't be satisfied with an official document detailing the council's decision that spelled out procedures for legal appeal. No. He embraced action. The physical.

Deep in the wilderness. No longer walking but standing with her naked legs spread wide and a trembling hand pressed to her chest. She'd become a trapped animal, a doe in heat waiting for a rutting buck to approach. Although she quivered and fear gnawed at her, she wanted this. Wanted the magnificent buck to rear onto her back and spear her. They'd mate under the canopy of trees, and her belly would swell with his seed. She might never see him again, but she'd never forget.

"That one gives me the creeps," Brad muttered, indicating Mato. "Reminds me of a junkyard dog. I wouldn't trust him as far as I could throw him."

Watching Mato as an elderly man joined him and they began speaking, she acknowledged that the reporter had pointed out an important point. Despite her momentary lapse of sanity, she didn't see Mato as a junkyard dog or even as a buck any longer, but more like a cougar or wolf. She'd be a fool to let down her defenses around that predator. He had to know his impact on women and had undoubtedly long used his raw sensuality to get what he wanted. If she had the sense she was born with, she'd drive out of his world without saying a single word to him.

But she couldn't because even now the memory of the hawk photograph haunted her. She *had* to have it. Had to paint it and bring it to life.

And what about the man who'd taken the picture? Did she have to have him as well?

Hell, yes. Nipples hard, back arched, nails clawing at his flesh as he drove her to the ground and made her scream.

"What are you staring at?" Brad asked. "Don't tell me he turns you on."

"Why don't you get your head out of the gutter," she snapped. She might have said more but something strange happened. Almost as one, those standing in the rain started forming a tight circle, with Mato Hawk and the older man in the middle. If Mato didn't want the attention, he gave no indication. Instead he seemed to embrace the others, to become one with them.

In contrast, she had never felt more alone.

More wanting.

Hearing a drumbeat, she stared until she spotted another man kneeling in the mud, a drum resting on his knees. This man's arms lifted and fell, lifted and fell as he pounded out a slow rhythm on what no doubt was a homemade instrument. The assembled townspeople were moving in time with the sound, as was she. Although the reporters she'd been talking to now spoke in urgent, staccato tones, she didn't try to concentrate on them. Even when one aimed his digital camera at the crowd and began taking flash pictures, her gaze and thoughts and emotions went no further than the group—or, rather, Mato Hawk.

Hawk?

Yes, he was that.

And more.

From the way he'd lowered his head, she had no doubt the wind was trying to drive rain shards into his face. Then the wind whirled in another direction, slamming into his shoulder and forcing him to turn with it. If she had been standing beside him, they'd fight the wind together, and once they'd won, they'd what?

Celebrate their victory.

Sink to the ground and fuck in the mud.

"Laxgebu," the older man said. "Hear me, Wolf People. The

sacred river of our ancestors is threatened. We place its protection in your hands."

Shoulders squared, Mato's boots beat against the sodden ground. Even from where she stood, she could sense his energy and commitment. He'd entered a zone, a space, a something she couldn't comprehend and yet ached to join him in.

"Look down on us," the older man—who must have been Mato's father, from what she could ascertain—continued. "Hear our prayer. This is your river, Laxgebu. Home to the sacred salmon. A sign—send us a sign. We entrust the river to you for safekeeping, as our ancestors did in ancient times. We pray for guidance. What, oh, Laxgebu, do you want from us?"

Action.

Alarmed, she looked around to see who had spoken, but the reporters all had their mouths closed, their attention riveted on what she believed should be a private ceremony. And yet the word or emotion or whatever it was had come from somewhere out in the atmosphere. She was trying to convince herself she hadn't heard what she had when the older man lifted his face and arms to the heavens. His eyes were closed, his aged body swaying. Mato touched a steadying hand to the older one's back.

"For generations you kept the river pure for us, your children," the speaker continued in a voice loud enough to battle the storm. "For as long as Salmon Spirit has returned to the water, it has been Salmon's home. Laxgebu, do not let that end! Look into our hearts and know we need the river as much as Salmon does."

"Hearts, hearts, hearts," the assembled townspeople chanted.

The older man nodded. "Without the river, our souls will die. Keep it as it has always been so our children and children's children will not forget those who came before them. So the sacred Salmon will live for all time."

She was drifting, no longer flesh and blood and chilled skin.

Instead of concerning herself with the logistics of getting behind the wheel and going to the small but cozy and dry cabin, she concentrated heart and soul on the words being said. And on Mato, who was intently watching the older man. A few moments ago his sharp gaze had unnerved her, but now it was all she could do not to beg him to acknowledge her again. Instead he remained locked in a time and space and emotion foreign to her. A new kind of hunger slipped through her, a craving for not just understanding but acceptance.

If she came to comprehend this ritual, this prayer, would he allow her closer to him?

Would he peel off both their clothes and kneel before her in the cold mud while they kissed and touched and she cried?

While she cupped her hands under her breasts and lifted them, silently begging him to take them into his mouth?

She was losing it—not just *it* but chunks of herself she'd always taken for granted. And unless she grabbed hold of herself again, she'd lose definition and distinction. She'd come to exist only for him.

And if he didn't want the gift of her body and maybe her soul as well . . . ?

Out in the rain, the wind again slammed into Mato, his father, and the rest of those he considered his family. The world around him was dark and wet, the school porch light barely penetrating the dense night. Beside the reporters stood the young woman who'd captured his attention back when he should have been focused entirely on what he needed to say to the hearing officer. Now her large eyes were wide, her mouth slack, her slender body so tense he wondered if it might shatter.

What are you thinking? he asked her in his mind. *Do you believe we're crazy, or does some part of you understand that certain connections between humans and their physical world defy logic? Do you care?*

I don't know what I'm feeling. He sensed her respond.

Something I never have before, not just about what's happening, but you—maybe you most of all.

I feel the same way about you—and I don't want to. A warning: don't trust me. There's more to me than you can possibly comprehend.

I know.

Her response sent loneliness and hunger arcing through him. He wanted her. Just like that, he burned with the need to throw her to the ground and mount her. It wouldn't matter whether she responded with a fierce embrace, a willing body, and a soft inner core or fought him—he'd bury himself so deep inside her neither of them would ever forget their union.

What was he thinking? He was a man, not an animal. He'd never forced a woman to have sex, not simply because women had always given themselves to him, but because he respected both women and himself too much.

And yet—and yet—maybe it was the storm and the duty ahead of him and his fears for this precious land, but he wanted to become something simple. Something primitive. Powerful.

And if she responded to the hard animal lurking beneath his outer shell . . . ?

Sensing his mother's presence, Mato held out his hand so she could give him the sacred trumpet that was his right and responsibility, but he continued to lock eyes with the woman. Thanks to the distraction his mother had afforded him, he was able to distance himself a little from the unspoken communication between himself and the stranger—and from thoughts he'd never shared with another human being. Yes, she was young and attractive and, if he could believe the look in her eyes, intelligent, but why, tonight, was she distracting him?

Because she senses something about me? Or because she represents danger?

Danger, he could handle. As for the possibility that she might somehow fathom that there was more to him and his world than outsiders would ever comprehend . . . Learning the answer to that could be vital to his survival. But the question wouldn't be addressed tonight.

Run, he warned her. *Otherwise I'll change you.*

Maybe we'll change each other, she responded.

Holding the mouthpiece against his lips and closing his eyes, Mato blew, the trumpet pointed toward the evergreens beyond the parking lot. He held the note for as long as his lungs could stand, finding peace in the thought that the sound he'd created was drifting out into the night.

His breath spent, he pulled in more air and blew again. The third time, the faint cry of a wolf drifted in. Although he thanked the earth gods for the gift, when he opened his eyes and sought her out, he saw that the young woman was silently begging him to explain what she'd just heard.

You cannot understand, he told her. *Only those who are of the Wolf Clan have that right, that responsibility. Leave. While you can.*

"Do not think of anything except ritual," his father whispered. "That and continuing the promise our fathers' fathers' fathers made to protect this land."

"I know what I must do," Mato responded. *What I will do to safeguard what is precious.*

Rain continued to drench him, but although he was shivering, Mato managed to block off his discomfort and focus on the rest of the Wolf Clan members as their feet beat out a rhythm as old as time. After the frustration of trying to get through to the hearing officer, he took comfort in their shared experience. As the chief's son, carrying the burden of responsibility for the land was falling to him, and he now understood why his father had told him the burden would be a heavy one. Sometimes duty came before his personal need for such essentials as warmth. And love.

When the wolf spirit again answered the trumpet, he allowed

his own spirit to drift into the trees. He couldn't see Wolf; that gift was seldom given. But Wolf had sent one of his fellow creatures to embrace him. Smiling, he acknowledged his personal spirit's presence in a nearby pine tree, but instead of taking wing and hovering over him as he often did, the hawk's beak opened, and his lonely warning cry filled the air.

Danger. Danger from the woman.

4

Mato was heading for the parking lot. Seeing him alone instead of surrounded by others should have made it easy for Smokey to approach him, but for too long she stared at that broad back. *It's not the right time,* she tried to convince herself. *The last thing he wants to talk about tonight is letting some strange broad make use of his photography.*

But if she didn't take advantage of the moment, would later be any easier? Besides, the thought of going to wherever he lived dried her throat. And then there was the matter of getting through the night with him on her mind, and more. No matter how many toys she'd brought with her, they wouldn't be enough. Hoping no one was paying any attention to her, she plodded through the mud after him. One thing about being drenched was she no longer had to worry about getting wet.

He'd opened the driver's door to a well-used four-wheel-drive pickup when she caught up to him. Working moisture into her mouth, she noted he hadn't locked his vehicle. Proof he trusted everyone?

What did that feel like?

"Ah, Mr. Hawk, please, do you have a moment?" If her hands weren't buried in her coat pockets, she might have touched him, just a light brushing of her fingers designed to get the feel of him. Nothing too intimate. Too dangerous.

He turned, graceful, slow, and measured, and she wondered if he was digging into his memory to see if he knew her voice. Instead of responding, he looked down at her with the rain running off his hair and his jeans plastered to his legs.

Swallow! Swallow. Get it out. Stumbling through the words, she managed to blither that she'd seen some of his photography today. "You've captured some incredible images. I do a little painting, nothing that's going to make me rich and famous, but I'd love to use some of your subjects on a few oils."

More of his silence. Now that people were turning on their headlights, she found herself staring up into the most arresting eyes she'd ever seen. Beyond black, they had a depthless quality, as if he could see beneath the surface to her core. A core that fairly screamed out its sexual strength.

"I'll pay you," she blurted, though she hadn't given remuneration a thought before. "I don't want to deprive the museum of any of your work, but maybe you have duplicates."

"What are you doing here tonight?"

Oh, shit, face-to-face his voice scraped her nerve endings. That accomplished, it dug deeper, probed through the layers. Forcing her brain cells to unscramble, she voiced her lie about being on vacation. He didn't nod or shake his head, but she had the feeling he'd seen through her deception.

"I've sold some of my work," she pressed on. "In a gallery near where I live. If I manage to do justice to your shots, I should be able to get double what I have up to now. We could work out an arrangement whereby I give you a percentage. Maybe you'd like me to donate to the art gallery."

"I asked you a question. What are you doing here tonight?"

He hadn't moved, not so much as a muscle twitch. It was a

good thing because if he'd done something as unnerving as lean toward her, she might splatter like a raindrop hitting the ground. Damn, but he was hot! Hot in a primal way she had no defense against and quite frankly didn't want to have. The cold night hadn't stolen so much as a degree of heat from him. It would take much more than rain to suck the life force out of him, a force that crawled over her skin and made inroads she prayed to hell he was unaware of.

"I learned you might be here," she finally thought to say. "I, well, I had no idea how you'd respond to my request, so I thought I should observe you first."

"And despite what you saw, you came looking for me?"

Funny, even with all those vehicles pulling out, she had no trouble hearing him. "It did give me pause," she admitted. "I mean, you're pretty intense."

"I have to be."

Did he want her to ask why or tell him she understood where he was coming from? Maybe he was burned out on the subject for tonight and only wanted to go home. But although her own simple but dry cabin called to her, a much stronger draw kept her in place.

Ah, shit, turned on. Lip-floating turned on.

Think, damn you! Think. "Look, why don't you sleep on what I said. If you'd give me your phone number, I could call tomorrow and—"

Up close she was smaller than he thought she'd be, not fragile but far from rugged. He didn't know her name or where she was from and whether she was alone, but right now none of those things mattered. The stranger was female, pure female. Giving off vibes as old as time and as new as this moment. The hot energy radiating from her might be something she had no control over, instinctive messages escaping from a primitive element she'd either spent years trying to tamp down or wasn't aware of.

He was aware, damn it, more than aware. Otherwise he wouldn't have bothered talking to her, an outsider.

In some respect he saw her as nothing more than a bitch in heat, a female giving off the ageless message that she was ready to mate. If they were both animals, the mating would have already begun, instinct-ruled strangers brought together by lust and nature. As soon as he'd deposited his seed in her, the union would end. He'd never know whether he'd impregnated her, and she wouldn't be able to recall which of her kind had fathered her offspring, wouldn't care.

Not an animal, damn it! Not now.

"Yes," he said.

"Yes, what?"

"You can do what you want with the photographs."

Her mouth started to open. To his relief and disappointment, she closed it before he insanely tried to cover those soft lips with his. No kissing! Nothing that spoke of instinctual intimacy. "Thank you," she muttered. "Ah, I didn't think it would be this easy. I don't know what I'm supposed to do next."

"Ask for my phone number again," he told her even as something warned him to walk the hell away from her. He kept his hands rammed in his pockets because he knew what would happen if he touched her.

At least what he wanted to happen.

He gave his number to her without waiting for the question, and although she didn't write it down, he had no doubt she'd remember. Before he could decide what, if anything, he should say or do next, a nearby horn honked. His uncle, barely visible through the rain-washed windshield, gave him a half-wave, half-warning gesture. "Call me tomorrow," Mato said to the woman. "We'll arrange to get together."

"Together?"

"So I can give you some prints. That's what you want, isn't it?"

"Yes." Maybe he was wrong, but he was nearly certain she was squeezing her thighs together. "The photographs."

Long seconds after her last word, she turned and walked away. She appeared unaware of her probably ruined shoes and wasn't trying to pull her coat against her neck, maybe because her mind was still on him.

Tomorrow. The thought took him far from what had dominated him for weeks and had brought him out into the storm. Tomorrow he'd decide whether to invite her out to his place or tell her he'd meet her someplace in town, someplace he wouldn't be tempted to rip off her clothes.

Dangerous! She's dangerous!

"Are you going to give her an interview?"

Pulled to the here and now by the unfamiliar voice, he spotted one of the reporters standing under an umbrella a few feet away. Like Mato, *she* hadn't had an umbrella. Maybe, like him, *she* needed to be as close to nature as possible. "Interview?"

"Don't dodge my question, Hawk," the reporter said. "It'll be easy enough to find out whether you're giving her an exclusive. Damn unfair, that's what it is. If I had breasts and a pussy, you'd talk to me, wouldn't you, 'specially if I looked like she does."

Rain pounding on the umbrella, to say nothing of the vehicle sounds, prevented him from being positive he'd heard everything the reporter had said, but he got enough. "She's a reporter?"

"She sure as hell isn't a hooker, which is a pity because she could make more money on her back than writing those award-winning investigative pieces of hers."

The reporter's attitude was going to earn him a fat lip if he didn't watch it. But, then, was he really angry at the man? Shouldn't his anger be directed at the woman who'd conned or nearly conned him? Telling himself not to give too much away, he looked around for her. Yeah, there she was, still walking in that sinuous way of hers, weaving around the largest puddles, her body small and controlled, ripe. Ready?

"What's her name?" he asked.

"You don't know? Haven't you seen her picture with her columns in *Northwest News?* Damn, you people are even more isolated than I thought."

Dismissing the put-down, he stared at the reporter until the man's jaws clenched. "Smokey Powers. And much as I hate having to admit it, she deserves all the awards she's gotten, and, yeah, she puts the word *investigative* into *reporter.* Word of warning: weigh every word before speaking 'cause nothing gets past her."

A chill that had nothing to do with the weather ran through Mato to kill his half erection. Well accustomed to sidestepping reporters' questions, he didn't believe he had anything to fear from those who were interested only in the current story about the proposed extensive development and local objection to it. They were all privy to the same hearings' records and thus would essentially write the same articles, articles the majority of people didn't care about.

But if someone—if she—dug deeper or into the past, everything he and those he cared about and stood for was in jeopardy.

Bottom line, he had to make sure that didn't happen.

Whatever it took.

Condensation kept Smokey from seeing out, not that it mattered. The cabin she was staying in was down a short, tree-surrounded path from the five-unit motel, which meant her view was limited to the dense vegetation the front porch light illuminated. She'd had to leave her car in the motel parking lot, but fortunately the woman she'd rented from had turned on the porch light, which had saved her from having to stumble around in the dark.

Now that she was inside and had turned up the heat, she could have extinguished the light, but then she'd feel as if she were the only human being in this part of the woods. Maybe she should have opted for one of the motel rooms, but the cabin had come with a kitchen and small living room, space to turn around in.

The TV was on—not that it had gotten between her and her thoughts. Maybe if it was capable of picking up more than five channels . . .

No, she admitted as she shucked out of the last of her soaked clothes and reached for her terry robe, TV wouldn't stop her from thinking about Mato Hawk. She should have been prepared for his impact, darnit! After what the young woman at the art gallery had said, she should have had her defenses in place.

Only, what defenses guarded against that kind of raw male energy?

Shaking her head in resignation, she slumped into the recliner and slipped her hand between her legs. Sooner or later she'd be going into the bedroom for her toy collection, but right now she wanted to keep things in as low a gear as possible so she could think.

Tomorrow. She'd see him tomorrow. They'd talk about photography and painting and the town he called home while sparks danced and her skin ignited. Every word he spoke would take on added meaning, every eye contact would have multiple layers, every touch—

Wet. Already wet. Labia loose and easy. Nipples hard.

Closing her eyes, she spread her legs and slipped a finger into what had been designed to house a man's cock.

It was entirely possible he took her for some damn bimbo without the sense to stay on the highway. He'd look at her in daylight, take his measure of her, put one and one together, and figure she was trying to hit on him.

She could let him believe that, she could! Send out messages that didn't need words. Let nature take its course. Get him to scratch her itches and do the same to his. Give him a home for his cock and not let him back out until he'd made her scream.

And once her muscles had been drained, she'd tell him why she'd come to Storm Bay.

Groaning, she pulled her finger out of herself. Certain reporters—she called them sleazeballs—thought nothing of trying whatever dirty tricks it took to get the story, but she never had. Granted, she sometimes had to work long and hard at getting reliable material from a source, but the upside was that once she'd forged a relationship, she could go back to that source again and again and know she was being told the truth.

Truth. That's what she needed to think about, not the smell of herself on her finger and her finger now going into her mouth. Somehow, hopefully through her honest admiration of Mato's skill with a camera, she could begin to break through Mato's barriers. They'd go from a discussion of how to keep a diving raptor in the viewfinder to a *casual* comment about why such a small community had had so many unusual deaths over the years. Maybe—

A muffled knock on the door brought her upright. Pulling her robe tight around her, she got to her feet but stopped before taking a step. Only one person knew she was here, and if the motel manager wanted to talk to her, she would have used the phone, right?

"Yes?" she said, making her voice sound as authoritive as possible. "Who is it?"

5

Mato Hawk. He's here, standing just outside.

Torn between wishing she was anywhere but here tonight and shaking at the thought of sharing this space with her, Smokey turned the knob. As she did, a simple fact registered: she hadn't locked the door, which meant he could have walked right in.

There he was, wearing a rain-painted jacket, his hair plastered to his head, droplets clinging to his too-long-for-a-man lashes.

"I didn't expect..." She indicated her robe. "I thought everyone would be home tonight."

"I'm not everyone."

No, you're not. You're the most bone-rattling man I've ever seen.

"Are you going to invite me in?" he asked.

Before she could put her mind to what her response should be, he stepped past her. Now that she was dry, she felt his humidity on her neck and the arm closest to him. Waves of heat and cold radiated from him, making her wonder if he was capable of countering weather's extremes. Just the same, she wanted him in here. Close to her.

"Do you want . . . The heat register's over there." She pointed. "Maybe you need to stand near it."

"No."

His arms were at his sides, fingers still, sending out the message that he was at peace with his body. In contrast, energy hummed through her.

He'd have to be dead not to feel it. To not know she was naked under the robe.

"Aren't you going to ask what I'm doing here?"

Think like a reporter. Control the interview. Somehow. "I was waiting for you to explain." Damn his wet jeans. The way they clung to his form and cradled—oh, shit, an erection! "But you're right, I do want to ask a question." She stood as tall as she could in her slippers. "How did you know where I was? If you followed—"

A lift of a dark eyebrow silenced her, that and the line of his jaw and width of his shoulders, and that bulge.

"There's only one motel in Storm Bay. I called Sandra. She told me you were staying in the cabin."

"Sandra?"

"This is her business. It supports her and her daughter, barely."

So that was the too-slim young woman's name. The way he said it made her wonder about the relationship between the two. Was it possible—no, surely he would have said "my daughter" if the girl had been his. And, she wanted to believe, he'd support his child no matter what his relationship with the mother.

A mental shake brought her back to the most unnerving man in recent memory, if not ever. "Why didn't you call me, then?" she asked, pleased because it was a reporter's question. "Whatever you had to say—"

His hand was on her shoulder almost before she knew it was going to happen. Living weight pressed against skin and bone, rooting her in place. And more, damn it, a hell of a lot more.

What came after combustion, after flames and fire?

Her mouth went slack; her eyes wanted to close. Longing for the feel of his fingers on her throat and from there to her breasts, she surrendered to the weakness climbing over her. He'd turned her female, nothing but female, a simple touch shaving off layers.

"You deliberately didn't tell me who you are." His low voice spread out to coat her, the deep tones saying everything that needed to be said about the male animal in him. "But someone else did."

"Oh."

"A reporter." He leaned back a bit as if trying to get away from what he'd just said, but his hand remained on her. Kept the connection going. Kept the fire flamed.

"You sound—you're making it sound as though my career's something I should be ashamed of."

"Am I?"

Oh, god, he was leaning close again, his breath on her hair and upturned face. She'd turned on only that one lamp, the bulb hardly up to the task of erasing the night. Maybe that's why he seemed to dominate the room.

But maybe it would feel that way to her no matter what the lighting.

Think! Just think! "I saw and heard you tonight, you and the other residents. I had a pretty good idea what your reaction would be if I revealed my profession; you'd tell me to take a hike instead of granting me access—"

"You came here for the same reason the others did, to report on our opposition to NewDirections and more than hint at our reasons for wanting Flann Castetter dead. To try to convict us because it makes for sensational press."

Anger, so much anger.

Or was that what *she* was feeling? Was it possible that his emotions were more complex, more in tune with hers?

Dangerous.

Exciting.

"Do you read my column?" she asked. Much as she wanted to clutch her robe, she forced herself to keep her hands at her sides. One thing she'd learned on the job was never to give away emotion. "If you do, you'd know I don't play that game. I'm about facts, not insinuation and sensationalism."

"No, I don't read your column, but I called some people who do, and I talked to your competition, not that the jokers who came here are capable of that."

She waited for the punch line. Instead she got his other hand on her previously untouched shoulder. *Locked in place,* his grip said. *Right where I want you.*

Right where I want to be, she came dangerously close to telling him.

"What did you learn?" she asked because the silence was killing her.

"That you don't write about backwater communities—not unless there are layers to the story other reporters don't pick up on."

He knows. Or at least he's guessed. "Tell your source I take that as a compliment."

Pressure on her shoulders, dangerously close to pain. "Tell me about the layers, Smokey. What really brought you here?"

"So that's why you hunted me down." The moment she said the word *hunted,* she wished she could take it back. "To find out what skeletons I'm going to try to dig up."

She'd already surmised that he wasn't a man for evasion or lies, so she expected him to agree with her. Instead he drew her closer, so damnable close that a single step would bring her in contact with his erection. She wouldn't, absolutely wouldn't!

"Let me go."

"It isn't that easy." When he went out of focus, she knew he was zeroing in on her, his mouth challenging hers, insanity speaking to insanity.

She wanted—hell, but she wanted!

Only she hadn't lost her mind—yet.

Teeth clenched against a whimper of need, she slid her hand into the space between their mouths and pressed her fingers against his lips. For long seconds they stayed like that, touching, breathing in each other's essence, sharing heat.

Then he flicked his tongue over her fingers, and she knew he'd had no intention of kissing her.

"You taste of sex," he said. "A woman who's been taking care of her needs."

Oh, god, no! Much as she wanted to pull back and preserve what little was left of her dignity, it was too late.

"What I was or wasn't doing is none of your business," she told the man who'd invaded her space and taken the taste of her juices into him.

More silence. A return on his part to that place she couldn't make sense of.

Things like this didn't happen to her, damn it! Her lovers were men with brains she respected—tax-paying, law-abiding career types who mixed sex with equal doses of intelligent conversation. She didn't lust after hard bodies—well, not really. The way she'd always seen it, if there wasn't a mind to go with the body, the package was incomplete.

Right now she didn't care if Mato Hawk was headless.

"Let me get this straight," she tried. "Instead of getting warm and dry on this miserable night, you decided that trying to grill me about my supposed ulterior motives was more important? What are you, paranoid?"

"I'm a man with responsibilities."

What did that mean? And did she care?

Not tonight.

"So am I. A human with responsibilities." If she lowered her head, his breath would stop washing over her eyelashes and upper lip, but she didn't. Couldn't. "Mine are to my employers and readers, not to you."

"Aren't they?"

Why were they talking when she wanted to fuck?

Fuck? Had she really thought the word again? Damn it, her world was politically correct, not earthy and uncivilized. She spoke of intercourse and sex, not fuck.

Something changed that pulled her off her thoughts and back onto her body. It took seconds to realize his grip on her shoulders had stopped feeling like restraint and had slipped into caress. He was stroking her, those workman fingers gliding over her robe. His heat, his life and energy slid through her layers, spreading out and spiraling deeper, touching her lungs, belly, cunt.

Cunt. Pussy.

Pure sex.

"What are you . . ."

"Tell me to stop." His voice was more growl than words; a man clinging to self-control? "If it's not what you want, say it now. Fast."

No logic or sanity. No clothes. Her skin warming his and sanding away his goose bumps. His hands roaming her while hers did the same, touching, feathering, pressing, mouths coming into play, bodies pressing.

She knew what he had in mind the moment he wrapped his fingers around the vee of her robe. Her body belonged to her, not to him. He had no right. And that's what made what he was doing even more exciting and unnerving.

Strangers. Strangers standing face-to-face, the truth sparking between them and words buried deep.

Her body spoke for her, her thighs weak and strong, wet heat coating her sex, nipples puckered, mouth hungry.

Hunger. All hunger.

His nail on her right breast shut her off from thought, and she became sensation. Nothing but wanting.

Her breasts were exposed, his if he wanted them. If she so much as shrugged, the robe would slide off. The tie no longer hugged her waist—a discarded length of fabric.

Unless he binds my wrists with it.

Where did that come from? she wondered, but the question evaporated before she could mold it. Before, his breath had had a measured cadence, but now his lungs clawed for oxygen in ways that mirrored hers.

Insanity! Two near strangers blasting through convention's barriers.

Feeling as if she'd been thrown into a whirlpool, she wrapped her arms around his neck and held on with all the strength in her. Hating the barrier his jeans represented, she pressed against him. His breath deepened, quickened. One arm went around her back and became a living restraint that held her tight against him. The other claimed her buttocks, not that she needed encouragement to tip her pelvis at him.

She wasn't simply offering herself to him, wasn't simply losing control. Instead, she insisted. *Us. Fucking. Now!*

Assaulted by a sudden shiver, she plowed her way through a sex fog. He was wearing his jacket, his wet, cold jacket, and beneath that was his equally wet shirt. Growling something beyond reason, she arched away and released his neck. Her fingers went in search of buttons. Finding snaps, she tore and ripped, not stopping until she'd shoved the garment off his shoulders.

"Get the hell rid of it," the bitch she'd become ordered.

He let go of her long enough to obey And before he could

capture—*capture?*—her again, she locked her fingers around his sodden, hot shirt and yanked. One button popped free. Another flew off.

"What the hell—"

"Get rid of it!"

Was that a laugh? Maybe a growl. Didn't matter. Nothing mattered except Mato's fingers on his shirt and the sight of his undershirt. She helped him rid himself of the flannel and then dipped her head and closed her teeth around the skin tight cotton. Rearing back with the cotton between her teeth, she looked up at the dark stranger.

Beautiful. Primal.

Are you crazy! What the hell is happening to you?

A powerful fever charged through her and killed the silent scream of reason. It centered and settled in her cunt, flames licking out from her sex to ignite muscles and nerves. Her head pounded. Her mind—her poor, splintered mind—screamed out another warning, but though she heard it, she didn't care.

Sex.

Fucking.

Working together, they pulled the T-shirt over his head. Before her strength could desert her, she clawed at the jeans' fastening and yanked down on the zipper. Then, exhausted or maybe disbelieving of what she'd done, she dropped her arms to her sides. One shiver-shrug, and her robe puddled on the floor.

Naked. Him still in his jeans but his navel exposed and his cock reaching for her.

She needed him to ask what the hell was happening, to admit he had no more control than she did, but give them a few more minutes and they'd find their way back to civilized. Most of all she needed him to tell her he'd respect her in the morning. But when he didn't say any of those things, she had no choice but to admit that respect had nothing to do with what was happening.

Animal. Only animal.

The moment his fingers settled around his waistband, her legs gave out, and she sank to the floor on her knees. She found enough strength to grasp denim and tug downward and then stroke his calves. They worked in tandem to bring the jeans as far as his boots would allow.

The wet leather laces challenged her, but thanks to her long nails, she eventually forced them to give up their hold. He balanced himself by resting a hand on the top of her head and lifted first one and then the other leg, wordlessly commanding her to finish the undressing. Exhausted and shaking, she watched him dispense with the briefs that contrasted spectacularly with his dark skin.

Naked. Both of them.

His cock inches from her mouth.

6

Heeding the insistent hum between her legs and nothing else, she flicked her damp tongue over his tip. He tasted male, aroused male. And his sigh forced a like sound from her throat.

Licking him, fingers circling the base of his cock and holding him in place, she felt equal strength, if not more, in his hold on her hair. His grip prevented her from moving her head more than an inch in either direction, but what did she care as long as she had access to his cock?

Licking him! Opening her mouth and closing her lips around him, sucking, experiencing!

The inner fire turning her senseless.

Her hands were on his knees, not only so she could take her measure of them but to keep her from swaying. She was vaguely aware of how damnably wanton she was, but it mattered little because his cock was in her mouth and she was tasting him.

Becoming part of him.

The tension on her scalp lessened only to be replaced by a gripping sensation on her left breast. Not releasing him, she nevertheless acknowledged his claim on her nipple. They held on to each in their own way, a rhythm starting only to end when he pressed on her breast or she all but swallowed him. It didn't matter that she had little experience sucking cock; she knew what she needed to feel, what she wanted to do.

Throwing caution aside, she sucked him deep. When he filled her, she became part of him, mouth fucking because she hadn't been able to wait. Just a little more and she'd—another inch and he'd be begging—

In what might have been the same instant, his tip all but slammed into the back of her throat and he pushed her away, tearing her hands off him. Instinct opened her mouth before she could do him harm, and she managed to throw her hands behind her to stop her fall.

Somewhere between anger and surprise, she took note of how she was presented to him, her torso and neck stretched and exposed, vulnerable, nipples hard and breasts flattened against her rib cage. "What was—"

"Not going to happen, Smokey, got it?"

The way he glared down at her put her in mind of a predator taking his measure of the prey he'd brought to the ground. Maybe she should be terrified, but the emotion would have to wait until others had had their turn.

Manhandled. That's what the shove had been about—a demonstration of his ability to manhandle her.

Did he have any idea how damnably exciting that was? How damnably sexy she felt?

"What isn't going to happen?" she finally thought to ask.

"You aren't going to get a story out of me that way."

No! That's not what this is about! It—I don't know what the hell it is. "Fuck you! I'd never resort to that." Her denial might have carried more weight if she hadn't felt as if she'd just pinned a giant welcome mat to her body. He could touch her wherever he wanted, straddle her, splay her out on the carpet, and she'd take it. Love it.

"Then what was what you just did about?" He shook his cock at her.

"You didn't like it? Go on, tell me you didn't want—"

"I'm a man. Of course I want. But I'm not stupid."

No, he was hardly that. At the moment, he wasn't just looming over her, he commanded her space. She should feel foolish and ashamed and scared, shouldn't she? She'd never done anything remotely like what she'd just done, but she wouldn't apologize, because given half a chance, she'd swallow him again.

Or even better, suck him into her pussy.

"Neither am I," she belatedly said. Words—specifically written words—had long been her strength, so why did she feel tongue-tied?

No, not tongue-tied. More like done in by her out-of-control body.

He was still looking at her—more than looking, leering. His gaze going from the top of her head to her kneecaps. She had no doubt he would have continued the journey if her lower legs weren't tucked under her.

There was something more than a little predatory about the way he lingered over the hollow at the base of her throat, her so-available-to-him breasts, what little there was of her belly with her pelvic bones sheltering it. And when, finally, he came to the dark curly hair standing pitiful guard over her sex, she swore she felt his tongue and teeth on her there.

Oh, shit!

Wanting it!

The carpet was old, that's what she'd think about. Old carpet with dirt undoubtedly embedded where a vacuum and shampooer couldn't reach. No one would want to have sex here, certainly not her.

As for him—

Something moved toward her. It took several blinks before she realized he was extending his hand. Good. He'd had the same thought about the floor covering. The moment he had her on her feet, she'd dust herself off, reach for her robe wherever it was, and get modest again. Show him the door.

Only, when he wrapped his arms around her waist and drew her upward and from there against him, the last thing she wanted was him out in the rain.

Crushed against him, breasts smashed flat, legs wide to keep her balance—and one of his sliding between them, thighs sealing to thighs—her arms dangling uselessly behind her, she kept her head back because kissing was for lovers and therefore out of the question.

He must have known what she was thinking and been determined to demonstrate his greater self-control; what other reason did he have for bending over her and biting at her neck? Chills raced through her, gathering her strength and turning it into nothing. She should be shivering, shouldn't she? All that cold should have stripped the heat from her.

Instead, flames licked. Everywhere.

"Damn you, damn you." She wasn't sure whether she was cursing him or herself, or, rather, she wasn't sure until it dawned on her that she'd looped her arms around his neck so he couldn't get away.

There. Let him deal with her nipples gliding over him and her pelvis again tipped toward him. Let him hold her and keep on holding her because surely he was too much of a gentleman to allow her to fall backward onto that filthy carpet.

"Damn you."

No, that wasn't her voice. Unable to put one and one together so she'd understand his anger, she rode out his long, hard breath.

She was still listening to him when he yanked her upright so roughly her head swam. A moment later she felt herself being lifted off her feet. Then he had her over his shoulder, head dangling, feet grazing his belly.

Captured by Tarzan?

The word *captured* again distracted her, and she paid no attention to where he was taking her until he tossed her onto the double bed in the postage-stamp-sized bedroom. There was no light on in here, nothing except what little made its way from the main room. Staring at the ceiling, her senses told her he was standing by the side of the bed and once more looking down at her, maybe seeing things she couldn't but then maybe trying to come to grips with what he'd just done.

"Tell me to get the hell out of here," he ordered.

Go. Leave me alone.

But she didn't say the words, because they represented the last thing she wanted. "Condom."

"I have—in my wallet."

But his wallet had to be in his jeans. "In there." She pointed at the nightstand. She waited to see if he'd say something about her being ready for sex, but when he only opened the drawer, she sent him a silent thank you and an equally silent message about how a teenage pregnancy scare had taught her an unforgettable lesson.

His weight on the mattress tilted her toward him, causing her to roll onto her side. Before she could brace herself, he grabbed an ankle and lifted her leg. An instant later he knelt between her legs. Although he lowered her limb, he kept a hand on her thigh, anchoring her to the bed. Unable to lift her pelvis, she gripped the thin coverlet. He might have given her the opportunity to tell him to leave, but since then things had changed dramatically. He was on top.

Feeling dwarfed by his size and untapped strength, she latched on to the moment. She wouldn't look behind or ahead, wouldn't question her sanity. As for whether she trusted him—

No, don't ask yourself that!

There was something she should say, something about whether they respected each other and knew what they were doing, but how could she form the words when she didn't respect or understand herself?

Didn't matter. How could it with his nails running down the space between her breasts? A delicious warmth rolled over her, settling in her belly before seeping lower, deeper. What was it she'd said about him earlier, that she wouldn't care if he were headless? Now, thanks to him, she wasn't sure whether she had a mind. Granted, a tiny voice whispered of danger, but the sound was too faint to break through the sensations tumbling around her.

Her world had become simple, so simple. A man capable of passionate speeches and deeply held convictions loomed over her naked body. His cock was sheathed, his hands both restraining and tantalizing her.

She could, wanted to do this! She might thrash about, might curse his strength, but it was all part of the spinning fantasy. Light-years away from the modern independent woman she believed herself to be, she was about to be taken by a stranger. Taken. Used. Not abused, but not cherished either.

Sex. Hard. Anonymous and stupid.

A bolt of what felt like a lightning strike had her gasping and trying to sit up. As her senses began to untangle, she realized what she'd felt was him raking her thighs with his nails. Instead of fraying her nerves again, he cupped large and cool hands over her breasts. Drawing them upward, he pressed inward until she wondered if they might meet. He had control over that one part of her body, and yet he owned and ruled everything. And she wanted it! Loved it!

Needing him to understand, she scratched his shoulders and thighs. Groaning, he leaned back. "You're pushing—"

"Don't talk!" she begged. "Just don't."

"What are you afraid of hearing?"

She wasn't afraid of anything, damn it. Fear didn't factor in. Determined to force him to concentrate on what he'd brought her in here for, she left a trail of marks on his chest. On a sharp intake of breath, he grabbed her wrists and pulled her arms over her head. Switching his grip so a single hand held her while the other served to brace him, he leaned so low she was compelled to deeply bend her knees to keep him from smashing her under his weight.

Some sound rolled out of him. She tried to lift her head, but whether she intended to kiss him became a moot point as he rocked forward. His penis, solid, hot, and heavy, slipped into her wetness. Shocked by the suddenness of his penetration, she struggled to blink him into clarity. But then her body loosened, muscles and bone oozing into nothing.

Her hands were free.

Confused about her sudden disappointment, she nevertheless lowered her arms. Sliding them between her body and his arms, which now bracketed her and served to support his upper body, she reached. Finding his buttocks, she grabbed hold and encouraged him ever deeper into her.

He plowed, invading her inch by inch. Even with her knees and lower legs caught between their bodies, she still found a home for her feet on the small of his back. She could barely make out his features and only guess at his mood. Surely he was feeling the same thing she was, the slick union, her soft, wet cave around his probing cock.

And when he rose up and became her personal living blanket, she closed her eyes so she could feel. Nothing but feel.

He was so big, long, and thick, hard as hell and yet like satin against her tissues. Whether he held still or pumped into her made little difference; her body loved it all. Needed everything he had to give.

Already! Less than a minute after coming in here, they were having sex. Fucking!

The smallest of voices, nothing more than a wind whisper, warned that she'd entered the predator's den and might never leave. But even as his cock brushed her cervix, causing a ripple of discomfort, she shut down the caution. She could stare at him and wordlessly tell him to slow down, to pace himself until her vagina had fully prepared itself for him. Yes, that's what she'd do, open her eyes and explain the facts of a woman's anatomy.

In the next minute.

Ah, another assault on her cervix. Only this time there was no hint of pain, only her wet heat easing his journey into her. Only her mouth opening to make harsh animal sounds.

Digging at his buttocks, she held him as deep inside her as possible. And she threw back her head and kept her eyes closed so there was nothing except the feel, smells, and sounds of sex. Close! Making a lie of everything she'd believed about her body's need for elaborate foreplay.

Tonight was her and a dark stranger in a darkened room, bodies straining and sweating, gripping fingers and straining muscles, his cock spearing and spreading her, making her pussy weep.

There! Climax. Nibbling at her nerve endings. Coming closer. Building. Insisting.

"Ah!" Without knowing why, she struggled to twist under him. "Ah!"

What!

Despite her short-circuiting system, she took note of what he'd just done. Without pulling out of her, he'd managed to straighten so his chest was longer married to her. Not only that, he'd grabbed her calves and lifted her legs as high as they could go. One was crossed over the other, the bottom one resting against his shoulder, both held in place by his damn capable hands. In essence he'd turned her into his prisoner because she could no longer move in any direction. She could try to scoot away using her hands against the bed as leverage, but he'd only come after her.

Trapped.

His sex slave.

Nonplussed by the thought, she shifted her own hold so she was gripping the back of his left thigh. Her other hand clung to his right wrist.

Him, shoving into her again. This time she could only lay there and take it. Even her attempts to clamp her sex muscles around the invasion were pitiful.

Had he known he was going to immobilize her from the beginning? If that had been his original intention, she was glad she hadn't been forewarned, because she might have panicked.

Might.

One thrust followed by another followed by yet more, each scooting her closer to the top of the bed. He came with her, their bodies fused, her legs high in the air and anchored in place. His grip completed her imprisonment, her incredible, exciting imprisonment.

Reaching the top of the frameless bed and her head sliding back and down into space changed little. She still held on to him as best she could, breasts exposed to the damp night air, pussy filled to overflowing, and butterfly wings brushing her throat, collarbone, and rib cage.

He could, if he wanted, bend her nearly double. He could, if that was his desire, lift her buttocks off the mattress and drive into her until only the wall just beyond the head of the bed prevented her from landing on the floor.

Let him. Let him do whatever he wanted to her because she wanted it all, everything, strength and dominance and her screaming cunt ruling her.

There, a series of explosions closing in on her again, flowing over her. Her body became something fierce and wild.

Something insistent.

Where was he, she wondered even as her inner muscles spasmed. Had he reached his own climax?

Didn't matter. She'd become selfish. Single-minded. Loud. Fierce and savage.

Long seconds after the explosion calmed, her head still thrashed. Her nails again raked him as she forced sensation on him and pulled him over his own edge.

And when he came, she came again.

Five minutes later, deeply shaken and afraid of both of them, she ordered him to leave.

7

It rained through the night, but morning brought the sun and slowly dissipating clouds. Fog clung to the surf and extended out into the ocean, but long accustomed to a storm's aftereffects, Mato paid it little attention. Besides, his journey was taking him to a cliff overlooking the ocean and not into the water. Within walking distance of his property and all but undiscovered by outsiders, the cliff was sacred to his people. Even the younger generation with their disinterest in much of what fascinated their parents spoke of Spirit's Overlook with reverence.

As he'd long done when seeking guidance, he worked on emptying his mind of the past and opened it to the future. Just the same, his body occasionally fought his orders. No matter that his need to make himself receptive to whatever wisdom his spirit might gift him with in the wake of what had happened at dawn was urgent—he still felt *her* on his skin. His nostrils remembered her smell, and his ears knew the sound of her voice. Most of all, his cock clung to memories of where it had been housed last night.

"Leave," she'd told him as thunder snapped and lightning

charged through the room. "I don't want to talk, don't want to think. I just need you gone."

He'd needed to be gone just as much, if not more. Separation, he'd told himself as he'd made his way back to his pickup, would return him to sanity, but though he'd fallen asleep a few minutes after reaching home, escape had lasted only a brief time. He'd awakened with an erection and memories of a frenzied fucking, not with memories of his failed attempt to get the hearing officer to listen to him.

Hawk Spirit, I need your guidance. If you were there when my father and uncle came to me at dawn, you know what they want me to do. But they spoke out of fear and a determination as old as time. Their pleas—I can't listen only to them.

The sound of the ocean attacking the massive rocks dotting the surf let him know he was reaching his destination, but even as he began the final climb to Spirit's Overlook, he remembered the look in his father's eyes as he spoke of dedication and loyalty. Instead of going straight home last night, his father and two others had gone to the town's only bar because they'd guessed that was where the reporters would congregate. They'd been right. And it had taken only a couple beers before the reporters had begun talking, not just about their reaction to the public hearing, but more importantly about their suspicions regarding Smokey Powers's reason for being there.

That's why his father and the others had come to see him so early. Afraid she'd probe where she had no right probing, they'd all but begged him to silence her as others had been silenced before.

I can't, he told Hawk Spirit. *Not the way they want me to.*

The old way had long been one of violence. He'd once accepted it because he'd been raised here and knew nothing else, but he was no longer an impressionable and obedient child. He was an adult, a man. A man who'd had sex with the enemy.

They're right. She's dangerous. She can't yet know every-

thing, but if she's as good as the other reporters say she is, the time will come when she exposes us. Unless I stop her.

It had to be him. He was the chief's son, heir to responsibility and tradition.

Hawk Spirit's human servant.

The sound of rocks and waves locked in ageless battle grew louder. He'd always found peace looking down and out at the vast Pacific, but today raw energy raced through his veins. Much as he wanted to believe last night's sex was responsible, he knew better. Today's energy wasn't any different from what he'd been feeling, and battling, since NewDirections's directors had declared their intention to build their obscene subdivision.

His world, his life, was under attack! Whether man or animal was responsible for his mood, he'd fight the danger with every bit of strength in him.

Spirit, I want to come to you as a child. To wait for you to direct me. I trust your wisdom; I always have. But I'm not a child, and the man I've become—

Pain slashed at his palms. Looking at his hands, he realized he'd been digging his nails into himself hard enough to draw blood. When he licked at a bloody indentation, the taste more than fascinated him, it drew him into its circle. Predators thrived on the taste of blood; death meant they'd live.

Was that what he was becoming? A predator? Had Hawk Spirit chosen him because he held the capacity for violence, even death deep inside him? If that was true, the time would come when he stopped resisting and would do whatever it took to defend this sacred land.

Even if it meant killing the woman he'd left his seed in last night.

I need your guidance, Spirit. It has always served me well and shown me the path I must walk.

A scent that wasn't of the ocean and surrounding forest

reached him, and he immediately recognized it as her smell. Somehow it had followed him here.

Don't command me to kill her! Whatever threat she represents, it can't justify ending her life!

Shaken by his heartfelt prayer, he stepped to the cliff's edge and gazed down into fog so thick he could barely make out the foaming surf as it crawled over sand and driftwood. For a moment, just a moment, he believed he was going to step into the void. Then he heard a sound.

Recognizing the lonely call of a hawk, he turned his back on the ocean and peered into the forest. After a moment, something drew his gaze upward.

There. Drifting weightless with the clouds as background. A hawk. *His* hawk?

No matter how many times Hawk Spirit had revealed himself to Mato, he continued to find it a humbling experience, and although it appeared only as a small and distant bird, this morning was no different.

The raptor was riding on unseen currents, looking weightless and free of human burdens. Envy settled in Mato—that and acceptance. He had no doubt his spirit had heard his plea and was answering in the way of all spirits. Shrugging off Smokey's essence, he lifted his arms and greeted what was both a simple living creature and the embodiment of something ancient, powerful, and passionate.

Thank you, my guide and wisdom. Whatever your expectations of me, I open myself to them and will hear them with an open heart. He couldn't bring himself to admit that for once he might not be capable of following orders. Even when his actions brought him sleepless nights, he'd always done what was expected of him, but to take the life of the woman he'd mated with?

No, not mated. Simply fucked.

The bird now reminded him of a fall leaf caught in a playful breeze. It drifted one direction and then the other, wings spread wide, small body resting between them, head slowly turning in all directions as it took in its universe.

How he envied the creature!

After a long and aimless time during which Mato's neck ached, the killing bird ceased to allow the wind to direct his movements. Now it stared at something he couldn't see, and a tension that hadn't been there before wound through it, causing Mato to rub his eyes. As a young boy, he'd learned to embrace Hawk Spirit's ways of imparting his wisdom, and now was no different. When the time was right, his spirit's message would be revealed.

Maybe Spirit was guiding him in increasing his awareness of the changing weather by playing in the gentle breeze. If that was so, he'd express his gratitude for the end to the rain because much as this land depended on it, he was weary of the claustrophobia that accompanied a coastal storm.

No, not the weather.

Expanding his lungs, Mato pulled sea air deep into him as the hawk headed in the direction he'd been looking. Tension in the predator made Mato wonder if Spirit was hunting prey.

Was that the message Spirit intended he understand? Smokey Powers was *his* prey? An enemy to be vanquished?

Not for the first time he was still trying to wrap his mind around this idea when he spotted a small, dark shape flying toward his spirit. A few more seconds, and he was positive he was looking at another hawk. The second wasn't as large as his or embodied with the supernatural, but there was nothing tentative about its approach. Obviously the newcomer didn't fear Spirit.

Female.

Fists and jaw clenched, Mato blocked out the rest of the world. The graceful movement of wings put him in mind of a dance, and yet he now acknowledged a darkness to what he was seeing, a finality. The female's movements slowed and nearly stopped, making him wonder if she wanted something else than the fate that had been handed her. He might have felt sorry for her if not for the way his spirit approached the female. Spirit was single-minded, determined. He knew what he needed and wanted from the newcomer; nothing would stop him.

Closer and closer, Spirit riding a wind current above the female. Her waiting, watching and waiting.

And then Spirit folded his wings against his body and dove. Even from down on the earth, Mato heard the wind rake past the predator's body and heard the female's heart race.

Time slowed and sped at the same time, the inevitable stretching out until Mato could barely stand the tension. Suddenly Spirit slammed into the smaller bird. For an instant they appeared as a single intertwined shape, but then the female broke free, half flying, half falling. Instead of pursuing her, Spirit hovered overhead until nearly a hundred feet separated them. Then the unearthly predator attacked again with outstretched claws and open beak. The female's scream was both high and weak.

The second collision sent the female spinning downward. Feathers flew. She seemed incapable of stopping her fall, making Mato wonder if Spirit had fatally wounded or killed her, but before she struck the ground, Spirit again caught up with her. This time when he extended his talons, there was a beauty to the movement, as though he was determined to cradle his prey.

They were together again, united in a way Mato barely comprehended. He expected the female to scream again, but she didn't. Instead the two flew just above him, Spirit clutching the smaller bird and thus controlling her movements. Her legs dangled, and her wings drooped. At the same time, she kept her head up, and her gaze was locked on her captor. Her killer.

Back when he had accepted that a hawk was his spirit creature, he had taken it upon himself to learn as much as he could. Hawks mated on the ground or in trees, not in flight, and yet something about what he was seeing reminded him of the sex he'd had with Smokey Powers. He'd taken her, forced his strength on her and rendered her all but helpless, and he'd reveled in the sense of control.

Just as Spirit was doing.

What are you telling me? he begged. *Are you showing . . . You want me to handle the reporter the way you did the female?*

Control her. Master her. Otherwise she'll destroy everything.

On the verge of telling Spirit he couldn't sink his talons into a human being, he clenched his teeth. A surge of anger against anything or anyone who jeopardized what was part of his people's heritage filled his heart and lungs, even his cock. This land had been entrusted to his ancestors by the ancient ones. It was his responsibility to safeguard the land, vegetation, and all living things so he could turn everything over to his children and grandchildren as his elders had done for him.

Nothing would stand between him and duty! Nothing and no one.

Even if it meant he had to become a predator.

If?

The single word slipped into him, where he turned it around and around in his mind until the truth could no longer be denied. Because Spirit had embraced him, he already was a predator. And he would soon become a captor and master.

Control her. Change her.

He had no choice.

8

Thank goodness for a little sunshine. Granted, she wasn't about to break out her bathing suit and suntan lotion, but watching the fog disappear had lifted her mood. Or maybe, she allowed, being able to see out the cabin window to the lush, deep green vegetation had helped her put last night into perspective.

That's what that damn stupid sex had been about—a combination of night and rain and this small, isolated cabin. If she'd been in her Portland condo with noise from the nearby boulevard warring with the music from her stereo, she would have been in her right mind. She sure as hell wouldn't have spread her legs for tall, dark, and strange.

When would he return? And when he did, would he want more of what he'd gotten in the dark? Maybe he considered a roll in the hay the reasonable and logical reward for letting her borrow some of his photographs.

Well, he was wrong! *It* wasn't going to happen again!

"No, it won't!" she protested when an inner voice mocked her decision. "I'm not an idiot."

Okay, the idiot label was up for debate, thanks to the way

she'd acted last night. The thing was, what she'd managed to forget the moment her clothes were off, but wasn't about to repeat today, was that she might well be better on Mato's good side because he was key to getting the information she needed for her article.

Ah, yes, the article, or, more accurately, a series of investigative pieces.

Shoulders squared, she sat at the table beneath the living room window and picked up a copy of a twenty-year-old newspaper clipping. BODY FOUND: COUGAR ATTACK SUSPECTED the headline read. The short and not particularly informative article revolved around a few quotes from the county sheriff, who'd explained that hikers had found the body of a man missing for several months. Given the corpse's condition, a definite cause of death was going to be difficult. Though thinking about the truth behind the words had turned her stomach, she'd picked through the article and had highlighted the sheriff's last quote. "My department's been looking for the deceased ever since he disappeared. He'd been identified by a couple hunters as the man they spotted near the logging road where the Hull fire started."

The Hull fire had burned over twenty thousand acres of timberland.

Pain stabbed at her temples, causing her to rub them. When she'd first became interested in the story, she'd spent a long and frustrating afternoon at the county offices in the town of Farrel, where newspaper archives were stored, looking for follow-up articles on the suspected cougar attack, but she hadn't found any. When she'd asked about it, the none-too-helpful employee had pointed out that what happened in Storm Bay was hardly front-page news. The fire had been the big news, not some fool hiker.

The next morning she'd gone to the sheriff's department and asked for access to their records of the man's death, only to be told she needed a court order. As she was leaving, none too calm and collected, a clerk had whispered that records from twenty years ago were either hopelessly disorganized or missing, thus the stonewalling. According to the clerk, the former sheriff's incompetence had led to his firing, and his replacement had given priority to ending the good-old-boy hiring system, not improving record keeping.

So where did that leave her? Nosing around until she found someone who remembered what had happened after the body was found and who was willing to talk to her? No wonder she had a headache. Finding someone around here who'd tell an outsider anything worth writing down wasn't going to be easy.

She wasn't going to give up, damn it, she wasn't! There was a story here. One hell of a story. The kind that got her reporter juices flowing and sent chills up her spine.

An unexpected creak outside made her start. Jumping to her feet, she hurried to the door. Thank goodness she'd locked it after Mato had left last night.

Mato?

Heart stumbling, she cursed the lack of a window that would let her know who or what was out there. If Mato knocked, would she let him in? Instead of the expected rap, however, someone was trying to turn the knob. Alarmed, she leaned against the door. "Who is it?" she demanded, trying to sound strong and determined.

"Open up."

Mato. After last night, she'd recognize that voice anywhere. "What do you want?"

"Open."

Who was he to be issuing orders—other than her *lover.* "You can't just come storming in. I told you I didn't want to be around you."

"Don't lie."

Mouth suddenly dry, she nearly back stepped before forcing

herself to stand her ground. "What makes you think I'm lying?"

His lack of an answer really was an answer, wasn't it? she reluctantly concluded. She wouldn't have done the things she had with him in the bedroom if she wanted no part of him in her life. Where were the ground rules, anyway? Whatever she'd been told or had learned about the interplay between the sexes, nothing covered this scenario. "What do you want?" she finally came up with.

"Let me in."

No! Do you think I'm stupid? Before she was forced to answer her question, a possibility occurred to her. Even with the way she'd shown him the door—how could she have done anything different, given the way her nerves had shredded—he hadn't taken back his promise to let her borrow some of his photographs. He'd brought them and was making her pay for last night's behavior by not telling her.

And yet when she unlocked the door and stepped back, pictures had only a little to do with the gesture.

He had on clean, dry clothes. Although it was a bit cool, he wasn't wearing a jacket, which meant only a brown T-shirt stood between her and his nudity. The jeans were twins of what he'd worn yesterday, his boots just as well used as the probably still wet ones. Now that rain no longer plastered his hair to his scalp, she couldn't help but note how thick it was. Not only did he have a full head of hair, but the strands were anything but fine.

He'd shaved.

Trying not to think about what it would feel like to run her fingers over his smooth jawline, she looked to see if he was carrying something. He wasn't. More uneasy than she wanted to admit, she clutched the doorknob. If he made a move she didn't want him to, could she slam the door into him?

Yeah. Right.

"I don't know what I'm supposed to say," she started and then chastised herself for letting him throw her off balance. Hadn't her career taught her how to control a conversation? "I appreciate the personal visit, but a phone call would have sufficed. I'm assuming this is about the pictures. Believe me, I'm looking forward—"

Ignoring her, he pushed past her and strode over to the desk at which she'd been sitting. Thinking to intercept him before he got his hands on her material, she followed, but he planted himself between her and the desk in a wordless warning not to try to stop him. Even though the next few seconds might spell the success or failure of her mission, she couldn't bring herself to yank the papers out from under his gaze.

Standing this close to him was a bad idea, bad and exciting. Her thoughts and more spun back to last night and fast, hard sex. She'd never climaxed that quickly, never! And she certainly had never thrown herself at a man. Feeling his body heat gave her some idea of how the impossible and carnal had taken place. He gave off—what, an aura, a presence, raw sexuality? There wasn't a single inch of him that didn't say male—more than just male, animal-man, more like it.

She'd heard of male members of the animal world who could make the females of the species ovulate with nothing more than a sound. Mato hadn't said anything for a while, but something was taking place, something she had no defense against.

Masculine energy, especially when presented in this package, was mind-blowing. Touching him made as much sense as placing her hand on a red-hot stove, but she was tempted. More than tempted—damn close to doing the deed.

That's what she'd do—trail her fingertips over his back and get that out of her system. Maybe she could make the contact so light he wouldn't know she'd given into insane impulse, though she suspected he was too tuned into her for that to work.

And when he caught her touching him, he'd do what?

Touch back. Take.

Buzzing from head to toe, she forced herself to focus. In whatever time it had taken her to come to grips with his magnetism, he'd picked up a notebook containing the notes she'd taken while interviewing a retired fish and game employee. She'd gotten in touch with Frank Murphy because he'd spent most of his career working on the southern Oregon coast. Over monster-sized hamburgers she'd paid for, she'd primed him about his working years. At first it had taken some directing on her part to get him to talk about more than complex policies and ignorant politicians, but by the time he'd downed his third beer, he was talking about things he'd seen that only his fellow employees knew about.

Gauging by the look on Mato's face, she surmised he'd come to her notes about a drowning death on the Spruce River some five miles before it fed into the ocean. Frank's voice had lowered to a whisper as he'd described what he'd come across.

"There weren't two feet of water in that part of the river, because the channel there was so wide. That man drowned facedown in two damn feet? I don't care what the coroner said, that damn fool could have gotten back up. He was in his forties, in good shape, wearing the best wading boots money can buy. He'd been fishing all his life. He's not going to make stupid mistakes."

"Then what do you think happened?" she'd asked.

"He got what he deserved," Frank had whispered. Then he'd told her that the carcasses of a half dozen salmon had been found on the shore near where the man "drowned." That time of year, salmon fishing was illegal. The carcasses were female, all laden with eggs. "He broke the law," Frank continued. "Someone made him pay for it."

"Who do you think it was?" she'd asked, but for once Frank hadn't voiced an opinion. Instead he'd said he'd known when to turn deaf because he wanted to go on living.

A moment ago, Mato's heat had her all but panting. Now suddenly she shivered. Heart in her throat, she reached for the notebook. "That can't interest—"

"You've been talking to Frank Murphy." He speared her with a glance.

A hawk's look, a hawk's eyes. Pulling her into a deep pit. Scaring her and more. Making her wish she'd never come to this part of the state. "You, ah, you know him?" was the only thing she could think to say.

He didn't answer, but every line of his body supplied the truth. Only, his mood had very little to do with a talkative old man and everything to do with her. The room wasn't closing in on her so much as the walls seemed to be thickening to imprison her in this room dominated by Mato Hawk. Part of her fascination with the predator he'd photographed had to do with the bird's capacity for violence, its disregard for life beyond its own. At this moment, Mato Hawk was no different.

Unable to move, she gaped as he dropped the notebook and swiveled to face her full on. Cougarlike? No, not that, and yet there was something—

His hands, reaching for her, slipped through the air before she could make sense of what she was seeing, clamping on to her arms and pinning them to her sides. Too shocked for a scream, she tried to twist away, which only prompted him to spin her around and pull her back against him. Both of his arms now wrapped her body, and his chest further hindered her movements.

"Let me go!" she ordered. At the same time, she kicked

back, hoping to strike something vulnerable, but because his legs were spread, she barely grazed a calf. Just the same, she straightened and kicked again. This time her heel connected with something solid. Grunting, he lifted her off her feet.

"What are you doing?" Struggling, kicking, she searched desperately for some part of him to bite. "Damn it, you have no right!"

"Right has nothing to do with it," he fairly growled into her ear.

She might have demanded an explanation if he hadn't been carrying her over to the couch. Still not fully comprehending that this was happening, she stretched her legs, trying to connect with the carpet, but, damn him, he was strong and tall enough to keep her in the air. Strong enough to make her feel weak.

Reaching the couch, he dropped her face-first onto it. Before she could twist around, he straddled her, a knee jammed between her and the back of the couch, the other leg braced against the floor. His weight settled onto her buttocks to anchor her in place.

He was reaching for something in his pocket, not that she could take advantage of his distraction. At least she'd been able to turn her head to the side, and one arm dangled off the edge of the couch, which made him capable of—of what? She was still trying to answer her question when he grabbed her arm and twisted it behind her.

Something closed around her wrist.

Not just something, rope! "No! No!"

Grabbing her hair, he pulled her head back and then down. This time her face was in the couch, her ability to breathe severely limited. His weight had shifted forward to immobilize her. Pushing at the panic about to swamp her, she paid little attention to what he was doing until he abruptly stood. At first she couldn't think of anything except getting enough air into her lungs, but finally her head cleared.

He had tied her hands behind her, one wrist over the other so she couldn't straighten her elbows.

Feeling as if she'd been gut-punched, she offered no resistance as he hauled her into a sitting position. Then he stepped back. "You're coming. With me."

"What? No! How can—what are . . ."

The bonds around her wrists were doing things to her she'd never experienced. The simple explanation was that she'd always been able to use her hands and she didn't know how to adjust to the change, but her reaction went deeper than that. Several times last night she'd likened Hawk to an animal. He was looking at her through animal eyes now, eyes that acknowledged his superiority. Something told her she'd find no humanity in him, no concern for her as a fellow human being.

Wild. That's what he was, wild. Primitive.

9

A thousand questions pushed against Smokey's lips, but the look in Mato's eyes left no doubt he wouldn't answer them. Neither would he heed her screams.

What was she supposed to do then? Wait?

For what?

"Don't do this," she fairly babbled. "We're two civilized . . ." But he wasn't, was he? Dangerously close to accusing him of being a sexual pervert, a perhaps even more frightening possibility struck her. "It has to do with that material, doesn't it?" She jerked her head at her notes.

Colder than she'd ever been, she strained to free herself. Instead, the rope tightened, threatening to cut off circulation. Wincing, she willed herself to stop fighting; the bonds continued to bite into her flesh.

He wouldn't care. As long as he had her under his control, what did he care whether she was comfortable? Battling the emotion that went with her belief made her slow to note what he was doing until he pulled her to her feet and forced her to turn her back to him. Something, probably the instinct for survival, railed at her to try to get away, but where could she go? She couldn't even open the door.

His hands went to her bonds, and when the pressure let up, she sighed in relief. Before she could decide whether to thank him, he wound another length of rope around her waist. Alarmed all over again, she tried to look back over her shoulder, but he forced her head down. A moment later he'd secured her wrists to the small of her back via the new rope. If she wasn't so overwhelmed, she might have complimented him on his ability to completely immobilize her arms. No way could she accidentally or otherwise do harm to herself—or to him.

She'd deliberately kept the cabin temperature fairly low because she'd wanted to be alert as she went over her material, but despite the chill in the air, she was sweating. Her reporter's mind made a note of the condition. If she ever had the opportunity, it would be interesting to see whether people in crises were more likely to feel hot or cold.

Oh, god, what did it matter?

"You—you knew what you were going to do before you came here." Fear, and another emotion she wasn't about to acknowledge, loosened her throat. "That's why you had the rope on you. But why? That's what I don't understand. Why?"

A sound she'd never heard rumbled up from deep inside him, and when he closed his hands over her shoulders, she froze. Life as she'd always taken for granted had ended. She didn't know what was ahead of her or whether she'd be alive by the end of the day, but those thoughts were taking second place to his impact on her.

She hadn't paid that much attention to his height last night, but now she didn't have to look at him to know he was some eight or nine inches taller than her. And stronger. So much stronger. He hadn't thrown his power at her earlier, but it was wrapped around her now, imprisoning her as much as her bonds did.

Small. Weak. Helpless.

"I'm not a danger to you and whoever . . . I can't be a danger," she babbled. "And I can't believe this is about sexual domination. You know—you were given a vivid demonstration of how easy it was to get into my pants." *Shut up! Just shut up!* But she couldn't, because the resultant silence might be more than she could handle.

"What are you going to do with me? Can't you tell me that? I—let me go. Just let me—"

A calloused hand clamped over her mouth. Shocked anew, it was all she could do not to collapse. She'd learned her lesson; she'd be quiet. The better part of a minute passed before he let up the pressure, but before she could adjust to the change, he started forcing something between her teeth. Fresh panic seized her and sent her head to thrashing, but as before, his strength left hers in ruins. All too soon, she was gnawing on the wide strip of cloth he'd gagged her with, and he'd finished knotting it behind her head. She could probably still make some kind of sound, but he probably wouldn't be able to understand what she was saying.

Bottom line, he wanted her silent. Silent and submissive.

More seconds slipped past before he turned her toward him again. Legs slightly spread, she stared up at her captor. Her beautiful, powerful, and maybe deadly captor. The animal-like quality she'd seen in his eyes earlier was still there. In fact, if anything, it was even stronger. He might stand upright and be capable of speech, but she didn't believe he was thinking with a human's brain.

What had he become? And why was she part of it?

When he again placed his hands on her shoulders, she warned herself not to think beyond this moment. She needed to be locked on to him and as ready as possible for whatever he had planned. Just the same, the last thing she expected was to be forced to her knees, but there she was. At first she couldn't bring herself to look up at him, but that left her with little to stare at except the well-covered mound between his legs.

Suddenly she was grateful for the gag because as long as it was in her mouth, he couldn't force her to suck him. Errant mental images of his cock touching the back of her throat again made her slow to realize he was once more on the move. To her shock, he had picked up her briefcase from where she'd left it near the desk and begun throwing her material into it.

That's what brought him here? My notes?

After closing the briefcase, he carried it over to the door and left it there. He started toward the bedroom and then stopped and stood over her. His presence said it all: she was to remain on her knees until he'd decided otherwise.

Of course she would. What choice did she have?

The moment Mato disappeared into the bedroom, she felt not relief but an unexpected loneliness. In a short period of time he'd become what, her world? Her master? She'd probably choke on the word if she tried to say it, but he was more than a man who'd thrown ropes on a woman. There was something about his presence, a dominating aura that went deeper than her imagination had ever gone. He was in charge of her, responsible for her, free to do whatever he wanted to her.

Rape?

No. Even with reality filling her mouth and encircling her wrists and waist, she didn't believe that was his intention.

Instead of wondering what he was doing in the bedroom, she examined her sense of loneliness. The career she'd chosen called for long absences from her condo, and she accepted that although she considered her coworkers and some of her neighbors friends, she wasn't truly close to any of them. Even lovers came and went without a profound feeling of loss. She'd lost her roots when both of her grandmothers had died within three months of each other when she was in high school, and she judged all other losses by those yardsticks. Her parents and siblings lived hundreds of miles away, and she stayed in contact via e-mail and phone calls, but they weren't part of her everyday life.

That was it, wasn't it? No one, really, shared space with her on a daily basis.

How had it come to that? Yes, she loved her career, but surely there'd been opportunity to build a personal life, so why hadn't she?

It didn't matter—not now, anyway. All that mattered was that she was waiting on her knees for her captor to return.

Although her thoughts had spun off into their own channels again, she knew Mato had finished whatever he was doing before he filled the narrow doorway. He was carrying her lone suitcase, and her cosmetic bag was in his other hand. In a few minutes he'd stripped the room of her belongings. When he deposited his burdens next to her briefcase and slipped her laptop into its carrying case, she shivered.

What was he going to do with her belongings? Even more important, what did he intend to do with her?

She started trying to scoot away the moment he faced her. Even when he shook his head, she continued backtracking. And when he crouched over her and planted a hand over the back of her neck, she screamed into her gag. The sound was garbled nonsense.

Down, down he forced her head until she lost her balance and probably would have hit her nose on the carpet if he hadn't grabbed an arm at the last second and eased her journey. She was lying on her breasts, her head turned toward him, knees still bent, silenced and helpless. Alive in unfathomable ways.

He was going to touch her, just touch, not force or dominate. But although he'd given her time to accept what he had in mind, she had no defenses in place when he began massaging her shoulders. Was he concerned that tying her the way he had might have hurt her?

But maybe that wasn't what he had in mind at all. Maybe he wanted to make sure she understood he considered her his property. His possession.

What had happened to a lifetime of independence and accomplishments?

The massage ended so abruptly she couldn't help but wonder if he regretted it. Worrying about what he had in mind tightened her muscles, but instead of trying to read his expression, she stared at the carpet. She should fight, try to yell, something! Damn it, what self-respecting human being allowed herself to be plunked onto dirty old carpet?

Fighting Mato Hawk?

An image of her going after him with nails, teeth, arms, and legs started to form, only to evaporate when she realized he'd grasped an ankle and was bending her knee so her heel was touching her buttocks. Fright exploded around her, and lifting her upper body as far off the floor as she could, she struggled to twist free. Although she managed a quarter circle turn, he settled onto his knees, grabbed her hips, and pulled her back against him. No sooner did he have her in place than he'd bent her leg again. More rope materialized. Even as she kept her leg in motion, he looped the restraint around her ankle. Keeping tension on the rope, he held her down while sliding the rope's loose end through what was around her waist. A quick knot finished the job.

When he slid back, she made no attempt to keep him in her sight. Soon enough she would put her mind on him, but for right now, only one thing mattered. He'd secured her much as a rodeo roper did to the calf he'd just brought down.

Sweat bloomed along her sides and in the small of her back. Her head filled with the screams she couldn't voice, and yet she was more angry than afraid. If he didn't like what she was doing, he'd let her know, but in the meantime she'd give him as much of a piece of her mind as she could without words. Using the flooring for leverage, she managed to get onto her side with her tethered leg under her. If the overpowering brute got too close, she'd land her free leg where it'd do the most good.

Then she caught sight of him again, and thoughts of violent revenge slid off into an unreachable part of her mind. He seemed caught somewhere between man and creature all right, a maybe unwilling participant in something larger than both of them. Though she was the one with ropes on her, he made her think of a wild animal in a cage. She'd gone to a zoo only once because she couldn't stand the look of mute resignation and despair in the eyes of lions, wolves, antelope, even elephants. The animals had been well fed, but they hadn't chosen that life. Even those who'd been born in captivity seemed to carry memories of freedom in their genetic makeup.

Mato Hawk had been free last night. When she'd seen him at the hearing, he'd been fierce and self-directed, a man ruled by his intellect and convictions. Now, however, that intellect seemed buried under something else. Something he had no control over and maybe couldn't comprehend.

She hurt for him.

Then he stood and walked over to the door, and she stopped thinking and simply watched as he picked up her belongings. He stepped outside without looking back at her.

That was why he'd tied her leg the way he had, she surmised. He'd been going to leave her for a while and didn't want her getting away.

Trying to stay on her side called for constantly tense muscles, and after a minute she rolled back onto her belly, her eyes locked on the door He'd abandoned her. Yes, surely he'd return and pull her even further into whatever existence he'd entered, but right now it was just her and her thoughts and helplessness.

Without him she might die.

Reminding herself that the motel owner would come to check on things before starvation set in, she tried to imagine what Hawk was doing, but instead of wondering about his destination, she thought about his long legs striding over the still damp path. He'd carry her belongings as if they weighed nothing, his mind maybe in neutral, maybe listening to whatever voices ruled him.

What had he felt while he was tying her up? Had it simply been a job he needed to do, or had he been turned on because he could whatever he wanted to her? Maybe her helpless body free for the taking had been nearly as good as sex.

Sex was part of the equation for her as well as him, wasn't it? Yes, that would undoubtedly change once reality grabbed hold of her again, but for now she simply waited. Immobile and available, she waited for the man who'd captured her.

He'd thrown himself at her last night. All right, there'd been equal amounts of throwing, but he'd left her with hot proof of his sexuality. No matter what spell he was under, he was still a man driven by hormones and nature.

And he had free and total access to a woman.

Heat born of her thoughts bloomed in her core. A moment of disbelief that his tying her up had turned her on faded, and in the aftermath she accepted where her mind and body had taken her.

Being helpless was so incredibly different from freedom. Maybe that's what was behind her not-so-random thoughts. Incapable of acknowledging her dangerous situation, she'd embraced her captivity as some kind of sexual fantasy.

A sharp stab in her temples short-circuited those thoughts. By the time the pain had faded to a manageable level, she'd forgotten much of what had been going through her mind, and she was left with the smell of old carpet and her shoulders starting to ache. He'd better return soon.

Please come back.

10

Though the motel wasn't near the ocean, Mato could still smell the vast body of water; either that or the scent had become a core part of his makeup. The same was true for the sound the breeze made as it shook the tree branches, and the constantly changing mix of sunlight and clouds overhead. He didn't simply live on the coast; this land had shaped him.

Not just the land, he amended as the small rental cabin came into view. He concentrated on his surroundings while placing Smokey's belongings in the back of his pickup because although his people would approve of what he was doing, they weren't the only ones in Storm Bay. Now, however, there was nothing to stand between him and thoughts of Smokey Powers.

And yet there was.

Something was touching him—no, not touching so much as sharing the same body/mind space with him. He'd had this sensation countless times over the years, so it shouldn't feel new, but in the past he'd simply and totally embraced what he believed were Hawk Spirit's messages for him. Now, although he didn't believe he'd ever oppose those messages, he was questioning them.

Of course he was. He'd never kidnapped anyone before.

The cabin seemed to loom ahead of him like something from a suspense movie, and if he could, he would have walked away. Instead, holding his breath, he climbed the two steps and opened the door. She was where he'd left her, an awkwardly placed woman in jeans and sweatshirt but no shoes with her hands roped to her waist and a leg hobbled, a gag saving him from her wrath and pleas.

That helpless body also reminded him of the sex they'd shared.

Taking her in, his half erection exploded until he was forced to adjust his jeans. The moment he did, he regretted it because she'd seen his every move and now knew he was far from some unthinking robot.

Why had he done this to her? What forces had driven him to break the law?

Granted, he was hardly the first member of his extended family to bow to demands that had nothing to do with modern civilization's laws, but that didn't make acceptance any easier. If anything, admitting he was following in his ancestors' footsteps made those steps harder to take.

Harder but inescapable.

Was this how his father, grandfather, and great-grandfather had felt as the weight of responsibility and loyalty had settled over them? Had they even tried to deny their heritage?

The closer he came, the wider her eyes grew until he was reminded of a wary deer. He'd never looked at a doe or buck without being struck by their shining brown eyes. Smokey's had flecks of blue in them, which served only to captivate him. Maybe if it hadn't been so dark last night he would have already prepared himself for their impact.

Your task. Don't forget your task. Everything depends on your mastery of her.

Shaking off his hatred of the insistent voice, he planted himself over her. He'd do what was required of him in order to keep certain secrets from the outside world. And what the male animal in him wanted, he added.

The moment he acknowledged that he'd risk his freedom and self-respect for a return to last night's fiery sex, he recoiled. Imprisoning her was one thing; raping her went against everything he stood for and believed in. And yet he couldn't deny where the impulse was coming from—the beast inside.

Overpowering the beast wasn't going to be easy.

Gathering equal amounts of determination and obedience around him, he knelt and untied her ankle. Although he wanted to apologize and explain, he remained silent. Eventually, if everything went the way the spirit forces demanded, he'd be able to tell her the truth and she'd understand, but for that to happen, he had to remake her.

Reminding himself that his people's future left him no choice, he helped her to her feet. She smelled of soap and the woods that were as much a part of him as his own breath, and he might have made the mistake of telling her that if she hadn't tried to twist away. Her defiance reminded him of the great difference between the two of them and the danger that difference represented. Gripping her hair, he propelled her toward the door. She resisted, but he pushed against the back of her neck until she was off balance. After that, she seemed to accept her fate. With him both forcing and guiding her, she stepped outside and then down the stairs. Looking at her bare feet, he cursed himself for not thinking of that, but the path was well packed and reasonably clear of debris. Besides, that she had to concentrate on her own footing seemed to fill her mind, for which he was grateful.

He'd deliberately parked out of sight of the motel and had

left the passenger side door open so he could quickly load her. She tried to plant her feet when she realized what he had in mind, but he grabbed her around the waist and lifted her onto the seat. After hooking her seatbelt and locking the door, he hurried around to the driver's side and climbed in. Though the key was in the ignition, he didn't immediately start the engine.

She was beside him, staring straight ahead, her body so tense he wondered if she might snap, leaning forward so her weight wouldn't rest on her hands. He'd done it! Made her his possession.

And now—

The ride took forever and didn't last nearly long enough. Although they traveled on the main highway for several miles, there were few vehicles out, and no one took note of a passenger with a gag in her mouth. Feeling utterly isolated, Smokey couldn't help picturing the vegetation reaching out to swallow her. She'd simply disappear from the face of the earth. Her family, though accustomed to infrequent contact from her when she was on a story, would eventually try to get in touch with her. Her editor wouldn't wait that long to start leaving messages on her cell phone, and when she didn't call back, he'd contact law enforcement.

But what if what passed for local law enforcement protected Mato?

The more she thought about it, the more she was forced to admit that such a scenario was not just possible but probable. During last night's meeting, she'd been given undeniable proof that Mato Hawk was a major figure in the community. When he spoke, people listened. The area's residents supported him. And they'd protect him.

Maybe that's why no one looked at Mato's truck as they passed it; they already knew what he was doing.

All right, she tried to chide herself, she was probably letting her imagination get the best of her. Surely an entire community wouldn't condone kidnapping and whatever Mato intended to do with her.

God, what were his plans?

A chill washed over her, but she refused to let it drown her as she risked a look at her captor. His hands on the large steering wheel had been designed for manual labor. Physical work had carved his body, and she'd already seen how at home he was outdoors. His lungs knew the taste of pure air, and his eyes were accustomed to trees and mountains, not city streets. She couldn't imagine him ever getting a manicure or having his hair styled. When he needed new clothes, he grabbed whatever fit him at an outdoors store, not at a mall. She wouldn't be surprised if he'd never been in an upscale department store. He didn't do the club scene and probably barely knew what the term meant.

Where was he taking her, and why?

By the time he turned off the highway, she had stopped asking the question and allowed lethargy to settle over her. Even knowing they were nearing their destination didn't alarm her. She did, however, take note of her surroundings. The single-lane gravel road wove through the trees, making her wonder if whoever had built it had followed a deer trail. Maybe the goal had been to leave as many trees standing as possible. Certainly reaching one's destination quickly hadn't been the priority.

After what she judged to be a half mile, they entered a small clearing. A maybe-two-thousand-square-foot log home was in the middle of it, a good-sized separate garage to the left. On the right was a shed filled with firewood. A man's home, she concluded.

Sensing a change in Mato's demeanor, she looked at him for the second time since he'd hoisted her into the cab. Before, his features had been tense, as though he wasn't entirely comfortable with his thoughts. Now, however, he appeared relaxed.

Realizing that being home had this effect on him made her envious because although she enjoyed her place, she'd never seen it as a sanctuary.

It might be his sanctuary, but it was about to become her prison.

Wiped from the face of the Earth. Spirited to this small piece of civilization in the middle of a rain-fed wilderness. Alone with not just a man but with *him.*

When, after pulling into the garage, he opened the passenger door, she wondered if he expected her to swivel toward him and maybe even step out on her own, but she couldn't make herself move. This wasn't happening, it wasn't! She hadn't become Mato Hawk's prisoner and responsibility and possession. She hadn't!

But she had, she was forced to acknowledge as he dragged her out of the cab. Acting instinctively, she tried to kick him only to have him easily avoid her foot. The moment she reached the ground, he hoisted her over his shoulder. His powerful arms locked around her legs. Afraid he'd let her fall if she resisted, she lay limp. He was so incredibly strong! His strength came from more than solid bone and work-carved muscles. There was a certain confidence about his body that made a mockery of her strength.

Unable to see anything except his back, she concentrated on his footsteps. The sodden ground muffled the sound of his boots, but her sensory system recorded the act every time he moved a leg. His arms encompassed her thighs as if hugging her—only, no hug had ever dominated her like this. Thank goodness for her jeans; if he'd been touching her bare skin, she might have lost her mind.

There was only one step to the porch leading to the front door. She was wondering if he'd have to dig into his pocket for his key, when he let go of her with one hand and twisted the knob. Then he brought both of them over the threshold.

She was in his place.

A sudden tremor had her gnawing at her gag, but if she was being honest with herself, she'd have to admit she was feeling more than simple fear. This was home to the most amazing man to ever touch her life. He'd hauled her out of her world and was depositing her in his.

And she didn't know why.

Step one completed, Mato forced himself to acknowledge that she was here—in the house he'd built with timbers from his land.

Because he'd never so much as considered putting up curtains, daylight illuminated his living room. At the moment, he was standing just inside and facing the large rock fireplace he'd built from stones he'd hauled down a mountain; his prisoner's weight pressed down on his shoulder blade, and his home accepted her presence.

On the log walls, the framed photographs he'd taken over the years helped to ground him. There was the small elk herd he'd come across one spring morning, the angry ground squirrel chastising him from the safety of an overhead tree branch, the hours-old fawn all but hidden by the mountain of leaves its mother had left it in, the bear with her half-grown cub fishing at a riverbank, the hawk staring down at something only the predator could see.

Those creatures had one thing in common: they were all wild.

Like him.

He had stoked the wood stove before leaving, but with the sun's impact growing, he didn't anticipate having to keep it going. Good, because he had other things to do. Things he'd never done before.

Setting the woman down, he backed up so he could study her. Her name no longer concerned him, and although he had a great deal more to learn about what had brought her to this part of the state, that would wait. Right now he existed for one purpose, to follow Hawk Spirit's commands. Whatever it took, whatever he had to do to her was for one goal—to put an end to the danger she represented. Secrets *would* be kept.

Staring openly at her, he centered himself. His spirit had told him that the key to defusing her threat without killing her lay in her weakness as a woman. Last night she'd welcomed him, a stranger, into her body because primitive need had overruled her intelligence. That's what Spirit had ordered him to build on.

By the time he was done with her, she'd exist for no other purpose. His pleasure would become her only goal and reason for living. She'd forget everything else, and there'd be no need to end her life.

Although he'd slipped into a mental space fashioned by powerful forces, acknowledging the task those forces had given him shook him, and the reasoning human part of him doubted and questioned. Yes, he'd kidnapped and brought her here, but those had been physical tasks. Now he had to start altering her very mind, something no human being had the right to do to another.

Let her go. Before it's too late, let her go.

Not taking his eyes off her, he fought the urgent message he'd just given himself. The command had come from a small portion of his brain that hadn't yet surrendered to his Spirit's will, and he didn't know what to do with it or even how to react. Neither did he know how to handle her impact on his senses.

Much as the wilderness's forces demanded he see her as less than human, he couldn't, not yet. She was a woman, slightly built but independent, intelligent, and sexy. Just thinking about taking her breasts in his hands made them ache. He wanted her breath warming his crotch, wanted her on her belly with her knees bent and her ass welcoming him in. Even before that union was completed, he'd slide a finger deep into her pussy. Or he might tease her labia, playfully slap her buttocks, even tickle the bottom of her feet.

She'd wiggle and laugh, push back against him, lift her head, and howl in delight.

Take her. Break her down. Remake her as your possession. Because if you don't, you'll have to kill her.

As the command spread throughout him, his rebellion blacked out, and the humanity that made him deeply appreciative of the creatures who'd allowed him to photograph them slipped off into a place he couldn't find. Something as old as the land he loved had taken control of his mind, and he no longer heard the warning to free her. Hawk Spirit spoke to him of loyalty and duty, and he saw not a woman capable of caring for him as a fellow human being but clay that needed to be molded into something compliant and safe.

There was only one other option.

11

Something fundamental had changed about Mato, Smokey acknowledged as she tried to back away from him. Only a few seconds ago, he'd looked at her with a man's eyes. She'd felt the heat of his sexuality and had responded to it, wanted his body around hers. Being his prisoner had made it easier to lose herself in the fantasy of repeating what they'd done last night, and she'd imagined them tearing at each other's clothes in their frenzied need to fuck.

Now, however, he was coming after her.

Risking a quick look behind her, she took note of a large leather couch and, next to it, an overstuffed chair and matching ottoman. If she wasn't careful, she'd run into them. Mincing more than walking, she continued her doomed retreat. With each step she ridiculed herself for thinking she could get away from him, but because her only alternative was to wait for the beast man to overtake her, she kept moving.

He smiled—not a man's smile but something primitive and possessive. Holding out his arms as if taunting her with possibilities, he matched her pace. She hated his mockery and considered stopping so she could land a foot where it would do her the most good. Kicking him in the balls would only enrage him, but for a few seconds she'd be the victor. It might be worth the consequences.

The backs of her knees came in contact with something and nearly caused her to lose her balance. She tried to slide around whatever it was. She was still searching for its end when he reached out. His fingers closed around her upper arms.

Violently twisting to the side freed one arm, but he easily spun her around so her back was to him. An instant later, he'd shoved her face-first onto the ottoman. She was now on her knees with her upper body pressed against the fabric and his hands splayed over her shoulder blades. Kicking her legs apart, he stepped into the space he'd created.

"There's no escape in here." His voice was low and drum-like, not quite human. "This is my space, my den."

Den, not home? Alarmed, she willed herself not to fight. The smell of whatever fabric covered the ottoman was some-how calming.

"There's no longer a reason for you to be gagged. My near-est neighbors are nearly a mile away, and even if they're home, the trees will muffle any sound you make."

And those neighbors are on your side, aren't they? she wanted to throw at him. *They'll condone whatever you do. Hell, they'll probably help.*

Stopped by the question of what Hawk had in mind, she blinked back tears, but even with helplessness pressing all around her, she remained acutely aware of his legs against hers and his hands on her back. He could, if he wanted, run his fin-gers over her ass until she couldn't think of anything else. Even with her jeans standing guard over her sex, the right amount of pressure in the right place on his part would break her down.

Too much, too much. If, somehow, she had a hint of how

today would turn out, she might not feel quite so in over her head, but damn it, nothing in her life had prepared her for this.

The feel of his fingers at the back of her head, followed by a slackening of the pressure on the corners of her mouth, told her he'd untied her gag. As long as silence had been forced on her, she'd been spared from trying to communicate with him. Now, however, a certain anonymity had been stripped away. It was back to man and woman.

She was still trying to come to grips with the change and new demands that had been forced on her when he reached under her belly. An instant later she realized he'd pushed the waist rope aside and was unfastening her jeans.

"Don't," she begged. "Please don't rape me."

"It'll never be that."

Confusion and maybe relief rendered her speechless. She was still trying to come to grips with what he'd told her as he started tugging her jeans off her hips. Although she tried to press herself into the ottoman, he had no trouble dragging the garment down to her knees. Instead of sliding out from between her legs and finishing the job, he hauled her to her feet and released her.

Gathering herself, she faced him. The confining denim circling her knees forced her to move slowly and deliberately, and yet she noted the wealth of wildlife pictures adorning his walls. The room seemed to be filled with living things, and she longed for the time to study the photographs.

His boots, in contrast to her shoeless state, accentuated the height difference between them, but that was nothing compared to the impact of her bound wrists and hobbled legs. He'd said he wouldn't rape her; she had to believe him.

And deal with her awareness of her skin.

"Why are you doing this?"

"I have no choice."

Shaking her head did nothing to clear her confusion. She

was truly and completely in this man's world, wasn't she? That's what kept running through her mind; she'd stepped into his universe.

Last night she'd pressed her body against his and screamed out a climax that had said everything about physical satisfaction. The time she'd spent in his arms and under him seemed a lifetime ago, and yet looking up at him brought it all back. She'd never felt anything like this for another man, never! No one had ever invaded her personal space in this way, and she didn't know how to handle it.

Or if she wanted to.

Maybe she simply wanted to experience.

No, damn it! You aren't some damn slut—or his sex slave.

The moment she labeled herself his sex slave, she rejected the notion. The last thing he needed was to bend a woman to his sexual will. Quite the opposite: he was more likely to be pursued by lusty females.

Then what was this about?

An image blipped to life, and she recalled how he'd concentrated on what he'd found on her desk. "What did it?" she pressed. "How did it come to be like this between us? Something you read?"

"What?"

She'd seen that look on a fox when she'd written a piece about a wildlife rehabilitation facility. In preparation for her article, she'd accompanied a staff member when he'd taken a fox into the wild to be released after its broken leg had healed. For nearly a minute after its carrying-cage door had been opened, the fox had stared out uncomprehendingly at freedom. Then the call of the wild had reached it, and it had raced away. Mato Hawk didn't fully comprehend her question any more than the fox had comprehended freedom—or maybe it was this moment in time he couldn't fully accept.

"Which was it?" she pressed. "The 1824 diary entry about

that wolf bounty hunter with his throat torn out? I came across that in the state historic society, in case you're interested. I had to wade through a dozen old family diaries that had been donated to the society before I found that. The writer said he was there when the body was found, so . . ."

What was going on inside Hawk? Whatever it was, the intensity in his stare silenced her. There was no need to tell him that wolves had once roamed this area but had been wiped out, surely he knew that. Neither did she want to quote what had been written about the condition of the bounty hunter's throat or the look of horror in his eyes.

"Why?" he asked after a long silence, "did you go looking?"

Maybe she should explain a reporter's curiosity about this area in the wake of Flann Castetter's disappearance and how a small newspaper article about a cougar maybe killing a man suspected of starting a forest fire a few years ago had turned curiosity into obsession, but she didn't.

"I did," she said instead. "Why do you care?"

"Because I have no choice."

Some day, when all this was over, she'd incorporate Mato into an article, and the power of the words she used to describe him would garner her several awards. When people asked what had been the inspiration for her eloquence, she'd smile a mysterious smile and—

Oh, shit, he was coming toward her again.

"You don't want to do this! Call it a mistake and untie me, and I'll—"

Her immobilized arms, she'd already realized, provided him the perfect way to propel her wherever he wanted. Despite her stupid attempt to struggle, he effortlessly dragged her over to the couch and dumped her belly-down onto it. The rich aroma of leather spread through her, and she couldn't help but notice how comfortable it was. She lay flat with no curvature to her spine. If he put a pillow under her head, she might fall asleep.

Sleep? What in hell was she thinking?

The couch height gave her a clear view of his thighs. If she had the courage, she could see more than that part of his anatomy. Instead, tense, she awaited his next move. And she made no attempt to pick up the threads of a conversation that hadn't been going anywhere. Instead she would concentrate on his every move, try to anticipate what he intended to do next. And if he started to slit her throat—

No! He wasn't a vengeful wolf.

Was he?

In the half instant before he touched the backs of her thighs, her thoughts locked on his last name. Then sensation shot through her and wrenched a gasp from her. Dismissing everything she'd told herself about the comfortable couch and a nap, she struggled to sit up.

Of course it took nothing more than pressure on the small of her back to end that insane attempt. And as soon as he'd made his message clear and she'd forced herself to stop resisting, he went back to trailing his fingertips over the sensitive flesh between buttocks and knees. She couldn't say he was tickling her, because he kept the pressure just strong enough that she felt his touch all the way to her leg bones—and elsewhere.

Over and over again he laid claim to her flesh there. Not sure how long she could keep from losing her mind , she struggled to think of something, anything except his fingers. Unfortunately the only other thought to reach her was about a bounty hunter who'd known he was going to die and that his death would be at the fangs of the very creature he'd set about to destroy.

Except for that thought, only Mato existed.

She'd never wanted to be a man's possession, but that's what she'd become, wasn't it? A man who had too many of his namesake's characteristics.

More than the backs of her legs was being touched. Maybe

not touched in the literal sense, but there was no denying the hot pinpricks of sensation throughout her pussy. She should tamp it down somehow, kill the heat, tighten her inner muscles and curse. But her body had been designed to celebrate this *attack.*

Unable to remain still, she rocked from side to side. Her toes dug into the couch, and she'd chewed on the leather before she'd known she was going to. When he pulled her jeans off, she rolled over as far as she could and looked up at him through heavily lidded eyes.

How beautiful he was, raw and masculine, his features darker than she remembered, and his hair like midnight. His intense gaze made her breath quicken, and she should have been afraid, but she was too deep into her body's messages for that.

When he drew her back down onto the couch, she was content to again study his legs. The flesh he touched was becoming more and more sensitive, desire and the need for respite warring with each other. Sanity said she shouldn't allow him ready access to her legs, that her will was in danger of melting away. At the same time, the female animal inside her begged him to continue. Much longer, and she'd forget she'd once had another existence, but maybe it didn't matter.

Maybe only the two of them mattered.

Then his fingers quieted, and she stopped breathing, wondering vaguely if she could start her lungs working again without him showing her how. Then he lifted his hands, and she sucked in a desperate and unbelieving breath, only to hold it again as he untied her hands. Pins and needles shot up her arms, making her gasp.

He pulled her to a sitting position; then, as she rubbed one wrist, he leaned so close she instinctively flattened herself against the back of the couch. Why, she wondered, when his touches had brought her to life, did she crave space? He kept staring at her with an intensity that mirrored hers, his silence and stillness hammering at her until she thought she'd scream. Instead she pressed against his chest. Rather than backing off, he captured a wrist and snaked the rope he'd just taken off her around it.

"Damn it, no!" she screamed, pounding him with her free hand.

It did no good because scant seconds later, he'd lashed her wrists together again, this time in front of her. Not content with that, he fastened them to the waist rope so she couldn't lift them off her body. Helplessness rose in a wave around her.

Taking hold of her hair, he lifted her head. Once again he closed in on her space, and though it would take little to bury her knee in his crotch, she only returned his gaze.

"Are you married?" he asked.

"What?"

"I need to know whether you live alone."

Damn him, he wanted to find out who would start looking for her and when. "Why would I tell you? After everything—"

"I can get that information. I just don't want to take the time. You aren't wearing a ring, but that might not mean anything." Still holding her hair, he cupped a hand under her chin. "What about your parents?"

"Keep them out of this! Whatever you do, don't involve them." *They're going to say I screwed up royally.*

"I might not have a choice."

"Yes, you do." Despite her attempt to keep terror under lock, it lapped at her. Though her parents had taught her from an early age to stand on her own two feet, she longed for their arms around her. "All right, all right! They aren't expecting to hear from me any time soon." She tried but only partly succeeded in taking a calming breath. "No one is." It wasn't the full truth, but close enough that her solitary existence weighed on her.

He looked at her—nothing but looked—and yet she had no doubt he was seeing beneath her outer layers. She couldn't be sure how deep he was going, but he was going much more than she wanted him to. And yet some part of her longed to open up to him, to tell him about the older brother who'd always expected her to keep up physically and mentally and cut her no slack, about the joy and satisfaction and sense of creativity her work gave her.

And of her dreams of one day giving birth to her own children and holding them to her breast.

"What about you?" she demanded when his stare became more than she could handle. "Does anyone else live here?"

"No."

As many times as she turned the word around in her mind, she couldn't find any emotion behind it. She was transparent while he kept everything inside. If that was the truth, she'd never survive their time together.

Survive?

Are you going to kill me? she needed to ask but couldn't. Her only alternative was to live in the moment, to wait for him to reveal his plans for her, to touch her, to control . . .

She'd forgotten that he'd taken hold of her chin, but when he turned her head to one side and then the other, she didn't resist. Perhaps he found what he was looking for because before long he released her. Keeping as much distance as possible between them, she tried to comprehend why he was no longer touching her. Yes, her arms were as helpless as when he'd roped them behind her, and he'd closed her up in his house and stripped off her jeans. But this momentary freedom made it possible for her to pull herself back together a bit. Just because his caressing the backs of her legs had been exciting and erotic was no reason for her to run up the red flag of surrender. Even if she couldn't keep his hands off her, she'd insulate herself against his impact.

Damn him for treating her like a living lump of clay, a nympho.

Once more his hands invaded her space as, using the ropes as a handle, he hauled her to her feet. She was going to try to twist away, she was! But when he pulled her against him and ran a hand over her buttocks, resistance slid off into a space she couldn't find. Maybe, by turning contortionist, she could scratch and pinch, but her hands didn't want to move. In truth, no part of her wanted to do anything except respond.

Nympho? Was it all that simple?

Hating both of them while at the same time slipping free and full into the moment, she locked her knees as his fingers and nails skimmed nylon. It was a touch, just a simple touch. Followed by another.

He worked her relentlessly, never attempting to slide a finger under the fabric but managing to make her feel utterly invaded nonetheless. By turn he traced the elastic around one leg and then the other, and like the damnable fool she'd become, she kept her legs spread so he'd have easy access. Over and over again, his *caresses* bordered on tickling, only to take her deeper. Her skin had never been so sensitive or felt so alive. Instead of studying him as she absolutely needed to, she stared out the window at the trees and sky that should have reminded her of freedom but only emphasized her isolation.

This was his home, his lair, and she was his prisoner. He, a predator, had captured his prey and hauled it in here to play with. Like a cat, he might grow tired of the game and kill her, but she didn't believe that was her fate.

As for what it was—

Oh, shit, shit, he'd planted his hands against her belly and was pushing her back. She fell awkwardly onto the couch, her buttocks near the edge, and her upper body supported by her shoulders. A superhuman effort might bring her upright, but how could she concentrate on that, now that he'd run his forefinger under the panties crotch and was tugging on it, drawing her toward him.

Her own weight kept her in place, but that didn't explain her now widely splayed legs and the way her toes dug into the carpet, her fingers curling inward, mouth open. "Don't, don't," she chanted, though she might crumble if he stopped.

Still holding the cotton off her pussy, he slipped a forefinger into the space he'd created. She was going to die, absolutely die! The only way she could keep on living was by fighting him, by denying his impact, but she couldn't begin to think how she might do either of those things. It was so much easier to let her head flop back and concentrate.

Ah, what was that, his nail kissing her labia? Yes, oh, shit, yes. He understood her so damnably well, understood her need for a light touch interspersed with quick pressure. As long as he kept doing that, she was off balance and hovering on the brink of something that went far beyond a climax. Maybe, if they hadn't had sex last night, he wouldn't be giving her what she needed, but they had, and he was.

Her eyes closed, dragged open, closed again. She kept curling and relaxing her fingers. No matter how many times she reminded herself that she couldn't use her arms, she kept tugging at her bonds, not so she could resist but so she could touch as she was being touched.

Such a simple touch, nothing more than feathery contact counterbalanced by pressure on her clit. She felt herself begin to flow, and the smell of her arousal killed the scent of leather and fine fabric. Even the aromas of pine and earth died.

He was milking her; she couldn't think of any other way to express what he was doing each time his finger slipped into her. It didn't matter that he barely reached beneath her surface and stayed there just long enough to stop her breath. A trickle of arousal was becoming a flood. With it came a stripping away of her strength and the inability to open her eyes. He'd tossed her into a warm, slow-moving river and was helping her float down. Her muscles, what remained of them, tingled, and her breasts kept expanding until the press of her bra became painful. In blind reaction to the pressure, she rolled her upper body about, but either he didn't know what was happening to her, or he didn't care. Not bothering to study her naked expression, he continued to tug on her panties, leaving his other finger free to stimulate. To tease and dominate.

Her legs started jumping, quivering movements that caused her feet to tattoo the carpet. No matter how she twisted and rocked and tried to free herself from the couch and him, he remained with her. And when, gasping, she tried to surge upright, he rammed a finger deep inside her, stopped her.

She hung on him, her juices flooding him, inner muscles clenching, sobbing, and sighing. Fearing herself.

There. Gathering. Rolling over her.

But just as her climax bit down, he pulled out of her and backed away. Heat burned her cheeks and throat. Her world was trimmed in red, exhaustion and disappointment swirling throughout her until she hated him with everything she had. In her mind, she pummeled him between the legs until his cock became a purple, swollen mass, but, in reality, the couch continued to cradle her worthless body.

No, not worthless! Not his to break apart!

Sitting upright took everything she had, but finally she achieved her goal. Her breasts felt as if they might explode, and her cunt still jumped. Convincing herself that her muscles were no longer stripped consumed too much time, and once reality settled itself around her, she wasn't sure what to do with it.

Stand. Show him what you're made of.

A rebel voice taunted that she'd already given him undeniable proof of what little fortitude she had at her disposal, but she nevertheless pushed herself to her feet. Her panties stuck to her wet labia, and her hard nipples rubbed against her bra.

"You damn bastard! What the hell do you think you're doing?"

He folded his arms across his too-broad chest. "What you want me to."

"The hell I do!" If only she could do something about her flaming cheeks. "You have no right."

"Right has nothing to do with it, Smokey. This is about survival, yours and mine."

That couldn't be regret in his voice, could it? The way he'd manhandled her left her with no doubt that he loved his superiority, didn't it? Confused, she came too close to feeling sorry for him.

The woods. That's where she wanted to be. Alone.

Acutely aware of how easy it would be for him to deny her, she walked over to the window and stared out. An amazing amount of sunlight reached the ground despite the surrounding trees, giving rise to thoughts of sitting outside in shorts and getting a tan.

About to turn around, movement stopped her. Something was in one of the closest trees, its coloring nearly lost within the dark green. One second passed and then another as she gave whatever it was her full attention. It was looking at her. That's what it came down to: it was focused on her.

A hawk.

12

Icy fingers killed the heat Mato had infused in her, and yet Smokey was far from terrified. The most intense eyes she'd ever seen continued to scrutinize her. In self-defense, she stared back. Asked the hawk what it wanted of her. If the bird heard, it gave no sign. Neither, she believed, was it judging her. Yet.

Sensing Mato's presence, she shot a glance at him before again concentrating on the predator. "What is it doing here?" she asked.

"Maybe hunting."

"No," she snapped. "It's not that, and you know it. Did you call it?"

"What makes you think that?"

"Because . . . the picture you took . . . it made me think you and the hawk were on the same wavelength."

"We are."

"Are?" she repeated. "Then you did summon it."

"It's more than that, Smokey, much more. Hawk is my spirit."

A memory of the ceremony that had taken place in the rain

outside the schoolhouse distracted her. At that time, she'd believed it was simply that—a ceremony—but if there'd been
something behind the *prayer* to the sacred salmon—no! What
was she thinking? And yet . . . "Your spirit? What does it want
of you?"

She should be used to Mato's silence by now, but his refusal
to respond to her sarcasm grated on her nerves and helped to
further dampen the flames he'd been responsible for. What
would he do if she told him his damnable plan had backfired? It
had, hadn't it?

"Don't bother answering," she said, her voice strong because she'd put effort into it, "because I don't give a damn
about that so-called spirit of yours. It's outside. We're in here."
She paused. "And I'm telling you to let me go."

"I can't."

Much as she wanted to pull a further explanation out of him,
she knew he'd tell her only what he'd decided she could and
should know. Righteous indignation seeped out of her to be replaced by fresh awareness of his body. It had become a magnet
calling hers into its inescapable strength.

Telling herself to resist was useless because suddenly she
wanted him as much as she had before. That's all—she wanted
him.

Once again he used her tethered hands to force her from the
window. The front door wasn't that far away, but it might have
been on the other side of the earth, for all the access she had to
it. She noted the way her feet glided over the soft carpet and
that she again smelled leather before Mato was done hauling
her to the couch. Much as she longed to be sprawling on the
couch again while his hands played her, rebellion filled her and
might have spilled over if she hadn't known how useless fighting him was.

He'd roped his prey, hadn't he? And now she was his.

After positioning her so the backs of her legs pressed against the sofa seat, he released her and stepped away. Again studied her. Her legs weren't model quality, her breasts average, her hair nothing more than hair. Why then did dark desire now rage in his eyes?

You're scaring me, she came too close to telling him.

Only when he abruptly pulled her sweatshirt up over her bra did fear melt into something both familiar and new. She looked down at herself, seeing her swollen nipples through the fabric and feeling the weight of her breasts. His latest goal achieved, he stepped away from her, leaving her free and yet not free while his gaze roamed over what he'd just revealed. Her breasts began tingling. All too soon the sensation became something more intense, not painful but a world away from anything she could ignore. She wanted to squeeze and fondle and, yes, worship her breasts, to lift and cup them and challenge Mato not to touch them. If her hands were free, her breasts would be hers, and he'd have no right to them.

But right now he did.

"What are you going to do?" she asked and then shook her head because hadn't she already thrown a similar question at him and not gotten an answer?

Turning quickly, he looked at the window where she'd spotted the hawk, giving her no choice but to ponder whether there really was a link between human and creature. Before she could make sense of it, she again had his full attention. Not only that, but he was once more killing the too-small space between them. She saw his hands reaching for her, felt electricity arc through her pussy and breasts, froze when he gripped her bra and pulled it up over her breasts, exposing her.

The combined pressure of her top and bra forced her breasts down and out. Although distorted, they represented one thing: sexuality.

Standing so close their feet nearly touched, he caressed not her breasts but the base of her throat. The gesture was nearly gentle, nearly something lovers would do. Could they become lovers? she irrationally wondered. Under other circumstances, would they seek each other out? Tentative, casual conversations would become deeper and more meaningful as they learned to trust, as interest slipped into love.

Love? No! Romance didn't begin with captivity.

But, then, hadn't he been a dark stranger when she'd fucked him last night?

Confused, she nearly handed him her questions only to swallow them because his fingers were no longer on her throat but brushing the tops of her breasts. A long, slow shiver snaked downward, and she unwisely pulled it deep inside her. Something pulsed between them. Her lips became numb; her vision again blurred. Weak, she spread her legs slightly but swayed nonetheless.

Feeling disconnected from her mind, she gave herself up to his gentle touches. There was something almost worshipful about the way his fingers explored the swollen flesh. Half believing he was no more sure of himself than she was made it easier to accept the lingering strokes. Wave after wave of something without a name traveled down her body to settle deep in her core. Her mouth sagged open, and she couldn't be sure, but wasn't she swaying in time with his breathing?

Gentle. That's what she couldn't wrap her mind around. When he could and maybe wanted to be rough and masterful, he continued to handle her as though she was precious to him.

He hadn't expected to feel this way. How she had come to this conclusion, she couldn't say. Neither did she understand why or how she'd been given access to his thoughts, but maybe it didn't matter. Maybe nothing did beyond the heating air around them and his fingers touching every inch of her breasts.

Dizziness washed over her, but although a niggling sense of alarm tried to make itself known, she shoved it aside because his thumbs and forefingers were closing down around her nipples. Another unsettling wave surged when he drew her breasts toward him only to fade as yet more heat channeled throughout her.

Although she'd drunk to excess a handful of times, alcohol held little appeal because she hated losing control. What she was experiencing now wasn't the same thing, and yet the similarities brought back memories of floating, of simply existing. Her brain existed, barely. Her body was hers to command, barely.

She didn't care.

How could she lose control with him in charge? she pondered. Not that the answer mattered. Maybe his gentleness was what made it so easy for her to turn ownership of her body over to him. He hadn't hurt her. Far from it—everything he'd done so far seemed designed to bring her pleasure.

So far.

Although she continued to feel as if she were drifting, she took note of the latest change. He'd already pulled her to him so her right side pressed against him, her leg sheltered and stimulated between his. One hand continued its sensual mastery of her breasts. The other . . . the other had slid beneath her panties and was gliding over her buttocks. Breathing deeply to forestall another wave of dizziness, she struggled to straighten only to give up the insane battle when he yanked her panties down around her knees and his fingers found the cleft between her ass cheeks.

How strange to be grateful for her early morning shower. How strange to wonder if this was really what he wanted to be doing. Most of all, what remained of her mind questioned her utter acceptance of him.

Cool fingers of sensation touched the back of her neck, giving her something new to focus on. The fingers—which were rapidly growing warmer—paused at the top of her spine and then began a downward journey that again opened her mouth and arched her back. Her temples began pulsing, the power there briefly alarming her. She might have shaken her head if not for the distraction of the fingers now pressing against her ass.

He couldn't reach her pussy with her legs this close together, he couldn't! If only she wasn't being tethered by her damnable underpants!

No! She couldn't possibly want them gone. They were all that stood between her and utter vulnerability. Not naked yet, she reminded herself as his embedded forefinger glided over her back entrance. She still had on her top and bra—not that they were doing what they'd been designed to do.

So much change, so little she could comprehend or control.

So little she wanted to?

Was her mind melting? Was that why her body now seemed to be made up of disconnected parts? Her brain was both swollen and nonexistent, her legs little more than liquid fire, her spine both cold and hot, her breasts hard and heavy, arms straining to either embrace or reject him. She hated and loved her bonds, hated and adored everything about Mato Hawk.

The hawk. Was it still out there watching, approving, maybe controlling Mato just as he was doing to her?

Stopped in midsigh by the thought, she tried to look into his eyes, but the two of them stood too close for his features to be anything except a blur. The pressure against her asshole increased as his finger made small and tight swirling movements. Her chest was on fire, but from that or from the fingertip lazily circling her left nipple, she couldn't tell.

Too much! The contrast between firm and light more than she could handle! Mewling like some lost cat, she tried to twist free, only to be shoved back onto the couch. Free! She was free of him!

A single look at the looming figure made a lie of her insane thought, but at least his hands weren't on her and she could think again. Barely.

"Don't," she managed. "Just don't. I can't take . . . I don't want."

"Yeah, you do."

Were his cheeks and throat flushed? And had his voice turned rough because he was warring with something inside him? She wanted to study his crotch but couldn't think how to drag her attention off his face. She'd thought of him as beautiful, hadn't she? Where had that thought come from, when the man was all dark energy and barely contained power, harsh and savage?

And though she damned herself, she wanted that savage.

Needed.

13

Despite the misfiring in his brain, Mato struggled to concentrate on his captive. He wanted to be doing what he was doing—he'd never deny that—but this task hadn't been of his choosing.

Maybe that's what made him feel as if he were drowning.

Even as he roughly yanked off Smokey's panties, a part of him stood off to the side studying what the stranger he'd become was capable of. It was the darkness, that's what made comprehension so difficult. Despite the welcome sunlight, night fluttered around him, and whenever he closed his eyes, it was as if he'd fallen into a deep well. Touching her kept him connected with reality. At the same time, her satiny skin and the scent of soap and arousal pushed him closer to the edge.

Walk away. Turn your back on her and keep going.

No, he admitted with his hands on her thighs and the smell of her swamping him, he could never do that, because Spirit waited outside.

Need screamed at him in a way he hadn't felt since his randy teenage years. Back then he'd been overwhelmed by sex's power and unsure of himself. Now he understood the primal drive, understood that it existed equally between the sexes. All the man he'd become had to do was send a wordless message to a woman, and she'd either respond or ignore his invitation. Most times she responded, though it had never been as Smokey had responded and was still responding.

Of course she is, he chided himself as his fingers moved of their own accord to the whisper softness of her inner thighs. He'd given her no choice; he'd forced himself on her.

Then stop! Don't make it like this between the two of you.

I can't; the choice isn't mine.

Made half sick by the internal argument, he shook his head. The fog lifted marginally and then settled over him again, forcing himself to toss his head while gripping her for balance. Though his surroundings came into focus, she remained in the fog, and he wondered if she was real or part of whatever spell had been cast over him.

Hawk Spirit was responsible.

And those who depended on him to safeguard their world.

Tension had roped her leg muscles, but he now sensed a lessening to her resistance. Even though he couldn't make out her expression, her sprawled-on-the-couch body spoke to him, gave up her secrets. Instead of her knees being clamped together, they sagged apart, and her cunt sent its aroma to him. As soon as it reached his lungs, it spread through his veins. The raging sexuality he'd thought he'd put behind him once he'd reached adulthood slammed into him and dropped him to his knees before her. He then pushed her knees apart and tugged her toward him so her ass barely touched the seat, placed his head between her legs, and commanded himself to taste her. To swallow her offering.

His tongue delved deep and bold, and he easily slipped it between her sex lips to the hot, wet place where everything was centered. She jumped and quivered, writhed about on the couch, cried like a lost soul.

And although he was again standing at the well's edge, he risked it all by licking her offering and bringing it into his mouth. Guided by that force he only half understood, he swirled his saliva and passion-drenched tongue over her labia until her shaking made that impossible.

Rearing back, he blinked repeatedly. She was coming into focus now, and seeing the helpless look in her eyes strengthened his resolve. He'd break her down as Spirit had ordered him, wipe out everything she'd been and believed before him, and turn her into his sex slave, his needy and willing prisoner.

Because if he didn't accomplish—

No! He wouldn't kill her; he couldn't!

"Don't do this," she whispered. "Please. I can't take . . ."

Determined not to let her know she wasn't the only one falling apart, he shoved her legs even wider and dove back in. As he did, she seemed to flow toward him. Did it frighten her to know she'd lost control, or was she too far gone to care? A twin of her weakness began flowing over him, but he ended it by gently closing his teeth around a labial lip and drawing it toward him.

"No, no, no. Oh, god, no."

He might have believed Smokey's plea if not for the wet heat that had made her flesh so slippery. That and the way her body now strained toward him gave away so many of her secrets.

Good. Force her to reveal everything while keeping your own secrets.

Maybe, he acknowledged, switching his hold to her other sex lip, but not if he couldn't manage a stronger grip on his emotions. He was surrounded by her, his head trapped by her soft fullness, and her helpless whimpering tapping into his own sense of helplessness. Seducing a woman had always called for respect and consideration. Not needing to concern himself with her expectations today freed the beast. Instead of empowering him, however, the inner savage was being weakened by fear—of himself.

No! Can't happen!

Briefly, only briefly, he wondered who or what had ordered him to wrap himself in a predator's mantle, but before he could think how or if he might free himself, the predator clamped hold of him. Powerful teeth closed around his soul and conscience, and he became one with his spirit.

Strength surging through him, he sucked her loose flesh into his mouth. He was still closing his lips around her gift when she shrieked and tried to wrench to the side. Not releasing her, he clamped onto her knees and hauled her even closer. Her buttocks slipped off the edge of the couch, forcing her weight onto her spine and upper body.

Good. She couldn't fight him now, could barely breathe.

He was more than a hawk now. Yes, Spirit's single-mindedness continued to rule him, but in his mind he took a cougar as his guide. The woman quivering beneath him was no longer human but prey. A cougar might immediately break the neck of whatever creature it had run down, but he would play with his. Dominate and play.

A deep breath pulled too much of her essence into him; if he continued to handle her this way, he risked losing the battle. Distance. He needed distance.

Releasing her soft outer flesh and backing away might have been the hardest thing he'd ever done, but he had no choice. Standing, he drew her out and away from the couch until only her shoulders remained on the couch and her knees on the ground. Not giving her the chance to regain her balance, he untied the rope from around her waist but left it knotted to her bound hands. If she asked what he had in mind, he wouldn't be able to answer, because that unholy force had hold of him, and he was nothing more than the instrument of that force's determination.

Giving up self-control, he draped the loose rope between her legs. "Stand up," he ordered.

When she only looked up at him, he slapped her flank. "Now! Stand."

Awkward and gasping, she struggled to obey. She was still in the process of standing when he tugged on the rope and forced her hands down to her crotch. Then he maneuvered the rope between her legs and up so it settled into her crack. Keeping the rope taut, he began walking toward the bedroom, which forced her to stumble backward after him.

"Stop, oh, please, stop! This can't—you can't—"

He silenced her with a jerk. "No more talking," he ordered. "If you do, I'll gag you again."

She was crying, not the kind of sobs he'd heard from a woman's throat before, but a mix of fear and anticipation. He had her, not all the way yet, but growing closer. Not giving her the opportunity to look where he was hauling her, he continued walking. Maintaining tension on the rope caused it to press against her cunt and forced compliance out of her.

When the bedroom's familiar surroundings were around him, he stopped, tugging up and lifting her onto her toes. He loved her futile attempts to pull her hands away from her crotch, and although he briefly let her think she might be capable of winning the battle, he soon ended it via another harsh tug that again forced her onto her toes. Reaching around her, he claimed a nipple.

"You're a wild horse," the man beast he'd become told her. "But by the time I'm done, you'll be tamed."

"No, oh, please, no!"

"Silence!" He slapped her breast. And when she tried to twist away, he slapped her again.

Maybe he should have praised her ability to learn when she stopped struggling, but right now he didn't trust himself to speak. Hated himself. Casting around, his gaze landed on the head of his four-poster bed. This time when he pulled on her leash, she dropped her head and backed up. Something perverse took hold of him as he knotted the rope to the top of the bed so she couldn't settle onto the balls of her feet.

Stepping away from his prisoner, he folded his arms over his chest and studied her. Her hands were all but between her legs, her legs spread as she fought to keep pressure off her cunt. Having to lean forward made it difficult for her to keep her head up, but maybe she was staring at the floor because she wanted nothing to do with him.

He wasn't a horseman, and he'd never so much as thought of capturing a wild animal. But seeing her like this filled him with dark heat. He almost believed he could fly like his spirit, fly and dive and tear and kill.

No, not kill her, but close.

Leaving her helpless and gasping, he went out to his truck for her belongings. Part of the force that had overtaken him told him to study her notes and go through her laptop now, but that would have to wait because he couldn't wait to get back to her.

On his way to the bedroom, he glanced over at his kitchen. There on the countertop stood a wooden block filled with knives. Selecting one, he took it with him. The moment he passed through the doorway, darkness again crowded around him. Spirit had claimed him, captured him as surely as he'd captured the female.

The cords pressing against Smokey's labia distracted her from trying to determine what her captor had in mind. Her leg muscles burned, but that was nothing compared to what was happening to her sex. Not painful, not really, something more, something she couldn't begin to wrap her brain around.

When her nerve endings warned her that he was back, she lifted her too-heavy head. Had he become larger? That was impossible, of course, but there was something different about him—more of the beast she'd sensed and seen before, less of the articulate human being who'd argued against development. Did anything of that intense and committed man still exist, or had everything funneled into the primitive? He hadn't harmed her, she reminded herself. Roped and tied and teased and taunted, yes, but no pain.

Knife! He was holding a knife.

"No! No!" The more she twisted, the deeper the rope bit into her; the sensation surrounded her with memories of sex and climax, but she couldn't make herself hold still. "Please, no."

"Shut up!"

What was that, an order or a growl? Whatever it was, it penetrated her fear—she was afraid, wasn't she? Shaking from the effort of doing as he'd commanded, she watched, fascinated, as he took one slow step after another. Closer, closer, his heat reached out to stroke her skin.

Looping his fingers around her bra, he drew her toward him. Memories swamped her of being gagged and having her legs tied, but maybe the restraints weren't responsible for her dumb compliance. All she knew was that her existence revolved around him, and she didn't want it any other way.

The knife should still have unnerved her, should have forced fresh screams out of her. Instead she watched and waited while he severed the bra straps and sawed through the bra in front. Tugging the ruined garment off her, he dropped it to the floor. She thought he'd do the same with her sweatshirt, but once he'd sliced it from neck to hemline, he only pulled it away from her breasts.

Idly stroking the dull side of the knife, he studied her until she thought she'd explode from his unblinking scrutiny. Growling like some demented animal, she kicked at him but couldn't reach him. Brought up short by fresh pressure on her pussy, she glared.

"Do it!" she demanded, though she wasn't sure what she hoped to accomplish by her order. "Just get it done."

His expression revealing nothing, he stepped to her side, where her foot couldn't reach, and cupped a hand under the naked breast closest to him. The instant he touched her, she lost a piece of herself. Maybe she could have tried to shake him off, but she wanted him to touch her, to manhandle, if that's what he had in mind. Not watching Mato freed her from a certain responsibility. She could simply exist, simply feel and anticipate.

A large area rug near the bed covered much of the hardwood floor. The Navajo design surprised her, but maybe he'd chosen it in respect for all things Native American. Where had he found it? That's what she'd think about: a wilderness man stepping into a store in search of something to protect his feet.

A pale, swirling fog slipped between her and images of him sorting through rugs. Even with the mist sliding through and around her thoughts, she was keenly aware of his commanding fingers. He could be gentle and firm at the same time, caress and control with a single touch. At first she wasn't sure why he kept lifting her breast only to release it, but she soon understood. Every time his fingers pressed against her she was reminded anew of how much she needed the contact. He was toying with her, wasn't he, a cat batting about a hapless mouse. Only, he was no cat.

"I don't want this," she lied. "Damn it, don't you understand! I don't—" His hand around her throat silenced her. Dropping the knife, he gripped her wrists with one hand, pulling her hands away from her body and increasing the pressure on her cunt. Despite her struggles, his hold on her didn't slacken, which taught her a vital lesson. As long as she remained his plaything, he'd allow her to breathe and think, but if she tried to take back ownership of her body, she'd be punished.

Punished? No, not that. Something delicious. Something that pulled her back into the fog where the words *captive* and *captor* didn't exist.

He must have achieved his purpose because as soon as she stopped resisting, he released her throat, and the tension against her pussy slackened. Her sex juices kept the rope glued to her, but she made no attempt to shake it loose. Instead she waited, anticipated, prayed he'd touch her again. And when he sucked a breast into his hot mouth, she nearly collapsed.

Having him suckle and nibble her sex lips earlier had nearly been her undoing, but she should be used to lightning running through her veins by now, shouldn't she? There was only so much stimulation the human body could handle, right? When the limits had been reached, the body shut down in self-defense, didn't it? Diminishing returns, that's what she'd tell him. *Give it up. I can't take any more, can't feel—*

Sucking her deep, opening his mouth as far as he could and all but swallowing her breast, he left the other neglected and crying. And then—and then slowly he released her but stopped with her nipple surrounded by damp heat and his teeth sliding over the hardened nub. She shivered, shuddered, fought to remain still, fought to keep her cries locked within her.

Oh, damn, his tongue now, repeatedly flicking her nipple. Heat and lightning flooding her throat and spreading everywhere. So much fire building beneath the damnable rope and needing him in her. Empty and weeping her pungent juices, afraid of but worshipping her body at the same time. Thanks to him, she felt things she had never felt, and she sensed the promise of even more ecstasy.

"Can't—I can't—can't. Can't."

His teeth locked around her nub to hold her breast prisoner while he bathed her nipple. The mist kept building, heating and expanding, spinning her into its center. No longer able to put words together, she used her hands to rub the rope over her labia. There. Just beyond her reach and vision, an end to wanting. A little longer, the rope massaging and drawing her deep into herself.

Let him think he's in charge. I'll show him, get off, teach him that he doesn't own me after all!

Lightning had turned the fog into a white-gold, and her pussy had begun to seize when he spat out her breast. A sound like a wounded and lost animal escaped her raw throat. Then he freed the rope from the bedpost. When he kicked her legs apart so he could draw the rope from between them, she couldn't kill her defeated whimper. She again began to care what he intended for her when he lifted her arms over her head. Short seconds later he'd spun her around and again tied her to the post.

Although she could turn a few inches to one side or the other, the short tether had her facing the bed. She could bend her elbows to keep strain off her shoulders, but that was scant comfort because her backside was now presented to him.

Her ass, within his reach. His to do with what he wanted.

Just thinking about the possibilities sent fluid leaking down her inner thighs. Though she'd never allowed a man to ass-fuck her, she'd given the act serious thought. Thought nothing! More than one session with her vibrators had come to a successful conclusion because she'd built a fantasy around having a cock in her bunghole. As for the fantasies themselves . . .

Wiping the sweat on her upper lip on her upraised forearm, she prayed Mato couldn't guess what she was thinking. How had it gotten to this? Her world reduced to helpless arms and an all-but-naked body because—because why? What did Mato want from her?

Hawk. Hawk Spirit.

His body pressing against her back and his arm clamping around her breasts ended the irrational thought. Before, she'd fought him, but now she was incapable of movement beyond letting her head loll to the side. The pressure on her breasts blinded her to everything else, and he handled them as if they belonged to him. Kneading and pressing by turn, he guided her into a place without form or end. She drifted, waves of sensation rocking her, his body's heat infusing her. Small whimpers escaped her, and she imagined the quiet cries rising until her mist engulfed them. She could no more fight his impact than she could stop breathing.

The hand not on her breasts tightly wrapped around her waist, making her wonder if he thought she'd try to break free, but there wasn't anything she wanted less. He had use for her, a use she didn't understand but that kept her close to climaxing. It would take so little to fly apart.

The thought of his hand between her legs started her panting and darkened the sensual fog she now believed would remain as long as he was around. To be possessed and manipulated, to have screams forced out of her, to beg—

Would she beg him to fuck her? She was that far gone?

No, a small and deeply buried voice screamed. She wasn't his slut, she wasn't!

14

Propelled by the insistent voice, Smokey tried to pull out of Mato's hold. But, his muscles tense and hard and wonderful, he effortlessly drew her back against his erection. Empowered by proof of his response, she set her mind and body to turning his weakness into her strength by pressing her buttocks against him.

"Damn you," he muttered, his breath boring into the side of her neck.

She thought he'd force her off him, maybe by swatting her all-too-available ass. Instead the hand at her waist switched to her belly, where he prodded and pushed until she sagged. A moment later, she planted her legs under her and surged forward.

The instant she did, the hand on her belly plowed between her legs. Cupping her mons, he pulled her toward him. His damnable jeans imprisoned his cock, making her wonder how he could stand the pressure.

Hoping to force his thoughts onto himself and off whatever he intended for her, she ground her ass against the hard lump, but though his quickened breathing said she was putting him through hell, his fingers continued their invasion. Her mons belonged to him, trapped within his grip, being shaken and prodded. And his fingertips! Damn them for breaching her wet folds and entering—entering her!

No, damn you, no!

She caught her breath, certain he'd gag her again, but when he started stroking her with a knowing finger, she realized she hadn't spoken aloud after all.

The mist was inside her now, warm and soft, living fingers gliding over her nerves and slipping into her veins, filling her heart with something she didn't understand, melting her. She didn't trust him, she didn't! And yet even as his nails brushed her labia and clit, she depended on him to keep her upright. It didn't matter that the touches were little more than butterfly kisses right now: they found their way to her womb.

His cock should be in her, damn it! That's what her pussy had been designed for, to house and shelter and sometimes torture a man's cock. He only had to touch her to send her careening off the edge. Much more, and she would no longer be able to stand.

Don't let it happen! Resist—resist everything!

Propelled by her rocketing thoughts, she twisted to the side and pushed her hip at him. Though she wasn't sure what part of his anatomy she'd connected with, she continued her assault. He was trying to get away, moving in counterbalance to her while still gripping her cunt. Sweat bloomed everywhere, and her head roared; she loved this! Loved it!

A bruising grip around her waist lifted her off her feet. Startled, she tensed, waited. Not letting her down, he slid a finger into her and with the invasion put an end to her resistance. Strength flowed from her to leave her rag-doll weak. His finger dove deeper until his palm pressed against her cunt lips to capture them as securely as her hands were. Fire lapped at the base of her throat. Letting her head fall back onto his shoulder, she stared without seeing at the ceiling.

What was holding a naked and turned-on woman like for him? Was his body control so complete that his erection was little more than an annoyance? *No, don't let it be like that for him, don't!* If she was the only one in trouble—

Assaulted by a fresh wave of anger, she tried to kick back. Though he had no trouble dodging her, he set her back on her feet. The hold on her waist slackened, so she no longer had to work at breathing, but he'd completed his task without his finger slipping out of her, and how could she cling to her anger with that going on?

Standing took a great deal of concentration, and she was slow to comprehend the reason behind the deep-seated stretching. A second finger was joining the one she was impaled on! Not a cock, not that ultimate of gifts and power, but wonderful just the same!

Wonderful and wanted? What was she thinking? A reasoning woman would call on everything in her to fight the sensations, to let the damn bastard know he wasn't going to win this battle, but she wasn't thinking. Fog encased, she bent her knees and rocked her pelvis forward in invitation.

He responded by pushing home, by then withdrawing a little only to again shove his fingers as deep as they would go. Yes, fucking her, finger-fucking his sex doll while she danced like some damnable marionette. She grunted like a pig, squeezed and rocked and sweated. Gone. All gone.

Release from the terrible and incredible, hot tension that preceded a climax was a millimeter away and well within her grasp. Squealing in delight, she clamped her muscles around those knowing, no-nonsense fingers and threw back her head so she could breathe.

And then—and then the damnable bastard did it to her again!

"Shit! shit!" she screamed as he pulled free. "Goddamn you!"

"Quiet, quiet," he crooned, stroking her heaving belly with the flat of his hand.

"I hate you! Why are you so cruel?"

"Is that what you think it is?" he asked and kissed the side of her neck.

Of everything he could have put her through, a kiss was the worst. And the best. "I don't know anything," she admitted when she could speak. Her anger evaporated to leave her, what, empty?

"I know you don't."

He wanted her like this, shattered and dependent. The why eluded her; maybe she'd never understand his intentions. And what was that in his tone—surely not reluctance. But maybe that explained the kiss. "Are you ever going to tell me?" *Ever let me go?*

Silence.

Instead of repeating the question, she let her thoughts drift to the hand on her belly. Wet and hot from her arousal, it spoke to an intimacy perhaps more profound than what he'd just put her through. It was one thing for a man to dive into and explore a woman's pussy—that's what fucking was all about, after all. But to stroke her stomach . . . why would he do that if his only intension was to taunt and torture until he'd broken her apart?

He could be gentle; that's what she couldn't understand. And when that side of him slipped out of the cage he sometimes kept it in, she became content in ways that went far beyond sex. They hadn't connected in the ways lovers did—nowhere close. She knew nearly nothing about him and had revealed as little as possible about herself. And yet . . . and yet . . .

Ah, that work-honed hand of his caressing her flesh was quieting not just her agitation but the boiling need that had nearly blown her apart. For reasons she didn't try to examine, she'd stopped worrying about being tied up and stripped and helpless within his home. Neither did she care whether anyone was trying to get in touch with her. She had no interest in the piece she'd come to Storm Bay to write and didn't give a damn whether developer Flann Castetter's body was ever found or if he might still be alive. Her rent and other bills—those concerns belonged to the woman she'd been before she had lain eyes on Mato Hawk.

No, she amended as a fingertip teased her navel, the change had begun when she'd seen the photograph he'd taken of the hawk in flight.

Flight. That's what had happened to her. She'd flown far from everything familiar and had entered the world he'd designed for her, and for as long as he touched and whispered, she was content to have that world embrace her.

He was no longer holding her in place. Instead his body had become a blanket enveloping hers. The same languid warmth had spread over both of them and maybe turned them into one. Wondering if that was true or even possible, she shifted so she was angled back toward him. His hands and arms stayed with her, gliding over her, increasing the heat.

She wanted back the use of her hands. If only he'd let her touch him as he now touched her, she'd guide him into the nothing surrounding her so they could ride it together. She'd linger over the act of disrobing him, and when he was naked, she'd lean over and brush her lips over his belly. An image of his startled and vulnerable look made her smile. This hard and sometimes harsh and always-in-control man would learn that his strength was nothing in the face of her determination. He'd learn that moist kisses could bring him to his knees.

That's what she wanted, she acknowledged even as his hands

met between her legs, for him to kneel on his Navajo rug while she forced him to stare up at her. She'd cinch a leash around his neck so her new possession would understand how fundamentally things had changed between them. She'd secure his hands behind him and tie him to the bed before grasping his cock. No matter how he fought, no matter what he said, she'd refuse to let him go until he'd obeyed her every command.

Service me, she'd order. *Bring me to climax over and over again. When I can't come again, I'll grant you access to me so you can experience the same release. Then I'll leave you spread-eagled on the bed. Waiting for me.*

Although it would be easy enough for him to accomplish, he'd made no move to again invade her core. Instead his hands remained between her legs, just touching her opening, waiting for what?

For her to surrender to him.

"I'll do it," she said. "Whatever you want, I'll do it."

"You already are."

Was she? And was that all he wanted of her? Maybe.

Eyelids drooping, she drew as far away from the bed as she could and then bent forward, extending her ass to him. There, the hard knot of his arousal! Rocking to one side so her buttocks glided over his jeans, she ordered herself not to cry out if he stepped away from her, but though his breath stopped and his arms tensed, he remained in place. She rocked to the other side.

His cock was so close. So little stood between her and that incredible mix of strength and silk. Surely he knew he could have her however he wanted, whenever he wanted, as often as he wanted. She'd do much more than run her naked ass over the shielded mass until he stripped off his jeans, and by the time she was done, maybe he'd never want to put his clothes back on.

Was that possible? she wondered as she continued her improvised assault. Her ability to satisfy him would convince him that he wanted her with him all the time, administering to him, reading and responding to his needs, putting his cock first and always.

Nuts, absolutely nuts. And yet, maybe because she hadn't succeeded in shaking off her near climax, she had spun a fantasy built around him. They might have to concern themselves with the mundane details of earning a living, but when the day was done, they'd reunite in this for-sex room. He'd throw her over the side of the bed so her buttocks hung over the edge supported by her bent and splayed legs. She'd wait, shivering, for him to tongue her to climax. Instead he'd fasten golden clips to her labial lips.

Captured in ways she'd never thought possible, she would prop herself up on her elbows so she could study what he'd done to her. After letting her satisfy her curiosity, he'd add a thin gold chain to the clips and take the chain between his teeth. On hands and knees, he'd back away from the bed, bringing her with him. Master and mastered, owner and owned, partners in the night's game.

Heat ran down her sides. Her breasts were in constant movement as she stroked him in the only way she could. Not knowing where his hands were was disconcerting, but she still didn't believe he intended to harm her. Although she wished she could read his expression, his raw breathing said a great deal. He could walk away if he wanted. A single backward step on his part, and her awkward attempt to tease him would end.

A deep rumble of sound made her wonder if he'd tried to speak. Not stopping her disjointed movement, she tried to look at him only to nearly lose her balance. Planting her feet under her again, she willed him to meet her challenge by stepping even closer.

Instead she heard the sound of a zipper tearing loose. Fresh heat burned her sides. Suddenly she couldn't find him. Alarmed,

she yanked on her bonds and once more risked her balance trying to see behind her. Sensing movement, she widened her stance.
A mental image distracted her. Now the clips were on her nipples, the chain dangling nearly to her waist. More game playing? Maybe he'd had enough of games and was punishing—

Flesh, his flesh! Something between a sob and a scream escaped her when she realized his naked cock was sliding along
her crack. He hadn't had time to remove his shoes, which
meant his jeans and briefs were around his ankles, hardly the
most dignified position a man could be in.

Although she strained to separate her ass cheeks, she failed
to create enough room between them for his cock to fit in. Besides, that wasn't where she wanted him.

"Fuck me. Please, just fuck me."

The words were barely out of her mouth when he slapped
one buttock and then the other. He'd put no strength behind
the blows, and she felt no pain, only a potent wave of desire.

"Do that again. Hit me again!"

"Hit?"

Hadn't he been aware of what he'd just done? Damning the
confining ropes, she willed herself not to fight them. As long as
she stayed bent over like some bitch in heat, could she keep him
with her?

"You've had everything your way." The moment the words
were out of her, she wanted to take them back. "You have," she
continued, the damage done. "Stripping me. Tying me up. Making me crazy with—with everything you've done." *And everything my mind has come up with.*

"I've just begun."

Oh, god, what was he talking about? Hadn't she already
come close enough to losing her mind, and hadn't she already
lost her freedom? An overwhelming sense of defeat stole through
her, causing her head to sag. Just like that, she no longer cared
about trying to get Mato to fuck her.

Maybe she didn't, but her body still did.

Unable to stop herself from quivering, she once more extended her ass toward him. His cock had settled along her rear valley during their brief exchange, and it was still there, a hot and heavy weight. Promising oblivion.

"Do more than begin, then, damn it." Despite the curse, her voice was soft and low. She felt both distanced from her body and more connected to it than she'd ever been. She'd never stood like this, never allowed a man to handle her the way she was being handled. Never bounced between such conflicted emotions. "What next, Mato? Me on my knees before you? Worshipping your cock?"

"I don't want you worshipping anything, damn it."

Despite the unexpected curse, she thought not about his anger but of the totality of his emotions. She could be wrong, but she was all but certain he, too, was in conflict. He might have had one goal in mind when he'd captured her, but it was no longer so simple for him. Suddenly sorry for him, she straightened and would have reached for him if she'd had use of her arms. Short moments later she realized her change of position had robbed him of a home for his cock and her of that delicious weight.

"What do you want of me, then?" she asked even though she'd posed the question before.

"Everything."

The man was going to drive her out of her mind! Hell, he probably already had. Gripping the wooden post her arms were tied to, she rested her forehead on the back of her hands. Enough talking! Words were getting her nowhere. Neither, obviously, had offering her body to him.

But if he was immune, why had he exposed his penis?

And did she want it in her?

Yes. The answer was yes. Simple and mindless.

Groaning in helpless frustration, she again bowed her back, which lifted her buttocks. She'd become like the mares she'd observed while doing an article on thoroughbred breeding. When it had been determined that they were in heat, the mares were led into a stall. With their halters tightly tied to opposite sides of the enclosure, they were unable to escape the stallion that had been selected for them. Granted, hormones had rendered the mares more than ready for mating, but their owners were taking no chances.

"Then take everything!" she challenged. "Unless you're afraid." Where had that come from?

She should have anticipated the slaps to her ass, damn it! After all, she might have done the same thing if the tables were turned. Far from intimidated, she lifted her head in a mix of defiance and anticipation. "Is that how you handle things when people oppose you? Violence makes you the winner?"

By way of response, he clamped his hands over her buttocks. Awash in the delicious sensation, she continued her tirade. "That's what it boils down to it, doesn't it? People like Flann Castetter disappear because they don't do what you believe they should. As for me—go on, tell me, what have I done to anger you?" Driven by the unrelenting grip, she sucked in more air. "What are you going to do to me, Mato? Kill me and leave my body in the wilderness? But not yet, not until you're done playing with me."

"This isn't play."

Oh, shit, he was pulling her ass cheeks apart! As for how much he could see . . . "You—you said you weren't going to rape me, but why the hell not? It's not as if I can do anything about it, or as if I'll live to charge you."

"Rape?" Mato's tone had dropped, causing her to shudder, to wait and try to anticipate. "Don't try to deny the way you've been acting." He slapped her right flank for emphasis. "You want it."

How right he was, only now she wasn't sure what she wanted, thanks to his constantly changing moods. "And you don't?"

His breathing raged, and his hold on her . . . Much stronger, and pleasure would become pain. Nevertheless, she wiggled her ass at him. She would not go down without a fight, she wouldn't! Only, a fight wasn't what she wanted from him.

"Do it, Mato. Just the hell do it."

Was something sucking the air out of the room? Because they were both holding their breaths; not so much as a whisper of sound remained, and in the silence she found something she'd never before experienced. Somehow she'd ceased to be a separate person, not because Mato had imprisoned her, but because for these moments they had the same needs and wants. She could tell him that but prayed he'd come to the same conclusion.

Sensing the change in him, she struggled to lock on to his thoughts. Something seemed to be breaking free of whatever wall he'd build or had been built around his mind, but then he lightly raked his nails down her spine, and she howled. Heat licked her from throat to thighs, causing her to toss her head like some nervous and excited horse. Increasing her hold on the bedpost, she concentrated on keeping her legs under her. The too-familiar heat had begun to cool when he raked her again. As he did, she sweated.

"That's all it takes, isn't it?" he demanded. "Whenever I touch you, you lose it."

She couldn't lie to him now; what would be the point?

"Nothing to say, Smokey? What happened?" One hand pressed down on the base of her spine while he used the other to lift her right leg. "You've been full of words since I ungagged you."

If this was what it was to be a prisoner, she never wanted to be free, especially because he was reaching between her legs. The pressure on her spine streamed through her.

"One thing I need to hear from you," he said as he cupped her mons and drew her close. "Is or isn't it going to be rape?"

"I want!" the wild animal she'd become screamed. "Want to fuck!"

Where had his hands gone? The moment of terror faded when she realized he was still behind her, but not knowing what he had in mind had her twisting toward him. She'd reached the limits imposed by the ropes when he forced her back around via a hold on her flanks. Muttering something she sensed she didn't want to hear, he scratched the base of her spine. She was trying to stay on top of the electric shot when he kicked her legs apart and pushed his cock home.

His cock, inside her. An end to what had felt like years of anticipation and loneliness and wanting. Because he barely penetrated, she shouldn't feel invaded, and yet she did. Invaded and fulfilled.

He doesn't want to be doing this.

What a ludicrous thought. After all, what male didn't want sex? But though his erection left no doubt of his arousal, his complexity ran deep.

And not just complex. He was more than a man.

Before she could free herself from the irrational thought, another image invaded her overloaded brain and body. This time she was given not glimpses of kinky sex but of a hawk darting in and out of the trees. Its made-for-death body was intent on something, but she couldn't see what it was. Something had disturbed its world, and until order had been restored, it would soar and dive, soar and dive, search.

That was Mato, too? He'd decided to fuck her as a way of relieving his tension? If only it were that simple for her.

Desperate to distract Mato from his dark and unsettling thoughts, she closed her cunt muscles around him, and he responded in the way she prayed he would.

Deeper. Slow. Unrelenting. His muscles straining to control the beast in him.

Staring unseeing at the ropes around her wrists, she followed his measured journey into her. A frenzied assault would have her already climaxing, while this, although barely manageable, allowed her to celebrate her womanhood. She was a vessel, his vessel. Cunts and cocks cared nothing about relationships, the past or present. They understood pleasure and nothing more.

This was her pleasure, reward, and promise, so her inner tissues welcomed him one inch at a time, and although she quivered in anticipation, she trusted herself not to lose control.

Did mares feel this delicious waiting, or was sex nothing more than the instinct for survival? How wonderful to be a human, a woman.

A captured woman.

What was that fantasy she'd had earlier? she pondered with him in her clear to his balls and his hands linked over her belly. Oh, yes, as her *master* he'd fastened clamps to her breasts and labia.

That's what she wanted, her breasts tingling and hot while the chain dangled between them, her labia still smarting from having the clips removed for sex. When he was done using her, he'd put them back on so she wouldn't forget the totality of his control.

No, she amended, the fantasy fading because he'd started pulling out of her, she'd never need clamps or ropes to remember her captor, her master, her man. Her body would never forget him.

The ropes and her wrists blurred as her pussy wept in anticipation. She was shrinking and becoming nothing more than a cunt, a cunt housing a great cock. Much as she wanted to keep him buried in her, she needed sleek friction, so forced herself to remain still while he drew free. Losing him was like losing a part of herself, but then he returned, her lubrication guiding him home.

His pace both maddened and relaxed her. How he could

keep himself under such control alarmed her because where she was all hot need, he seemed disconnected from his body. He intended to slowly work her into mindless frenzy while calmly recording her responses? As for what he intended to do with his information and superiority . . .

Low gear shifted into second, and with his increased speed came hints that he wasn't in as much command as she had first thought. Although she needed more than those hints of what he was going through, how could she concentrate in the wake of what he was putting *her* through?

Fucking was suppose to be a joint activity, right? The reality of being allowed to do nothing except wait for him had her off balance. More than unbalanced, she admitted as his nails left trails of sensation from the back of her neck, over her shoulder blades, and then down to her waist. She was a hapless leaf in the grip of a hard wind, tossed about, being torn apart, flying here and there.

Third gear. Sometimes holding her in place via the powerful hands encircling her lower belly, sometimes releasing her so she was forced to brace herself. Her legs shook. She could escape the impalement by straightening and hugging the bed, but that was the last thing she wanted to do. Granted, she wasn't fool enough to think he wouldn't haul her back into place, but more important, she *had* to climax!

Teeth grinding, she forced her mind off her still heating body and onto what little she might learn about him. The measured breathing was gone; he now hauled in air as if desperate to keep his lungs inflated. She smelled his sweat—though maybe it was hers mixed with what drops leaked from him. When he was this deep in her, she half believed his head could reach her throat, his balls flattened against her buttocks, their wet heat reinforcing what his labored breathing was telling her.

Sex was messy and loud, awkward. As embers burst into flames inside her, her arms glistened. Not thinking, she licked a forearm and ran salty sweat around in her mouth. Far from satisfied, she licked again. She'd stuck out her tongue to lap from her other arm when he slammed into her with such force that she jammed her nose on the back of her wrist. Pain shot into her temple.

"Fuck," she moaned. "Fuck."

Either he didn't know what had happened or didn't care because, shifting into overdrive, he hammered into her. Even before the pain in her temple receded, he caught her. The point of no return was here, spreading over her, claiming her cell by cell. She wanted to wait, to have him come first, because that way she wouldn't be so vulnerable, but the brakes were off. And she was spinning, spinning.

"Ah! Ah, shit!"

Her mouth hung open, but she didn't know whether she was still screaming or had found the strength to be silent again. Her legs shook anew, and her locked-in-place knees felt as if they might shatter. Furious and rejoicing her body, she willed herself to remain anchored to him.

Then her climax struck. Sounds spilled from her. Sex muscles spasmed and clenched, trapping him inside her. Riding him, she wrapped her mind around her climax in a effort to keep it going.

To bring him with her!

A shudder, running through him. A deep voice spewing nonsense.

And then he pulled free.

"No!" she screamed. "No, goddamn, no!"

Hot cum burned the small of her back, his hot essence running down her sides. And she understood.

He'd forgotten a condom but not responsibility.

"Thank you." She wasn't sure she meant it.

15

A few minutes ago Mato had either been asleep or nearly so, his long, hard body motionless beside Smokey on the bed, but now he was standing at the window with his naked back to her. Although he'd freed her from the bedpost, he hadn't untied her hands, prompting her not to make the mistake of trying to convince herself that their relationship had changed.

The tension now running through him was in such marked contrast to the essence of a man at rest following sex that it distracted her from her own climax-created lethargy. Telling herself she wasn't afraid of him, she nevertheless was careful not to do anything that might draw his attention to her.

He was a man on the edge, but on the edge of what? The muscles on his arms and legs seemed to be growing tauter by the moment, forcing her to contemplate what she could do or say if whatever was building inside him exploded.

The hawk. He was either looking for or communicating with the damnable hawk! Hating the bird as she'd never hated anything, she forced herself to concentrate on her breathing. Wanting to wreak havoc on a bird made no sense, but she now understood that the predator was far from simply being one of nature's creatures. She'd entered a world and an experience she'd never known existed and now had to accept it for what it was: her new reality.

So this man who'd both fulfilled and imprisoned her was in tune with a bird, was he? What might happen next—what might whatever the hawk was want of Mato?

Shaken by the question, she let go of the lingering aftermath of sex and faced reality. Mato wasn't in tune with his *spirit* after all. Instead the predator controlled him in some unfathomable way. It had commanded the man to capture her, and he had. Bottom line.

If the *spirit* wanted her dead, Mato would obey.

"Is it out there?" she asked.

"Yes."

Having anticipated that he'd sidestep the question, it took her a beat to absorb what he'd just said. "What does it want?"

"Me."

Tears burned, though she'd already known what he was going to say. For a moment she felt sorry for Mato, but if he'd wanted nothing to do with the mysterious *thing*, he could have left the area, couldn't he? True, his roots were here, but if *her* survival depended on fleeing, she'd do so in a heartbeat.

Her survival?

Shoulders squaring, Mato spun and faced her. He was magnificent in his nudity, and intimidating. How could she just have had sex with someone so dark and hidden? And yet wasn't his savage night quality part of his appeal?

A flicker of movement outside the window distracted her, and though she knew what she'd see, the outstretched wings of the hovering creature dried her throat. The hawk was so close she half believed it was about to crash through the glass. Needing reassurance, she turned her attention back to Mato.

For a length of time so short it might have only been illusion, she was looking at not a human being but a bird of prey. Cold and intense eyes bored into her. Before she could think how she might defend herself, the human returned, and yet his eyes retained an unnerving, cool detachment. If he'd looked at her like this earlier, she couldn't have handed her body over to him.

"Talk to me," she tried, unsurprised to hear her voice shake. "What are you thinking?"

Though she tried to prepare herself for any response, his silence left her adrift. His gaze stayed on her, and yet she wasn't sure he was seeing her or even knew who she was. When he started toward her, her heart skipped beats. Chilled and hot at the same time, she struggled to make sense of the changes in him. In some respect he resembled a stalking lion. A hungry lion didn't concern itself with anything except satisfying its hunger. Whether his prey was a newborn gazelle or a heavily pregnant zebra or some animal much larger than himself meant nothing to him. He'd kill by tearing out the hapless creature's throat and begin feeding before the heart had stopped beating.

She was no longer a woman to Mato, no longer Smokey Powers.

Terrified, she scrambled onto her knees and held out her hands as best she could to protect herself, but even as she contemplated the manner of her death, she couldn't help admiring the man. Savagery suited him. He'd been designed for strength and, yes, violence. Rules and laws meant nothing to him; he'd do what he had to. And he wouldn't regret his actions.

I don't want to die! Not at your hands.

A low, rolling cry spilled from him. His fingers clenched, making her think of a cat retracting its claws. His nostrils flared as though pulling her scent into him. Could he smell her fear?

Then his head snapped back and his eyes widened, and she had no doubt he was reacting to her fear. Instead of attacking as she half expected, he whirled and stalked away. His retreating body appeared tense enough to shatter. She didn't breathe until he'd walked out of the room. A floorboard creaked. Something thumped against the bedroom window. Her hands at her throat, she stared but saw only an indistinct shadow.

"You're out there, aren't you, damn you," she hissed. "Waiting for him. Tearing the humanity out of him."

You don't understand.

Shocked speechless, she curled into a tight ball. Up until now she'd managed to cling to the edge of actually believing what was happening, but the three words resonated as clearly as if they'd been screamed into her ear. And they hadn't come from a human throat or mind.

Hawk Spirit existed.

The front door slammed shut, pulling her from the pit she'd fallen in. Mato had left her. What was so compelling he hadn't had time to dress? Despite the unsettling image of him striding naked through the forest, she couldn't deny that it also turned her on. Only a man who was more animal than human would expect the wilderness to embrace him as God had designed him.

Where was he going, how long would he be gone, and what would he do to her when he returned? A glance at her hands reinforced how easy it would be for him to tear her apart. At the same time, it wasn't as if she'd been left tied to the bed with no way of avoiding the inevitable.

"Get up," she fiercely ordered herself, abeit in a whisper. "Get the hell out of here." Instead of following through, however, she stared at what he'd done to her hands. If they were long-time lovers comfortable with each other, they might have mutually designed bondage as playacting, but there was nothing fanciful or deliberately arousing about having been tied up by a near stranger, a stranger ordered about by a *hawk*. It didn't matter that he'd been careful not to cut off her circulation—the purpose had been to impose his will on her.

On the heels of another "Get the hell out of here," she un-curled herself so she could plant her feet on the floor. Her mind fairly swam with possibilities and complications until she spot-ted the knife he'd used to cut off her clothes. Crouching, she snatched it up. Although the knife had been created to accom-plish mundane cooking chores, it was sharp enough for any propose, including slitting someone's throat.

No, damn it, he hadn't planned to kill her!

Had he?

Despite the tremors assaulting her, she forced herself to face yet more facts. The civilized human being others called Mato Hawk wouldn't so much as think about spilling anyone's blood, but he was much more than a mortal man, and that creature, that beast, might do whatever his *spirit* ordered.

Sawing through the cotton strands while grasping the knife in her fingertips ate up time she needed to be spending getting out of there, but finally her arms dropped to her sides. Some-thing shifted in her as the rope fell to the floor. She was free— yes, still naked and in his lair, but free.

Unwilling to entertain the thought of fleeing in her birthday suit, she opened dresser drawers until she found a faded sweat-shirt. It fell nearly to her knees, protecting and sheltering her. His shoes were in his closet, and though they were many sizes too big, after jamming a pair of socks in the toes, she slipped on a pair of slippers. Then she started toward the door, only to stop and snatch up the knife again. She didn't ask herself what she was capable of using it for.

Though she knew he wasn't in the house, it took all the courage at her disposal to walk into the living room. She wasn't going to look at his paintings, damn it, and yet she did. Condi-tioned by her last memory of him, she expected them to be dark and brooding. Instead the majority of his photographs had made liberal use of sunlight. Some, like the fawn pushing against fallen leaves and pine needles with its nose, were whimsical. Maybe Mato Hawk could laugh after all. How incredible it would be to hear his laughter and see joy in his eyes!

Blinking back unexpected and yet necessary tears, she tiptoed to the front door. Gripping the knife so tight her fingers threatened to cramp, she slowly turned the knob and pushed. As she did, crisp and wonderfully clean air swept over her. A gentle breeze had the trees waving in welcome. With her eyes scanning her surroundings and her heart tapping wildly against her chest wall, she hurried down the stairs and stepped onto damp earth.

Run! Run!

The forest he'd been born into and raised in cradled Mato as he made his way to the cliff he'd been coming to for as long as he could remember. He walked with purpose, and if whatever littered the path dug into the soles of his feet, he was unaware of it. No part of him was concerned with his nudity, and he thought only briefly about the woman he'd left behind.

Spirit had called to him. Spirit needed him.

The remnants of last night's storm steamed up from the ground, adding to the sweat already on his skin. An insect landed on his right shoulder blade and either bit or stung, causing him to slap himself there. Something about the instinctive act penetrated the haze wrapped around his mind, and he remembered another touch, the slide of flesh against flesh, his cock housed in a woman's warmth. After brushing off the insect he'd killed, he ran his fingers over his cock, rekindling more memories.

He'd wanted to be with her; he remembered that. Looking at her had stirred dormant longings for someone with which to share his life.

Don't think of her! Obey me, only me!

Familiarity with Spirit's commands should have made his acceptance easy, but for the first time in his life, he resisted. He didn't fully understand the inner war, just that he'd always regret it if he didn't fight. Concentrating on walking failed to clear his mind. If anything, he became more confused.

There was Spirit, whom he loved and respected and had always obeyed, just as his relatives and ancestors had obeyed their spirits. And then there was the woman: softness and large, expressive eyes and a body made for his. The scent of sex on her, and his seed on her skin.

Not *on* her next time! Inside her, filling her, turning them into one and maybe giving him a son or daughter.

The thought slowed his steps and cleaned yet more of the confusion from him, but then the smell of the sea seeped into him, and he remembered what his spirit had ordered him to do. Although Spirit occasionally guided his thoughts, regardless of where he was, most revelations and commands came while he was standing at the ocean's edge looking out at the vastness of the world beyond Storm Bay. Despite his inner conflict, he'd been heeding those commands all his adult life and couldn't comprehend doing otherwise, so he lengthened his stride until he stood looking down at the restless surf. The storm's aftermath was still evident in the higher-than-usual waves and piles of debris that had washed up on the beach. At this spot, the beach was more than a hundred feet below his perch, and he wondered if he might, like his spirit, take flight before he crashed to the earth.

Would Spirit give him the gift of flight?

I'm here. Again turning myself over to you.

Have you? his spirit demanded. *I see a man weakened by a woman's body.*

Not weak, never! I am your strength, your servant.

Do not lie to yourself, Mato Hawk. You tell yourself that loyalty to the spirits still makes your heart beat, and you have blinded yourself to certain dangers.

What dangers?

Her! She has crawled into your mind and heart.

A tension unlike any other flowed through him. This wasn't the first time he'd questioned the spirits' commands, but that, he'd convinced himself, had come from his independent nature. He had a brain and insisted on using it, unlike some of his fellow clan members who mindlessly obeyed the spirits. More than once he'd begged the others to think for themselves, but in the end he'd always fallen in line because the spirits spoke with the same soul he did. This time was different.

You ordered me to capture her, he pointed out. *Surely you saw what happened. Taking away her freedom and imposing my will, my sexuality, on her has changed her. Now she craves me.*

No more than you crave her.

Was there no end to what Spirit saw? *I'm a man with a man's weakness. Surely you knew—*

You're more than a man, Mato Hawk! Without you and others like you, the spirits are helpless. When this place we love is in danger, all we can do is fear and mourn. You are our hands.

Spirit was right because even as he stood motionless, he sensed fresh strength seeping into his muscles. But instead of being grateful for the gift, he longed to run from everything it represented. *Say it,* he forced. *Tell me what you want.*

She is more dangerous than I anticipated. Her will has not been destroyed; she has not become your slave.

He didn't want a slave. He wanted . . . what? Surely not a partner.

You are silent, Mato Hawk. But behind your silence I sense your struggle. She has touched you and weakened you. That cannot be! It must not, because we need you.

Impressions suddenly bombarded him. He cringed at the *sight* of massive equipment felling countless trees and tearing at the earth, and he *heard* the frightened cries of birds and animals as they fled the destruction.

At the same time, the Smokey Powers part of his mind kept

trying to fight her way to him, her arms outstretched. Remembering the feel of her sweet body, he mentally pushed at the enveloping fog. He was reaching for her when he noted that she held a laptop in one hand while the other effortlessly carried a large power saw.

Even as Smokey hurried down the dirt road leading from Mato's place to the highway, she wondered if it would do her any good. She might reach the highway before he discovered she'd escaped, but what if someone from Storm Bay spotted her? Instead of helping her, that person might run her down.

Was it possible that everyone who lived around here knew what the other residents were doing? In the past she would have laughed at the notion of a large conspiracy, but Storm Bay was unlike any place she'd ever been, and Mato was a highly respected member of the community, a leader.

More than a leader, she acknowledged as she slogged along in the too-big shoes. He was the alpha male.

So what did that make her, the alpha female? According to her admittedly limited wolf knowledge, the primary male mated only with the lead female. That might have gone to her head if not for the not-so-minor matter of his having kidnapped her.

Maybe she should have remained at his place. Instead of cutting and running like some scared rabbit, she should have waited for him to return to explain his bizarre actions. Once he'd dumped on her, she'd soothe the savage beast in ways that flooded her throat—and more—with heat and in so doing establish her role as alpha's legitimate mate.

How in the hell could she be contemplating such nonsense? The man had captured her, a member of the press. He might not have spelled out his reasons for doing so, but she'd gotten the point. He didn't want her writing certain things about Storm Bay. As for how far he'd go to keep her from doing her job—

The wind had been all but nonexistent, but now a gentle breeze was rustling—oh, shit, not the breeze! For an instant she half expected a wolf or cougar to attack from the underbrush, but then Mato emerged.

Mato, striding toward her, his eyes burning with a hunter's intensity. Screaming, she broke into as much of a run as the damnable slippers allowed, but even as she plowed ahead, she knew she was doomed.

All too soon she realized he wasn't overtaking her. Instead he was matching her pace and stalking her. Glancing behind her, she chilled at the lack of humanity in his eyes, where always before they had revealed his determination and passion. Berating herself for not bringing the knife with her—could she really use it on him?—she planted one foot after the other because she had no choice.

The too-distant highway became her salvation. Some vacationer would come around a corner the moment she stumbled onto the asphalt, stop, and let her in. Maybe her rescuer would be a trucker. Yes, a hardworking man accustomed to watching his own back who kept a tire iron or baseball bat next to him and knew how to use it. The moment the big, unshaven trucker spotted her fleeing her savage-eyed pursuer, he'd come to her defense. Swing his weapon at Mato's head.

The horrid image faded as she caught the distant sound of an approaching vehicle. The highway! Freedom!

16

Stumbling more than running, Smokey willed herself not to panic. In many respects, Mato had become an animal and as such might have little comprehension of the world around him. He was still stalking his prey, concentrating on her, not caring about civilization's sounds.

Though a part of her knew he wasn't that simple, when she caught a glimpse of the dark ribbon of asphalt cut through the vegetation, she cried out in relief. Then, before she could reach the shoulder, Mato leaped at her, his arms clamping around her waist. Spinning both of them, he propelled her back the way they'd come. She screamed as he half lifted and half shoved her into the forest to their right, effectively hiding them from the unseen driver. He set her back onto her feet and then pushed, knocking her to the ground.

More terrified than angry, she scrambled onto her hands and knees before looking up at him. Any hope she might have clung to that he wasn't as wild as she'd feared died because those eyes belonged on an animal, not on a caring human being.

No, she amended, not an animal, but a hawk. He'd driven his talons into his prey and was on the brink of tearing it apart.

"Mato! Mato, it's me!"

A low, chilling howl rolled from his throat as he stepped closer. His legs were widespread, arms extended toward her with his fingers curled clawlike. His flaring nostrils left no doubt that he sensed her fear. Taking advantage of a prey's terror might be a predator's greatest strength, but how could she force herself to calm down, to meet strength with strength? The last time she'd been with him, despite everything, Mato had been a productive member of his community, a homeowner. Now he was all predator.

Hawk Spirit's doing.

Hatred of the being that had taken away the man she'd believed she knew washed away much of her fear. How dare that force or element rob her and Mato of something rare, exciting, and overwhelming! Yes, the sex had been incredible, but it had been more than that—deep and life-changing. Even though a part of her screamed that she had to try to get to the road, after standing, she stepped toward him. Only inches separated them before she acknowledged the energy all but exploding in her. So she'd become primal herself, had she? Even in the possible face of death, she wanted to mate.

His hands still reached for her; his fingers indeed reminded her of deadly talons, and his stance left no doubt she could never escape him. Fine. A female wild animal didn't flee her mate. Instead she matched strength with strength, need with need.

"What do you want?" she demanded because she needed to hear his voice. "Just the fuck tell me what you want from me!"

If anything, his second growl was deeper than the first. Every bit of awareness in his system was locked on her, and yet he wasn't looking at her. Instead she suspected he was seeing legs and breasts, a neck and a cunt, something living to mate with. And if the female wasn't willing, she became something to take. To rape.

"Goddamn it, no!" Propelled by fury, she slapped him with all her strength. His head snapped to the side. "It's not going to be that, understand? I'll never let—"

Lowering his head, he rammed it into her midsection. Gasping, she fell backwards, arms and legs sprawled. When she could breathe again, she stared up at the naked man now straddling her. Maybe, if she was stupid enough to try, she could kick him where no man wanted to be kicked, but not only wasn't she sure she could maneuver the damnable slippers into position, hadn't she just learned that he met violence with violence?

"Can you hear me?" she asked as calmly as possible. Speaking made her midsection burn.

Something, maybe awareness, glittered in his eyes. But before she could be sure, a curtain of some kind settled over them, and she found herself looking at an unsettling gray that made her think of dense fog. Was he deliberately distancing himself from her, or had a force beyond his ability to fight come between them? Drinking sometimes did that to her. With a buzz going, she might be able to carry on a conversation, but she honestly didn't give a damn about the other person, and she couldn't access her emotions.

Hawk Spirit had taken over Mato's mind.

Would Mato truly do whatever he was ordered to do—even kill her? The possibility was real; otherwise she wouldn't keep asking herself the question.

"What are you going to do?" Clamping down on the fear that accompanied her question, she tried another tact. "Are you trying to decide how to kill me?" Propping herself on one elbow made it easier for her to keep an eye on him. "Can you do whatever you're contemplating without feeling anything? I'm no longer anything to you? Maybe I never was."

She'd never seen anyone become so utterly motionless. Even

the occasional breeze seemed to leave his hair alone, and if he was breathing, why wasn't his chest rising and falling? For reasons she wasn't about to probe, she found his quiet erotic and arousing. His cock was flaccid, evidence of how remote and untouchable he was.

"Do you remember what happened between us?" Desperate to get through to him, she tugged up on the sweatshirt hem so her upper thighs were exposed. "The sex."

If only he'd blink, at least that way she'd know he was present in more ways than his physical body, but his stillness continued.

"We had sex, fucked, mated, whatever you want to call it. And although you kept my hands tied, I wanted it as much as you did. Doesn't that count for something?"

Her muscles had been so tense they hurt, but now they seemed to be softening, tautness slipping from them as another sensation pushed its way to the forefront. She knew what it was; she just couldn't quite believe she was turned on by this man who might have run her down so he could kill her. Her world consisted of one thing—him.

"You aren't the same man I saw at last night's meeting." She intended the words for both of them. "Something happened to him, took him away. I don't—I don't know what to do with what I'm looking at now." Feeling exposed by her admission, she debated sitting up, but maybe any movement on her part would trigged the attack instinct in him. Was that it? she considered. The only way she might reach him was by treating him as if he were an animal?

The sexiest animal on earth.

"I'm afraid of you," she admitted. "If that gives you a feeling of power, so be it. I think that's what you want anyway."

When had he started breathing? she again wondered. And he'd just shifted his weight onto his right leg. Now if he'd only give some indication he heard her—but those eyes of his remained devoid of emotion, and there was still no life in his cock.

"If it were me, I wouldn't be proud of myself. What's manly about throwing a woman to the ground? Maybe you think I'll see you as this macho hunk and fall all over myself trying to do whatever the hell it is I think you want."

She had to shut up! She wasn't making any sense.

When he reached down and grabbed the sweatshirt, her first instinct was to try to slap his hand away, but a glance at his features warned her not to try. She didn't fight as he hauled her toward him. Holding her in place, he studied the oversize slippers, but she wasn't sure whether he realized they were his. Neither did she know if he recognized her. Being this close to him was exactly what she didn't want, and yet she'd give anything to get just a little closer, to press her breasts to his chest and stroke his cock.

A man in turmoil? Or a man too far gone.

"Where did you go?" she tried. "You didn't even take time to dress. The way you left me, it didn't occur to you that I'd try to leave, did it?"

She was speaking, and yet Mato didn't try to make sense of her words, because it took all his concentration to comprehend that he'd run down his prey. He didn't remember making the decision to stalk her, and although he must have been responsible for her being on the ground, he couldn't recall touching her. His vision and thoughts spinning, he struggled to make sense of the sounds and sights inside his brain. Because he'd heard his spirit's commands before, he knew what was expected of him, and yet today he questioned instead of blindly obeying.

Why? It had something to do with the helpless female and his body's lonely ache. If he spread her legs and buried himself in her, if explosion and release followed, maybe then he could think.

Struggling to ignore his spirit's strident voice and stirring cock, he crouched before his captive. Seeing her try to shrink away filled him with power, but then he read fear in her eyes and hated himself. *It shouldn't be like that,* the inner beast insisted. A predator cared nothing for the feelings of those under its control. Only domination mattered.

Not a predator—a man, a man whose body has been fed by this woman.

Unsure of what he had in mind, he tightened his hold on her and pulled her even closer. Doing so made the too-big garment ride further up her legs, giving him a glimpse of the fine matte of hair over her sex. She made no effort to cover herself. Neither did she try to sit up or kick free. That curling hair had been so soft to the touch, part of the whole woman.

Kill her!

Shaking his head failed to dislodge Spirit's order. Giving up, he relaxed his hold but gave no thought to freeing Smokey because he needed to feel her skin, needed her close. Otherwise he might become a monster. Hunger more powerful than anything he'd ever experienced raged through him, and though he knew he was lying to himself, he refused to admit he preferred death to never fucking her again.

She was more than his captive, more than his prey, but what?

Confused by the labels he'd tried to place on her, he dug deep into what little there was of his mind. As he did, he took off the one slipper and threw it away because barefoot she couldn't run. He was someplace between a man and a bird of prey, his brain splintered, and she was responsible.

Angry at her and yet not, he roughly bent her knee outward. Grasping her other ankle, he dragged her closer so he now knelt between her legs. Her woman scent invaded him. The raging hunger directing him, he released her, but only briefly.

Of its own will, his middle finger pushed her folds apart, exposing the wet opening.

"Don't do it, Mato, please, not like that."

Mato. Yes, that was his name. As for how she knew it—

A memory. Her naked and on her knees with her back to him, her hands bound in front. He was fucking her, his cock so deeply buried he couldn't see it. Long, thin marks marred the flawless skin over her spine, and he knew he was responsible for them. Had he forced her, ignored her pleas as he was doing now?

Wrapped in confusion, he dipped into her. The moment he did, her muscles loosened. Now she stared at the sky with her lips parted and her breasts heaving. A woman. She was a woman.

And he a man.

No, he hadn't raped her earlier; she'd wanted sex as much as he had.

Kill her.

Clenching his teeth, he again shook his head, but the inner voice repeated its harsh command, and he fought it in the only way he could think of by running his free hand inside her garment until he reached her breast. Yes, more softness, more of the sweet heat that was part of being human. Squeezing her breast as if it were a lifeline, he began a circular motion. Her eyes wide, with too much white showing, she squirmed under him.

"What are you doing? Mato, I can't—oh, god, I can't—"

Those breasts, in his mouth, his cock buried between them. Her body under and over and next to his, licking and kissing and nipping, drawing his cock into her mouth and holding him there until he exploded. He might kiss her in gratitude then, might tease her into her own climax, holding her over the flames until, exhausted, she begged for relief.

Was that what he wanted of her, to hear her beg and watch her helpless squirming, to know he ruled everything about her?

Wet heat between his fingers brought him back to reality, and he realized he now had two fingers inside her while continuing to massage her trapped breast. She kept opening and closing her mouth but was no longer speaking. Instead the sounds coming from her belonged to an animal.

Like the one he was?

She wouldn't want that—what woman would? Unless he existed fully as a man, he'd lose her, and could he survive?

Though he'd long embraced the link with his spirit, he now fought the connection. He wanted Smokey to be human, and he needed the same for himself.

Smokey. Yes, that was her name. As for why she'd come to Storm Bay . . .

Kill her.

"No!" he cried and then started, shocked by the desperation in his voice. Turmoil tumbled in him, and although he kept his hands on her, he couldn't concentrate on more than that. Even when she again squirmed and moaned, he did nothing more than stare at the treetops. True, a hawk been there earlier. Maybe Spirit was testing him, taking away nature's creation until he'd proven himself worthy of the responsibility that had been bestowed on him.

How weary he was of the responsibility! How tired of worrying about safeguarding the forest he loved.

In an attempt to stay on top of the sensations rocketing through her, Smokey had looked at anything and everything except Mato, but now, brought back to a semblance of sanity because he was no longer sexually working her, she focused on him. She was relieved to see life back in his eyes, but she wished she understood why he'd yelled "no" a few seconds ago. She knew he wasn't talking to her, which left only one possibility. Hawk Spirit was here in some form, maybe directing Mato's actions, maybe trying to take control.

She couldn't let that happen! She didn't dare.

Half expecting him to slam her back onto the ground, she drew his hand off her breast. Although he studied her intently, she wasn't sure he was fully aware of what she'd done. Then, even though she hated doing so, she planted her heel and remaining slipper against the ground and scooted backward. Pine needles and decaying twigs scratched her legs, but that was nothing compared to the wrench of losing his fingers inside her. Freedom from him made it somewhat easier to think, and yet the memory of his manipulation continued to heat her thighs. His cock carried more blood than it had earlier, which was proof of what?

Finally she sat up.

"Talk to me, please," she whispered. "Let me know you're here."

His short nod prompted her to continue. "What would you have done if I'd gotten away? If I'd found someone to give me a ride, would you have given up?"

"You didn't get away."

Point taken. There was no ignoring the tension riding through him, and she couldn't pretend she wasn't awash in her own tension. It had taken so little work on his part to arouse her sexually, and though he was no longer massaging her breast or searching for her G-spot, she was far from putting those sensations behind her, not that she wanted to.

"Where did you go? What prompted you to leave?"

A quick jerk of his head warned her that she'd ventured into territory where he didn't want her, but she had to push, had to try to comprehend. "Hawk Spirit—I can't think of anything else to call it—was responsible, I'm sure of that. And the way you're acting now, almost as if there are two of you . . . Hawk Spirit—is he, or it, here? Can you at least tell me that?"

A darkness that reminded her of a moonless night flickered

in Mato's eyes, making her suspect his damnable spirit was behind it. If only the powerful being had a physical form, she'd take Mato's knife to it. Kill.

"He is, isn't he?" she continued, abeit softly so as not to add to whatever he was going through. What kind of conversation would they have if she were dressed in her own clothes and in a familiar environment? "Your spirit wanted you to himself; that's why you took off, right? But then he—he ordered you to go after me." On the brink of asking the all-important question why, she stopped because icy fingers had touched her heart. "He wanted you to kill me, didn't he?"

Oh, god, what was that expression? She'd never seen anything like that on a human being; it was a primitive determination better suited for a wolf or lion. Even though he hadn't moved, it was almost as if he were stalking her, closing the gap between them so he could sink his teeth into her throat.

"Don't, damn it!" Much as she needed to jump to her feet and flee, she remained where she was. "Don't let Hawk Spirit win!"

She was still speaking when he threw himself at her, knocking her back onto the ground. This time he wasn't content to let his size alone dominate her but straddled her, his hands near her shoulders and his knees pressing against her outer thighs. A single, inescapable thought flooded her mind. She was Mato's prey, and he was about to tear out her throat.

Fighting panic, she reached out. There was only one way of stopping him, and after a frantic moment, she found his cock and began stroking him. As she did, he tilted his head in a way that reminded her of a wolf she'd seen on TV. The creature had been trying to make sense of the cameraman and was simply curious, certainly not afraid. So Mato was still more animal than human, was he? It didn't matter, because man or animal, she'd reach him. She had to if she wanted to go on living.

Caress him! Feather your fingers over his length and make him even harder.

By the time he was fully erect, his mouth was scant inches away. Much as she wanted to believe he intended to kiss her, his teeth so close to her throat told the true story.

"You're incredible," she whispered, her fingers steady on him, and her heart trying to kick out of her chest. "I never had any idea someone like you existed. I—I interviewed a survivalist once who had lived in the woods for years. Although I admired his independence and tenacity, he was half crazy. And in jail for trying to kill a forest ranger."

Something rippled through Mato, causing her to half believe she'd gotten through to him, but it also could have been Hawk Spirit trying to take back control. If she was in Mato's position, and some otherworldly force was determined to compel her to do something, what stood the greatest chance of returning her to sanity? The answer, the only one, was simple. Sex.

Still cradling his cock, she trailed her forefinger over the raised veins. In her mind, her finger became an instrument of worship and pleasure giving, and yet she had to fight the mix of fear and fever racing through her own veins.

"Have you thought about that? If you kill me, will you get away with it? If you don't, you might spend the rest of your life in prison. Think about it, Mato. Never seeing these evergreens again or feeling the sun on your back. No more listening to rain on the roof of your own home or holding the hawk carving your father created." Shifting her hold, she cupped his satiny tip; hopefully he'd remember what fucking her felt like. "Touching cold bars instead of a woman's warm body. No longer participating in the ceremonies I believe are so important to your people. Being shut off from them, forgotten."

He began shaking his head, and although the movement was barely perceptible, it gave her the encouragement she needed to keep going. "The sex you and I've had . . . I've never experienced anything like it, and I'd like to believe you haven't either. There's been no courtship, no getting to know each other, and yet there's a bond between us."

Changing her grip so one hand was on each side of his twitching cock, she extended her fingers to encompass as much of him as possible. If she was still afraid of him, she couldn't tap into the emotion. Maybe she'd given him a lifeline.

"What is it like to have Hawk Spirit trying to take over? Maybe you so believe in his message that you're a willing participant, but what about when you want to chart your own course, to live your own life?"

What was that? Another change in him? Wondering at the absolute insanity that had brought them to this time and place in their lives, she let his cock slide through her fingers, only to cup her hands around him again just before he slipped free.

"You have to want self-determination. Who doesn't? Why do you think I fought the way I did when you caught me? Because this is my body, my responsibility and right."

Concerned that she might be going too far, she willed indignation out of her voice. After all, what did she know of the relationship between Mato and Hawk Spirit?

"I don't want to die. There are so many things I want to do with my life, articles to write, vacations to go on." Not being able to add to the list struck her as incredibly sad, but then she dug deeper and found the courage to tell him more. "I want to become a mother, to raise my children. To love a man and have him by my side while those children are growing up."

His cock was so swollen she wondered if it was causing him pain, but wasn't that a lessening of tension in the rest of his body? If something she'd said was responsible . . . "I want sons," she whispered. "I'd love my daughters with all my heart, but when I think of my children, I have images of watching them play football, trying to solve disagreements with their fists. I'm not particularly feminine, so maybe that's why—"

"You're a woman."

He hadn't spoken for so long, seconds passed before she truly heard him. He could have said anything, made fun of her or ordered her to be silent, so those words brought a lump to her throat. Increasing her hold on him, she nodded. "And that complicates things between us, doesn't it?"

17

A twitch of Mato's mouth had Smokey thinking he was going to respond. Instead he lowered his head until she could no longer see his features, and though his teeth were closing in on her throat, she made no attempt to free herself. Just the same, she flexed her fingers in silent warning that he wasn't the only one capable of inflicting damage.

A touch—nothing more than his strength brushing against a vulnerable place and every molecule of her body instantly focusing on the sensation, nerves sparking, bones melting, pussy flooding. *Don't,* she wanted to order him, but because she couldn't lie, she remained silent. The treetops: she'd look at them and think of a wilderness wind, birds singing, leaves rustling, her heart beating.

Then he again ran his teeth over her neck, and she heard herself whimper. Her legs started twitching, and she tried to lift her buttocks off the ground in a wordless and ancient message. As she did, a hawk settled onto the top of the closest tree.

Leave him alone! she silently ordered. *Don't make him into your hired gun; don't turn him into a killer!*

More concerned for Mato than for herself, she released his cock so she could lock her arms around his waist. She tried to pull him down to her, but with his breath dampening her throat, he remained in place, dominating her.

Whatever the hawk was doing made its feathers ripple, but even when it spread its wings and slowly flapped them while still clinging to the branch, she wasn't afraid. This small creature wasn't Hawk Spirit, and though Hawk Spirit might be directing the bird's movements, there was no warning in what it was doing. Maybe it simply wanted to watch the humans below.

Dismissing the predator, she turned her attention back to the man looming over her. Keeping his mouth so close to her had forced his shoulders into an unnatural position. This time she succeeded in lifting her buttocks off the ground, and though her spine felt the strain, she pushed upward until his cock prodded her belly. It would take so little effort on his part to change the alignment so he could reach her opening and push home.

Sex. Yes, that might be her salvation.

What she needed.

Despite the possibility that he'd make her pay for inflicting pain on him, she released his waist and dug her nails into his buttocks. Hissing, he tried to rock to the side, but she refused to let go.

"I'm waiting for you," she said. "Ready. Do it, just do it."

"Damn you to hell!"

That wasn't Mato speaking; she refused to believe that. "Let me open my legs, please. That's all I'm asking, all I want."

Instead he reared up and back, causing her to lose her grip on him. Before she could guess what he had in mind, he lifted himself off her. An instant later he took hold of her calves and lifted her legs into the air. Barely aware of what she was doing, she gripped his wrists. Then he was on the move again, sliding close so his knees pressed against her buttocks. When he released her legs, they fell forward until they were stopped by his chest.

Ignoring her vulnerability and cursing the oversize sweatshirt covering them, she drew his hands to her breasts. She was sinking into the ground, weakening, heating. What was it she'd said about not thinking of herself as particularly feminine? She'd never felt more female than she did now, wonderfully helpless and controlled.

Then, although she tried to keep them on her, he lifted his hands from her breasts and shook free of her grip. She was trying not to cry out when he slid his fingers between the ground and her buttocks and lifted her ass a few necessary inches. Doing her part by hooking her legs over his shoulders, she clenched the sweatshirt and waited.

He'd slide effortlessly into her in a marriage of two bodies. Everything that had happened between them before this moment would evaporate, and there'd only be her pussy embracing his cock. She'd know or want nothing else, and it would be the same for him. Perfect. Complete.

But when his cock pushed along the valley between her ass cheeks, fantasy gave way to reality. Trying not to laugh, she waited for him to realign. The second time he easily found her, sliding past her wet folds. There was nothing gentle or tentative about the swollen cock plowing into her, and if anticipation hadn't loosened her, discomfort would have come between her and pleasure.

He was in her; that's all that mattered.

Blood rushed to her head, and she was already losing circulation in her feet, but in some respects she'd been waiting all her life for this moment. The watching hawk had taken on a red cast, and she could no longer see the sky, no longer hear the wind. There was only Mato's harsh breathing and her equally rough exhalations.

Unwilling to serve as a passive receptacle, she reached out.

Finding his thighs, she clawed. The harsher his thrust, the more determined she became to leave her impact on him. Never before had she thought of harming a sex partner, but, then, she'd never been in this place. There were no rules, no guidelines, only her mind roaring and her cunt threatening to explode.

A missionary position of sorts! Just like earlier, he'd insisted on taking her instead of achieving a partnership, but even as she silently railed, she wanted it no other way. This was fucking, not lovemaking—strangers and enemies taking from each other because they could. Just the same, having her legs lifted robbed her of the self-determination she'd always insisted on with her sexual partners. The longer he plowed into her, the more she sank into herself until the world beyond her body didn't exist.

She'd dove into a swirling pool. Yes, he was part of what she was experiencing, but for now she controlled the timing and tempo of her response. Much as part of her wanted to drown in her just-out-of-reach climax, she held back so the sensations would continue. These moments were about floating, about swimming in heat, about sinking beneath the surface and finding herself in a world of reds and blacks, of music even.

Perhaps Mato was responsible for the subtle yet increasing change in the flames licking her flesh; perhaps she was. Either way, the water she imagined herself in was becoming steadily deeper. The red and black hues became more vibrant and now swept over her as if colors and water were blending into a whole. And the music—lilting instruments she didn't recognize punctuated by powerful drumming that vibrated through her.

What was that she'd said and believed about being in control of her release? That had been true of the woman she'd been moments ago, but now everything was in motion, churning and changing. She felt his body attacking and pleasuring hers, heard herself scream and scream again. Her fingers ached from attacking him so she rested them on his flesh and pulled his heat into her veins.

Fire and night, the still vibrant hues rushing together, splintered thoughts shooting from one place to another, one sensation followed by the next.

Drowning! Something was pulling her deep into a pool or pond or ocean, closing her off from the world and yet embracing her. Still heating her and adding strength to her voice.

Then something shifted, another gear reached, and everything was streaming past her. Determined to catch the flow, she dove again. Fire and ice swallowed her.

And when it was over, she cried.

"You're sure you want to put it back on? I could carry you."

Shaking her head, Smokey held out her hand for the slipper Mato had thrown into the underbrush. She was sitting up, his sweatshirt pulled over her buttocks to protect her ass from the ground, her legs tingling, now that the blood flow had been restored, postsex weakness slowing her movements, and lethargy quieting her mind. Just the same, she knew she didn't want to be any more dependent on this naked man than she already was.

"What happens now, Mato?" she asked because putting off the question would only make it harder. "Do we go back to your place so you can tie me up again?"

"We're going back, but not for that."

"Why then?"

Although experience had taught her to expect lengthy silences from him, she had to grit her teeth to keep from saying something she'd probably regret. Mato looked every bit a man comfortable with his surroundings. Only heightened color in his cheeks gave away his recent exertion—that and a certain quietness in his eyes. The look of contentment caught her attention and gave rise to compassion for a man who seldom was at peace with himself. He still might be more wild than tame and under his spirit's influence, but she'd take what she could of the man.

When he held out his hand to help her stand, she took it. Then, instead of retreating back into her own space, she wrapped her arms around him. He smelled of the forest and sex, and she hoped he was breathing in the same scents. "I don't know what's going to take place between us," she said. "And I don't think you do either, but I want to thank you for what just happened, the sex."

"You climaxed? I wasn't aware of anything except what was happening to me."

"It was the same for me," she admitted, at peace because he'd hugged her back. "I was pretty single-minded, more than I ever remember being." She might have said more if it hadn't occurred to her that her self-absorption might have been deliberate. By concentrating on her own drive toward sexual release, she hadn't had to think about her partner.

A partner who hadn't used protection this time.

Because an animal doesn't think of such things?

Reminding herself that she was the one who faced the greatest risk—if bearing Mato Hawk's child was a risk—she debated mentioning the lack of a condom, but she didn't want to spoil this moment.

"What do you remember of how you acted?" she asked, still snuggling against him.

Once more silence defined their relationship, and as she waited, she gave herself up to the task of returning to the here and now. It might be a sunny day, but yesterday's rain had left countless puddles. The sweatshirt she was wearing was damp and muddy, and she was already feeling chilled. A blister was developing on her right big toe, and she was hungry. Mato hadn't eaten either. How could he be oblivious to his nudity?

"I'm trying," he finally said. "But so much is a blur."

"I think I know why, but I'd like you to say it."

His chest expanded and then expanded even more as he drew in a deep breath. She waited.

"Spirit," he answered.

"He took over."

"Yes."

"Does that happen often?"

Instead of answering, he turned them back toward his place and started walking. Unwilling to step out of his hold, she matched his pace. And though she warned herself that he might be taking her back into captivity after all, she felt no fear.

The hawk she'd seen while they were having sex might have been following them, perhaps directed by Hawk Spirit as a way of intimidating her. Could the spirit be afraid of her? If so, why?

The tall, strong body beside her supplied the answer: Hawk Spirit feared her impact on Mato.

"Do you know when it's going to happen?" she tried. "Something changes in you as a warning that Hawk Spirit is here?"

"Not a warning—a gift."

He'd spoken with just enough force that she couldn't help wondering if he was trying to convince himself. Maybe it was akin to paying taxes: much as she hated forking over a goodly chunk of her income, she accepted it as the price of living in a free society.

Mentally chiding herself for comparing taxes to what had happened to Mato, she concentrated on her surroundings. The damp, dark, living curtain had intimidated her when she was trying to flee it, but now she felt as though she was being sheltered. Maybe Mato was solely responsible; maybe she was becoming accustomed to the sight, smell, and sound of the forest.

And maybe Hawk Spirit was spinning his web over her.

"I think I understand why you consider your relationship

with your spirit a gift, but aren't there times when you want control over your mind? To make your own decisions?"

Stopping abruptly, he yanked her around so she faced him. "Is that how you see it? I'm Spirit's slave?"

Acutely aware of how carefully she needed to form her response, she tried to shake off his impact, but how could she when he'd become part and parcel of their surroundings, organic to this land? She easily imagined him walking here thousands of years ago, a primitive and primal man totally in tune with the world of his birth. He knew he'd die here, and when he did, his body would help replenish the soil, but until then, he'd embrace and be embraced by all living things.

As would any woman who fell in love with him.

No, not love! Hardly that!

And yet she had never before wanted to crawl inside a man so she could see his world through his eyes, never wanted to give birth to a child with those features and that passion.

"I don't expect you to understand," he said, his words slicing into her thoughts. "This isn't your home; the land isn't precious to you."

"No, it isn't," she admitted. "But I understand that even without Hawk Spirit, you'd love it. That said, what he made you do . . . Kidnapping me is a crime. You broke the law because he ordered you to, and as a result you could spend much of your life in prison."

If her words made any impact, he gave no indication. Trying to get through to him had exhausted her so she simply waited for him to make the next move. After a moment, he started walking again.

His phone was ringing when Mato stepped inside his home. His initial impulse was to ignore it while he went in search of something to wear, but no one called him unless it was important. Then he took note of the slight body so close to his and debated closing her inside the bedroom first, but she was no longer his prisoner, his captive. Unsure what she was to him now, he picked up the receiver.

"Where have you been?" his uncle Tal asked before he'd finished saying hello. "Where is she?"

"With me. What do you want?"

"You haven't heard, have you?"

"Heard what?"

"The news. Senator Gradbery held a conference this morning. He's calling for a renewed investigation into Castetter's disappearance, saying that as a result of what he learned about the objections to NewDirections expressed during the hearing, he's concerned someone here hated him enough to want him dead."

"Did he name names?"

"He didn't have to, Mato. You're—"

"At the top of the list. Did he reveal what the investigation's going to entail?"

"Not really, but he's demanding what he calls a 'professional' search of the area."

"Who's going to conduct it?"

"State police. Apparently they're already calling in their search-and-rescue people."

"In other words, he doesn't believe the locals really looked for Castetter."

"He didn't say the words, but it was there."

Smokey was listening intently, her deceptively strong body on the alert and looking ridiculous in the oversize shirt and slippers. Shutting down the impulse to strip her and carry her into the shower, he concentrated on learning as much as he could. According to his uncle, there was no public time frame for the state people to arrive, but Sandra had already received several calls about whether she had vacancies, and RV sites in the local campground were being reserved.

"They're pulling out all the stops," he said.

"What did you expect? A top state politician has spoken."

"This is about more than working toward a body recovery," he said, his gaze on Smokey. "There are going to be detectives, investigators."

"Yeah."

Are you afraid? he wanted to ask the man he considered his second father, but Tal wouldn't reveal his feelings any more than he would. This *thing* he and Uncle Tal and their relatives and ancestors had been part of as long as anyone knew demanded certain standards, courage, and commitment.

"Mato?" Uncle Tal said. "We've already talked about this, but I'm going to do it again. You were the most outspoken last night; you know what that means."

"I did before I opened my mouth."

"They're going to come after you."

"I'll be ready for them."

Hanging up, Mato scanned the room before locking on Smokey again. He'd fallen in love with this place even before he'd gotten the roof up. The wood and leather furnishings spoke to the man in him, while the photography reached him on an even deeper level. He'd never admit to having a poet's soul, but something came out in him when he studied what his camera and instincts had captured. The pictures of elk, coyotes, deer, and cougars reminded him that he was part of something far greater than himself, while the hawk carving from his father had forged a link between the generations. More than that, the carving stood as testament to his role in this universe.

Was Smokey Powers capable of understanding that?

And even if she was, did he dare trust her with the truth?

Studying him as intently as he was studying her, she kicked

off his slippers, walked over to the couch, and curled up in it, lightly massaging her feet. Her makeup was gone, her hair limp, and his old gray sweatshirt hid her curves, but it didn't matter, because his body remembered those things.

"You're in danger," she said.

"I need to be cautious."

"That's not what I said. You're in danger, aren't you?"

Wondering how deeply her reporter's directness was engrained, he sat next to her. Much as he wanted to take over her task, he didn't trust himself to touch her toes, let alone the rest of her body. The forest had always been a living, breathing creature to him, more alive than any of the women he'd known, but this stranger to his world had become a part of his world— and that might represent the greatest threat to his freedom and future.

"The state police are going to try to learn what happened to Flann Castetter. I have no doubt they'll want to talk to me."

"Because you oppose everything he and NewDirections stood for."

"Yes."

Some unfathomable emotion passed over her, and as it did, he lost touch with the inner calm that had embraced him once they'd finished having sex. Already his cock was stirring back to life.

"Did you kill him?"

"I'm not going to answer that."

18

Rolling her knuckles over an instep, Smokey wearily shook her head. "Because you're afraid I'll turn you in?"

"Because it'll only lead to other questions I can't answer."

"Can't or won't?"

"Maybe both."

"All right," she muttered. "All right. Only, you know why I said that, don't you? Because I have no choice but to accept your boundaries. One thing I want you to think about: how would you feel if you wondered if the person you'd been having sex with might be a killer? Wouldn't you need the truth?" Releasing her feet, she rubbed the back of her neck. "To hell with the truth—I need a shower. And food."

Despite himself, the change to the mundane made him smile. She must not have expected that, because she gave him a puzzled expression. "You find something amusing about my need to be clean?"

"No." His hands aching to touch her, he stood and angled his body away from hers. "I was just thinking that you're issuing orders."

"Not really. I just don't feel like a prisoner anymore."

With that, she stood. Even looking at her over his shoulders, he was keenly aware of the difference in their heights and how little of her there was to fill his sweatshirt. One step, one move, and he'd have it off her.

And maybe she'd feel like his captive again.

Keeping his tone measured, he told her where to find extra towels. He wished he had some of the expensive, flower-smelling shampoo women seemed to be drawn to and that her clothes were in his dresser instead of crammed into the suitcase he'd taken along with her. But he was still trying to get used to the change in their relationship, and he was looking for answers to how he would handle it.

She'd started toward the bathroom when a thought all but froze his throat. "The last time, did I use protection?"

"You don't remember?"

So much of what had happened once he'd overtaken her on the way out to the highway was a blur, including why he'd been out there naked. He held memories of Hawk Spirit's demands that he kill her and his refusal, her quivering body, and the scent of sex in the air. "No, I don't."

"For the record, you didn't."

Staring at what he could see of her belly, he imagined the life he'd helped create taking hold in there. She'd said she wanted sons, and though his desire for one had always been tempered by the roles and burdens that boy would someday have to shoulder, he longed to hold his child. "I'm sorry," he finally remembered to say.

"I don't know if I am."

For a bachelor, Mato's kitchen was well stocked. Dressed in a green blouse and brown slacks but still barefoot, Smokey pulled together an easy meal of turkey sandwiches and a fruit salad while he showered and dressed. As she worked, she kept her mind off the bedroom in which she'd both been imprisoned and fucked by Mato. She just wished she was as good at harnessing her memories of his unabashedly naked form and her fears for him.

It made no sense, she tried to reason. The damn man had kidnapped her and turned her life on end. His having to pay for his misdeeds should be at the top of her list, and if he'd killed Castetter—

Was Mato capable of murder?

Maybe not the human Mato, but she was starting to comprehend that he existed as Hawk Spirit's physical form in many respects, subject to his spirit's will and commands.

What kind of legal defense could an attorney make out of that?

"My grandmother did things to a roasted turkey that should be a crime," she said as they were eating at the kitchen table with the sun streaming in. All she had to do was keep the conversation casual, two relaxed and comfortable-with-each-other lovers shooting the breeze. "I held out for the dark meat because it was so juicy. Even now I can barely stomach sliced white meat; it isn't the real thing."

Mato stopped with his sandwich halfway to his mouth. "My grandmother's specialty was venison. She'd smoke it and—"

"What?" she asked when he sat up and cocked his head. "You heard something?"

He seemed unwilling to respond, so she concentrated. "My cell phone. That's the sound it makes when I have a message. Where did you put it?"

"In your suitcase."

Although she'd spotted her belongings in the living room, she was reluctant to go for them. The whole time she was walking, she half expected Mato to stop her. Opening the battered suitcase that had logged as many air miles as she had, she dug around until she found her cell. It was in need of charging.

"Put it on speaker."

Of course Mato had followed her, she reasoned, despite the way her heart quickened. She should be thinking about his order, not his closeness, but that was easier said than done. Instead of immediately obeying, she walked back into the kitchen and lingered over several bites of salad. Doing so calmed her a bit and, hopefully, sent Mato the message that she wasn't about to bow to his wishes.

There were three messages, all from her editor. The first, sent early this morning, was straightforward: had it been worth her time to attend the meeting, and were reports of a heavy rain last night accurate? He'd left the second one early this morning and the third not long before she and Mato had returned to his place: "Where the hell are you? This is not funny, Smokey. And it isn't like you not to stay in touch. I called the managing editor of the *Statesman Journal,* who gave me the cell number of the reporter they'd sent to the meeting. According to that reporter, all hell broke loose last night, with you in the middle of it. And now the search for Castetter has become top priority. I'm giving you exactly thirty minutes from now to call me back. If you don't, I'm calling whatever passes for police in that burg."

Closing the cell phone, she studied Mato. And despite her illogical urge to apologize for this new complication in his life, she simply waited for his response.

"It's been a half hour," he said.

"My editor is a punctual man. He expects the same of others, especially those he's worried about. Tell me something: do you have any influence with the police department? If you tell them to ignore a request to look for me, will they do it?"

"No."

"In other words—"

"In other words, unless you stop your editor, there's going to be a search, starting with contacting me."

Although she was still hungry, she didn't trust her stomach

to handle any more food. "Because people saw us talking last night."

"Yeah."

Mato didn't look trapped so much as resigned. "I have to call him and ease his mind."

"What are you going to say?"

Not what I should. "That I'm all right."

His look of resignation lifted to be exchanged with puzzlement. She could almost hear him ask if she truly believed she was all right; she was glad he didn't ask, because she wasn't sure how she'd answer. Half expecting him to take away the phone, she punched numbers.

"It's me," she said as soon as James, her editor, picked up. Because her phone was still on speaker, her voice fairly echoed.

"Smokey, thank god! Where the hell have you been?"

James had been more than pissed—he'd been scared. "Busy," she said. Then, her mind spinning, she apologized for worrying him.

"Busy doing what?"

Could Mato guess what she was about to say? His expression was one of caution, distrust, and yet hope.

"Earning my salary."

"Don't play games, Smoke. Give it to me straight."

Straight? If only it were that easy. "I can't give you all the details because I'm still working on them, but . . ." Swallowing, she continued. "Unless I've lost the instincts that led to my career, I'm on the biggest story of my life." *Bigger than anyone outside Storm Bay will ever understand.* "Not what I thought I'd be writing, but I don't care."

Fighting the impact of Mato's intensity, she waited for James to calm down. "Of course I'm serious," she said. "I might joke about some things, but never this."

"So you say, but I don't know what the hell you're talking about. What story? Let's get specific. Is it about Castetter?"

Determined to concentrate, she closed her eyes. Just the same, Mato's image stayed with her just as her skin remembered his touch. "You know why I came here—the strange deaths I uncovered and wanted to try to build on."

"Yeah. So?"

"So, what could have turned out to be a wild goose chase has landed me in the middle of a gold mine of information." Knowing James would push for specifics, she hurried on. "One thing I didn't count on was that my being here has the other reporters trying to find out what I'm up to. I'm having to sneak around while trying to find people who'll tell me the truth and not then run out and blab to the competition."

"What's this information you're digging up? Are you saying there's more—"

"I'm not saying more than I already have until I get it pulled together," she said, praying James wouldn't push.

"That's telling me damn nothing, and you know it. What about what's-his-name, the guy who threatened violence at the meeting?"

I've been fucking him when I'm not wearing his ropes. "What about him?"

"Damn, you know what I'm asking. Are you hiding from him?"

It's too late for that. "I can handle it," she said because she couldn't bring herself to lie any more than she already had.

"I hope to hell you can. I don't like this, and because I don't, I'm insisting you call me morning and night for as long as you're there. I trust you to do your job, but you're the only one there I trust. How long do you think whatever it is is going to take?"

The answer to that wasn't up to her, prompting her to admit she didn't know. Studying Mato, she agreed to the twice-daily contacts and then hung up before her editor could ask more questions. Tension seeped out of her, replaced with a growing awareness of whom she shared this room with. This man had become nothing less than the center of her universe. "I've bought some time," she said. "How much, I don't know."

"He isn't a patient man."

"No, he isn't. Mato, what's going to happen?" She fell silent. The longer the silence hovered between them, the less certain she became that she wanted an answer. She didn't want to believe he'd lie to her, but, then, did he dare tell her the truth? And maybe Hawk Spirit was keeping Mato's ultimate role from him. If Mato had to wait for Hawk Spirit's orders, would he tell her what they were? Was it possible he'd defy or try to defy those orders?

"Tell me what you know, damn it!" she blurted. "You were commanded to grab me and, what, turn me into something mindless? But if I turned out to have a will, or if you got too close to me . . . Is he here, listening to us?" Even as she shook her head at what she'd just said, she couldn't help looking around for the small bird she took as the embodiment of Hawk Spirit.

"He isn't."

"Are you sure? Do you always know—"

"My spirit is patient. He will wait for me."

To do what? she came within a breath of asking. Instead, abandoning her meal, she again walked out of the kitchen. At first she was aware of little except the distance between her and Mato, but bit by bit the room calmed her. If she lived here she might make a few minor changes, such as placing some plants near the windows and using a few light-colored throws to ease the impact of the solid leather furniture, but other than that, she'd leave things as Mato had designed.

The windows.

Not trying to stop herself, she headed toward the large one to the right of the front door. She could see the porch and below that the gravel driveway, even the beginning of the road.

What equipment had he used to carve out the road, and had he done all the work himself, or had his friends and relatives lent a hand? The notion of something akin to an old-fashioned barn raising lit a small fire in her heart, not just because she loved the idea of people with a common task and goal, but because the image reinforced what she now believed about this close-knit community.

Outsiders might laugh at the backwoods residents, but that was because they missed the essential element—unity. Enough unity that the residents would protect and defend each other, even the killer or killers among them.

There wasn't enough fresh air in the room, damn it! She needed to breathe, to stop thinking!

Dismissing her bare feet, she opened the door and stepped outside. A breeze heavy with the scent of evergreens and ocean met her, followed by a prickle of awareness across her shoulders. Without looking behind her, she knew Mato was in the doorway, but that wasn't what had alarmed her.

"Where is he?" she demanded. "I sense him."

"Today Hawk Spirit is the wind."

What the hell are you talking about? she ached to throw at him, but maybe he'd given her the only answer there was. If she tried to leave the porch, would he stop her? "It's so complicated," she whispered. "I've been threatened because of some things I've written, once by a drug dealer, another time by a so-called investment counselor who was stealing from his clients. I wasn't scared so much as mad. When I called the police, they tapped my line and discovered who had been leaving those disgusting messages, but even if I could call the police right now, they couldn't do anything."

How many speeches had she made? Maybe they'd only taken place in her head, but just the same, they'd given her a headache. Words were supposed to be about something concrete, yet what she was trying to deal with defied description.

"If I picked up the phone, would you let me complete the call?"

"No."

On the brink of asking why, she closed her mouth because what did she need with more conversations that went nowhere? The notion of being imprisoned here wasn't frightening; in fact, she could almost imagine spending the rest of her life in Mato's home. That was nonsense, of course, because she'd always wanted to jump headfirst into everything the world had to offer, and yet . . .

"I've bought you some time," she said. "Not much, but maybe enough that you should be able to decide what you're going to do next." *If you can make that decision.*

"Thank you."

So Hawk Spirit sometimes existed in the breeze, did he? It was somehow fitting—unnerving and yet right.

What, she wondered, could she possibly write about the world beyond the concrete world she'd always believed in? Many readers would make fun of her for buying into the whole woo-woo nonsense, but others might nod in agreement. Backed by all the facts she could pull together, the end result would resonate in ways her writing never had. She might even be awarded—no, this wasn't about some damn literary award. Instead it had everything to do with opening people's minds to other possibilities.

How would you like that, Spirit? If you read about yourself in my column, would you feel that everything you stand for has been justified?

Or would you feel betrayed?

"What is he saying?" she asked. "Does he want you to kill me?"

"Not anymore."

Staggered by Mato's response, she stared up at him. Was he expanding, becoming larger and more powerful, or was that nothing more than her imagination? Suddenly unnerved by her surroundings, she admitted that she was afraid to look around. "But earlier he was—that's what you're saying, isn't it?"

"If necessary, yes."

He revealed more in a single word than she could in an entire book. "Why didn't you?"

"I don't know."

You have to know! Head spinning, she gripped the railing. "Have you ever defied Hawk Spirit?"

"No."

"What was different this time? I have a right to know."

This wasn't a man who would ever allow someone to push him into a corner. At the same time, he'd committed himself to following Hawk Spirit's guidance about whatever it was, so how did he reconcile the two? The answer came as she dug her nails into the wood: for the first time, he'd disagreed with his spirit. Because of her?

Even though she wasn't sure she trusted her legs to hold her, she let go of the railing so she could stand before Mato. Her hand seemed to belong to someone else as she reached out to touch his cheek; at the moment of contact, shared warmth ran between them.

"I couldn't," he whispered as he covered her hand with his.

Much as she wanted him to elaborate, she sensed he'd gone as far as he could. For anyone else, refusing to murder another human being would be a simple moral choice, but everything was so complex for Mato and, as a consequence, for her.

"Maybe you can answer something for me," she said to fill the air. "If state law enforcement came looking for you, what would you tell them?"

"About what?"

"Castetter. They're going to be turning over every rock."

"I have to hear their questions before I can answer yours."

He was avoiding, damn him. "What about me? Are you

going to hide me in the woods, leave me tied and gagged to some tree?" The image made her shudder. "Of course, if you're arrested—"

"Don't go there."

"Why not? Because you're guilty?"

"Is that what you believe?"

As part of a series she'd once done on juvenile delinquents, she'd interviewed a girl who'd been arrested for breaking into the house of a family away on vacation. The girl had reminded her of a trapped animal, defiant and scared at the same time. She'd admitted to the break-in but little else, and it had taken Smokey more than an hour to break through her defenses. A runaway because she'd refused to be raped anymore by her stepfather, she'd taken refuge in the only place she could find.

Mato was hardly that desperate fifteen-year-old, and yet there was something in his eyes and a backed-into-a-corner air about him. But if he was a murderer?

Even with the question stalking her, she again touched his cheek. This time her fingers lingered until he drew them away. "What was that about?" he asked.

"I'm not sure. Mato, you should be able to do what you want with your life, not what some damnable force orders you to."

"It's more than orders, Smokey. In many respects Spirit and I share the same heart."

What about Castetter? He'd told her he'd had nothing to do with the man's disappearance, but could she believe him? Again overwhelmed by everything they were facing both separately and together, she wrapped her arms around her middle. "I'm trying to understand what you mean by what you just said. Maybe if I knew more about what Hawk Spirit stands for—"

"You can't because your roots didn't stem from here."

And that meant there'd always be a wall between them? Perhaps, she acknowledged, but in one elemental way Mato's heart and hers shared the same beat—sex. Standing on her toes, she pressed her lips to his throat. As she did, it dawned on her that they'd yet to share a kiss. And that no matter what he meant to her, she couldn't forgive him if he'd had a hand in Castetter's death.

"What was that for?" he asked.

"Maybe for not killing me." The moment she'd said the words, she wanted to take them back.

"You should want me behind bars."

Shaking off the frightening image, she debated tucking her hands in her back pockets so she wouldn't be tempted to touch him again, but the need was too great to deny. Someone reckless took control of her; that was her only explanation for what she did next. But even as she struggled to comprehend that she'd actually hooked her fingers over the waistband of his jeans, she eagerly anticipated her next move. Rocking forward onto the balls of her feet, she again kissed his throat. He was so soft there, so vulnerable and alive. The essence of that life flowed into her until it filled her, and yet, far from satiated, she ran her nails over his waist.

Grunting, he caught her wrists but didn't pull her off him.

"That tickles?" she asked as stroked him there again.

"Yeah, tickles."

A glance downward reinforced what she'd already sensed; his cock was swelling. "Looks like being ticklish has added benefits," she observed.

His hold on her wrists strengthened a little. "What's gotten into you?"

"I don't know, Mato. That's the hell of it—I don't know." Worn out by her admission, she rested her head on his chest, where she could listen to his heart's steady *thump-thump*. "I need something different between us. Not so complex and dangerous."

So do I, she almost swore she heard him respond. She wasn't the only one who wanted to start over, but how could they possibly make that happen? Mato was controlled by the otherworldly force she'd never fully comprehend, and he refused to examine that right now, but it was different for her. If she couldn't direct their course, at least she could start in the direction she wanted things to go.

Light. Simple.

Buoyed by unwise and yet needed possibilities, as well as the familiar energy spinning through her, she tilted her head so she could nibble the tendon at the side of his neck. He shuddered, and his grip shifted so he had ahold of her forearms but didn't try to stop her. Determined to make the most of her freedom, she licked where her teeth had been. The taste of him sent a hot shiver through her, so she licked again, which left her hungry for more. She was debating nibbling his earlobe when he pushed her back and gave her a look that nearly made her laugh.

"What are you up to?" he asked.

"As much as I can get away with. What's the matter, Mato? Don't you trust me?"

"I never said—"

"Then let me do my thing."

"Which is?"

Give me time; I'll think of something. Anything. "You're so serious. Don't you ever just embrace life?"

Instead of answering, he drew her hands off his waistband and settled them on his chest. The instant she felt it rise and fall, her fingers twitched.

"There's a good deal I embrace."

"I know you do. I'm sorry I said what I did."

After a moment, he released her arms, and she set about unbuttoning his shirt, somehow keeping her fingers steady as she did. Unfortunately she couldn't do anything about the heat in her cheeks or tingling throughout her crotch.

Light. Keep these precious moments light.

"Think of this as part of my education," she said once she'd finished with the buttons and had pulled out the shirttail. "You are aware that the male anatomy comes in endless varieties, which makes cataloging and classifying those differences difficult. I've had enough experience with you that I'm tempted to at least preliminarily place you in the well-hung category."

Her cheeks now flaming, she pulled the shirt apart. Oh, damn, how was she going to think, let alone talk with that dark, broad chest within reach? One step in her direction, and she'd be all over him.

"The problem with placing a man within a category," she continued, "is that there's a broad continuum, everything from fat and flabby but well hung to stud-studly. Hmmm. Yes, yes, indeed, I'm going to need to do a more thorough study before I can complete my evaluation."

Much as she wanted to look to see if he was buying into her nonsense, she kept her attention fixed on that made-for-action chest of his. And much as she wanted to press more than one part of her anatomy against him, she didn't trust herself to do more than cling to the shirt that still retained his heat.

"Measurements," she came up with. "That's what I need, accurate measurements. And photographs. Nude photographs taken from all angles."

The words alone were enough to send her imagination to flight, and in her mind she saw him standing naked and proud with the forest all around while she circled him, snapping shot after shot, her trembling fingers making her wonder if any of the pictures would come out. She'd stop to wipe her sweating hands on her hips, and he'd gift her with a knowing, inviting smile, and she'd put down the camera and hold out her arms and he'd—

Distracted by movement overhead, she held her breath before daring to look. As she suspected—or was it feared—a hawk had settled into a tree to watch her and Mato. Whether it was the same one she'd seen before was immaterial because the message remained the same: Hawk Spirit and Mato were connected in incomprehensible and inescapable ways. And most times Mato bowed to his spirit's commands.

"What is it?" he asked.

"You know," was the best she could come up with.

"He won't hurt you."

How can you be sure? But of course he knew everything he needed to about his guide and the living creature or creatures that represented Hawk Spirit. There was a fierceness to today's predator's glare, a cold calculation that made her question what Mato had just told her about being safe.

19

_____

"I want to go inside." With that, Smokey turned toward the door, tugging on Mato's shirt as she did so. To her great relief, he didn't resist, and yet even though the inhospitable hawk had chased her from the porch, she hated being inside again, cut off from the sun's warmth and invigorating breeze. Instead of apologizing for her cowardice, she drew the shirt off his shoulders and threw it as far as she could. Not long ago Mato had done whatever he wanted to her, his prisoner. She wanted to believe things had fundamentally changed between them and that she wouldn't share what she believed had been Castetter's fate, but she wasn't a fool. After all, she'd been given abundant proof of Hawk Spirit's role in Mato's life.

"Your shoes. Get rid of them," she said.

Quirking an eyebrow, he did as she ordered. Then he stood gazing down at her, his body seemingly at rest while she felt as if she were about to fly apart. Most people didn't know what to do with their arms, but he looked content and natural with them resting by his sides. The only thing making a lie of his body language was a bulge capable of focusing all her attention on it and it alone.

Swallowing, she debated *ordering* him to dispense with his jeans, but that would have been the coward's way out. Mato had turned her body into his plaything, and it was her turn to attempt to do the same to him. Stimulating him would give her something to do, something to concentrate on and hopefully to silence her inner turmoil.

Her hands extended toward him without her being aware of having made that decision. Maybe courage had nothing to do with her actions; maybe the light dancing throughout her was responsible. She'd seen him naked before, so a repeat shouldn't be so hard to contemplate, should it, but she'd been stronger back then. Either that, or somehow she's been less involved than she was now. No matter what the explanation, praying for the courage to expose him said a great deal about how far she'd fallen from the in-control woman she'd been.

Sucking in a lungful of courage, she fumbled with the jeans' fastening. When it finally gave up its task, she turned her attention to the zipper. The first inch or two wasn't that hard, but then she reached the potent mound, and her head swam. More air, that's what she needed! And an air conditioner because she was suddenly too hot, her jaw refusing to stay closed, and the top of her head tingling.

She was practically drooling by the time she'd finished with the zipper, and though she would have given anything to guzzle a glass of ice water, because she might not be able to get going again if she stopped now, she once more took hold of the waistband. Running his jeans down over his buttocks called for trailing her thumbs over the taut flesh, and try as she did to come up with something to say, only a moan escaped her throat. Arching her back brought her pelvis dangerously close to him.

What if he's a killer?
No, not now! I won't go there. I can't.

All right: jeans clinging to his thighs, naked chest begging to be caressed, cock visible through the slit in his briefs, goal nearly reached.

Against her better judgment, she glanced at the front window and then caught her breath; a hawk, surely the one that had chased her in here, was just outside, clinging to the windowsill. Its wings were outstretched as though about to take flight, its beak open, its intense eyes boring into her.

Leave us alone!

Mato must have sensed her shock because he followed her gaze. Gripping her shoulders, he said, "I should have known."

"What?"

"That this isn't about you and me."

"I don't understand."

Something was happening to him, the change subtle and yet impossible to ignore. His already hard, athletic body became even more so, as if he were drawing strength from some inexhaustible source. Although he wasn't changing from his human form, she sensed the potential and possibility. If she stripped away his skin and exposed the next layer, she'd find not a man but a wild creature—a predator.

Hawk Spirit was responsible! Robbing Mato of the right to simply be a man and turning him into his instrument, his slave!

She'd come to that realization before, so it should have been easier to accept the second time, but it wasn't, because Mato Hawk was much more than someone she'd just met, the subject of her current assignment. She'd had sex with him, fucked him, and wanted to again. Needed.

Sex! Sex might keep him with her.

Dragging her attention off the window and what waited beyond it, she shrugged off Mato's hold and yanked off her top. She hadn't bothered with a bra, and the sight of her breasts with their hardened tips drew Mato's gaze there. Aware of how much she was risking, she cupped her mounds and lifted them. No words were necessary. Playing with herself, stroking the heated mounds and rubbing her nipples, tamped down unwanted thoughts and fed the fire in her belly. She did so not just for her own sake but because she hoped her arousal would flow from her to him. His arms, which earlier had looked so natural by his sides, were now roped with tension, proof—she hoped, that he had to fight to keep them off her.

Determined to make his struggle with himself even more self-absorbing, she pushed upward on her right breast and lowered her head, extending her tongue as though trying to lick herself. She'd seen a porno movie with a big-breasted woman who could suckle her own nipples, and although she couldn't pull that off, she could pretend. And he watched.

When her neck began to ache, she abandoned her doomed-to-failure act, but the pretense had left its mark on her—or maybe it was thinking about Mato drawing her breasts into his mouth that made her blood race anew. The power of suggestion where he was concerned was heady and exciting!

Letting her arms drop to her sides, she kept them there even when her fingers curled into fists and her nails dug into her palms. Pain, she was learning, bore similarities to sexual arousal, and both sensations called for her undivided attention.

He was touching her again, not taking hold of her shoulders this time but placing his hands where hers had been. The contrast between her soft palms and his calloused ones on her breasts made her belly clench. Holding her breath and loving the warmth spiraling out and down, she made short work of her slacks' button and zipper. Being freed from the constricting fabric around her waist was wonderful, and she rewarded herself by stroking her belly. Smiling just a little—a wonderful thing to see—Mato ducked his shoulders and head, pushing up on her left breast at the same time.

She knew what was going to happen, felt his moist breath slide over her breast even before the contact was made. He had her, had imprisoned her in his mouth, and being a captive made her want to howl with delight. Grinding her knuckles over her belly, she pushed her response into high gear. Her legs were weakening, in danger of giving way! But if she started to fall, surely her captor would catch her.

Captor? Hopefully now only in her mind.

He was picking her up, holding her against his chest, striding over to the couch and dropping her onto it with her slacks clinging to her hips. Even before she stopped bouncing, she tried so sit up so she could tug at the unwanted garment, but he beat her to the act and yanked with such force that he nearly pulled her off the couch. Gripping the cushion, she struggled to concentrate on his expression. Her earlier belief that an animal lurked just beneath the surface slammed back into her, alarming and exciting her.

Mato was on the edge, standing on the brink between rational human and wild instinct, but was she any more civilized? Throwing caution high and far, she again tried to sit up. This time she managed to wrap her arms around him and pull him down on top of her.

Granted, he was kneeling on the carpet, but his upper body blanketed her, pinning her down. Letting loose a faint growl, she ran her teeth over his chin. The pressure on her chest increased, letting her know he was determined to control her, but even as a thin slice of fear chased through her, she met him fierce for fierce.

Squirming under him, she ran her nails down his spine while he arched upward. Wanting and yet not wanting freedom, she clung to him as she continued her assault on his chin. Then his weight shifted, and suddenly her mouth was on his.

Rough and harsh, she gave and took, whimpered and moaned. Over and over again he pressed his lips against hers as if trying to crush her, and when she was on the brink of begging for release, he suddenly turned gentle.

His lips now barely brushing hers undid her, reduced her to a quivering puddle of need and hidden tears. Whether he was more man or beast now didn't matter—nothing did except these rare, tender moments. Eyes closed against the tears trying to break free, she sent him her gratitude via light caresses on his spine. Could he tell she was growing weaker and softer and more pliable? Her body flowed and floated, heated by need. She no longer contemplated the past or questioned the future because her world consisted of the larger body covering hers and the exquisite tattoo of kisses.

He cared, no matter what Hawk Spirit had done and might yet do to her. Mato cared about her, and she thanked the man by offering him everything.

When he finally put an end to the heady exploration of mouth to mouth and drew her upright, she wrapped her arms around his neck, hearing his heart beating and feeling his lungs' give and take. Even with the strong need for sex, she was content to float in the heated pool they'd created. There was no watching mortal hawk, no powerful spirit creature with its talons buried in this man's soul—just male and female.

Sex, she needed sex. With him. Gentle and frenzied, the extremes flowing into one and feeding both of them.

Reluctant but determined, she pushed back and planted her feet on the carpet. When she stood, her head spun, forcing her to briefly close her eyes while his hands, now around her waist, kept her upright. Then, need pushing her on, she sank to her knees before him. If her fingers hadn't become numb, she would have made short work of his jeans. As it was, she tugged awkwardly until he took pity on her and completed the job, taking his shorts down at the same time.

Naked. Both of them.

She'd taken hold of his cock and was about to place her

mouth around the gift when he joined her on the carpet. Then, somehow, they were both stretched out on their sides, limbs tangled, his cock flattened between them and her pussy pulsing in anticipation. Fire danced through her, igniting flame after flame to keep her in motion.

Moments later he rolled onto his back and brought her with him so she now lay on top of him. Infused with even greater need and courage, she straddled his thighs so his cock rested, sleek and potent, against her belly.

Could she? Would he let her?

To hell with questions and doubt—it was her turn. On top. Calling the shots!

Sitting upright and then lifting herself as high as her legs allowed, she guided his rod between her legs. Then, although ruby fire lapped at her senses, breasts, and throat, she counted off the seconds with his tip at her entrance. Waited. Lived through the sweet torture.

As soon as she started to sink down, he'd slide into her and she'd be lost, wonderfully, hopelessly lost. For now she wrapped anticipation around her. Small but insistent sparks rocked her, and she took the mini climaxes as gifts from the man who'd changed her world.

"Do it," he hissed. Gripping her hips, he pushed her onto him. There. That delicious and always new invasion, tissues being stretched, privacy stripped away.

Joined. Two bodies into one.

Her hands splayed over his chest for balance; she looked down at her captive, the male animal she'd pushed to the ground and now controlled. Only, even as she ran the erotic notion around in her mind, she acknowledged that she was the one owned, not the owner. She might be on top, but his strength was greater, and her throbbing need had rendered her helpless.

Didn't matter. Fuck. Just fuck.

Why hadn't she considered this, she acknowledged seconds later with her thigh muscles burning from the effort of gliding her pussy up and down his cock. Being on top had been a worthy goal, but now that she'd achieved it, she might not last until the explosion. Just the same, the primal beast she'd become whipped her on.

Sudden pain, sharp bursts grinding against her hips. Yanked from the everything that was sex, she realized his fingernails were digging into her flesh. She couldn't, wouldn't entertain that he might be deliberately hurting her. Rather, his own needs must have rendered him oblivious to what he was doing. Grabbing his wrists, she pulled them off her.

As soon as she released him, he wrapped his arms around her and pulled her chest down to him. He remained in her, his hard strength now pressing against the front of her channel and giving her exciting new sensations to deal with. Concerned she might be bending his cock in ways cocks weren't designed to bend, she tried to straighten, but instead of letting her do so, he rolled onto his side, taking her with him.

Now they lay facing each other, her leg looped over his, her breasts skimming his chest, and his breath slipping into her hair. Whether it was day or night didn't matter—neither did her nearly empty stomach, thanks to her interrupted meal. There was just the two of them primitively bound together, skin sealed to skin. Not moving.

That couldn't be, shouldn't be! Not with her inner fire raging.

"All right, all right!" she gasped. "Just—do it."

"What?"

"Get on top." She almost added *damn it,* but it wasn't his fault that she lacked the finesse to get the job done with her in that position. At least she'd issued the order, right?

Holding her so close and tight she couldn't breathe, he pinned her under him. He was still in her, still the invader; that's all that mattered!

Pulling his arms out from under her, he planted his hands on the carpet and rose up, robbing her of so much. Staring up at the formidable form over her, she ran her fingers over his taut forearms. Instinct arched her back and bent her knees and was responsible for the high, bleating sound she kept making when he pounded into her.

Rough, yes, hard and fast, sweat blooming on both of them, her back and thighs straining with the effort of matching him. Her pussy filled almost to bursting, only to all but empty as he drew away. Again and again he came at her, his greater strength shaking her and changing her bleating to harsh cries.

Her body became a blur, every inch of her caught up in the act of fucking, and even when her back and thighs begged for relief, she dug deep for the power to match him.

There! The reason for everything! Proving herself—courage and strength and determination all flowing together. And the explosions. A harsh, sudden one followed immediately by another. Then everything ran into a whole, gasping and sweating and holding him deep and tight within her while she broke apart, splintered and evaporated.

Exhaustion gripped and then shook her, causing her to sink, panting, onto the carpet like some rag doll.

But he wasn't done. He kept after her, pounding until suddenly he became a tightly coiled spring.

Then the spring snapped. And he erupted in her.

Howled.

20

A little after nine the next morning, Mato was outside when he heard a familiar vehicle bouncing over the gravel road leading to his place. Knowing his uncle was coming made him clench his teeth and returned weight to his shoulders. How long had he been lost in Smokey Powers's spell? He remembered, vaguely, yesterday, followed by a night of almost no sleep and so much sex he now felt as if he'd been in a marathon. He'd left her sleeping in the bed—that would never feel the same to him—because, tired as he was, he needed to be out where hopefully his head would clear.

Now, however, he wished he could hide from the responsibility represented by his uncle's old pickup.

Too-short seconds later, he was forced to face not just Uncle Tal but his father as well. The two climbed down from the high cab and walked toward him, matching step for step. Uncle Tal had been little more than a year old when his father was born, and the two were so close in appearance and mannerisms some people took them for twins.

Instead of accepting Mato's reluctant invitation to come inside, the two older men stood at the bottom of the stairs, prompting him to join them. As had long been their way, he hugged his father and then his uncle, the air of age in both men warning him of how soon he'd have to pick up the full mantle of responsibility.

"Where is she?" his father asked in his direct way.

"Inside." Mato deliberately didn't look back at the house.

"Doing what?"

"Sleeping," he said because he couldn't lie.

"As your captive?"

"No. Not any longer."

"Why not?" Uncle Tal asked, his eyes saying he already knew the answer. "We know what your spirit demanded of you."

"She isn't what I thought she'd be," he started and then stopped. How could he explain what he'd been through when he didn't understand it himself? "Maybe it's me who isn't what I thought I was, what my spirit needs me to be. I'm a man, and as one . . . my flesh is weak."

"No weaker than any man," Uncle Tal said softly. "Mato, I know what you're going through because I've stood where you are."

In many ways, yes, but his uncle's loyalty to this land and his spirit had been different in one key respect: a compelling and sexy woman hadn't been at the core.

"Why are you here?" he asked. If he were still a child, he could ask his elders for advice, but because those years were behind him, trying to shift the subject was easier than exposing his weakness.

The brothers exchanged a look. Then his father pulled a folded newspaper page out of his back pocket and handed it to him. He recognized it as the paper Smokey wrote for. It bore today's date. "Have you read this?" his father asked.

A newspaper had been the last thing on his mind, which he

suspected his father knew. Not bothering to respond, he read the piece the editor-in-chief had written.

Our own award-winning correspondent, Smokey Powers, has been keeping a low profile lately, for good reason. She's been pursuing what she has assured me is the most comprehensive and thought-provoking story of her career. The result of her meticulous interviewing and research skills will soon grace the pages of this newspaper. As a result of a little arm twisting on my part, I am delighted to attest that she's about to knock our socks off. Not one to spill the beans, I'll leave readers with one small hint:

Things are not as they appear on the outside in a small coastal community. The truth will have you locking your doors, and more.

The overwriting aside, Mato was convinced the editor had accomplished his goal because people would be buying the newspaper in anticipation of a rare piece of journalism—about Storm Bay's secrets.

Gathering courage and more around him, he faced his relatives. No, he hadn't imagined the weary resignation in Uncle Tal's eyes, and he believed it was because if Smokey wrote her article, everything their ancestors had done and risked would be for nothing. His people's right to this land would be forced to end. So-called progress would destroy it.

All because of her.

"I don't have the words," Uncle Tal said. "My whole life I accepted my spirit's need for me and am proud of the time I chained myself to trees to protect them from loggers, but it isn't my role to command you to do the same. I'm not walking in your path."

Sensing his father's piercing gaze, he turned to him. "Say it. I need to hear what you're thinking."

Uncle Tal had looked resigned; in contrast, his father's face radiated commitment, as it always had. Strange that two men who shared so much faced the most compelling commitments in their lives so differently. Where Uncle Tal had always struggled with his responsibilities, his father had been defined by them.

"My phone started ringing at dawn," his father said. "It was still ringing when I left the house. Everyone who called said the same thing."

Used to his father's measured speech, he waited for him to continue. As he did, his thoughts slid to Smokey, who he prayed was still sleeping, still oblivious.

"The article can't happen."

"I know," he whispered.

Other people might ask how he intended to back up his words, but not his father. How well his father knew him, he acknowledged as the silent seconds stretched. Yes, this man who'd held him as a newborn read his mind, but it was more than that because in many respects he also shared his son's emotions—as Mato hoped to do someday with his own children.

"At times you've called your position here a curse," his father said. "And when you first comprehended what being a member of our family meant, you—"

"I put my fist through your door."

The brothers nodded in unison, causing Mato to belatedly note their similar attire—jeans at the end of their lifespan, flannel shirts thin at the elbows, cracked boots. The message was simple: their lives were hard. And yet neither man would ever want anything except what Storm Bay offered.

"Your spirit commanded you to kill her," Uncle Tal muttered.

How did you know? he nearly asked, but Spirit was a predator. Of course that would be his response to a threat.

If I fail in my mission, my father or uncle might be forced to kill her. Or me.

His father placed his smaller, dryer hand on Mato's forearm, drawing Mato from his thoughts. "We didn't come here to repeat your spirit's wisdom. Even with what's developed between you and that woman"—he jerked his head at the house—"my brother and I will never doubt you carry your spirit's words in your heart. What we want," he squeezed, "is to help you understand how powerful the spirit's hold is."

So I'll stop fighting it and become my spirit's warrior?

Suddenly so exhausted he didn't trust himself to continue standing, he sank onto the bottom step. After a moment his father and uncle joined him. The sun was high enough that it was pushing shadows into the corners, and as such nothing stood between him and his visitors' expressive, lined faces. They weren't old, but their strength was fading, and so they'd begun turning certain things over to the next generation—him.

"Our father, your grandfather, died when you were a young boy," his uncle started. "We tried to keep him alive in your mind, but we're not sure how much we succeeded."

Loving his uncle for the way he'd taken over what his father had begun, he nodded. "I remember Grandfather showing me how to fish using a spear. I wish I'd had more patience, but I wanted to use what everyone else was using."

"You know why he insisted, don't you?"

"So I'd know what the old ways were like." Although he tried to conjure up memories of his grandfather, his mental images of the man remained fuzzy. Not only had Grandpa died when he was seven, the older man had been distant and preoccupied. Mato had sometimes wondered if his grandfather had been clinically depressed because he couldn't remember him ever laughing.

"You know," His father cleared his throat. "You know his spirit was a cougar."

So that's where this was going; he should have known. Wishing with everything in him that they didn't go down this road, he nevertheless nodded.

"And what his spirit commanded him to do."

Don't say it! If you don't, maybe you'll be spared. "To kill," he said because he had no choice.

His father nodded, the gesture causing his thinning hair to fly about. "I know you've read what little's been written about that death; we all have. But it is never talked about when we get together; have you ever wondered why?"

Of course he had. At first his youthful imagination had worked to fill in the blanks, and then later he'd forced himself to try to put himself in his grandfather's position in preparation for the same mantle of responsibility, but his older relatives' silence had sent the message that he wasn't to ask for details. "No one was with him when it happened," he said. "And I don't believe it was something Grandfather wanted to talk about."

The brothers exchanged another of their intimate glances. As they did, Mato experienced a prickle of awareness at the back of his neck. He could be wrong, but he couldn't help wondering if Smokey was watching them. If so, she'd think they were talking about her, but she was wrong—at least right now. She was sleek sex, energy, and heat, more ethereal than real to him right now, and he desperately wanted to keep her that way.

"For many years he didn't," Uncle Tal said. "But when he knew he was dying, he called his sons to his side."

Despite the sun's warmth, Mato became chilled as the two men took turns telling him what they knew. Grandfather had gotten drunk right after Cougar Spirit had come to him with his desperate plea for justice, but when he'd sobered up, he'd turned himself over to his spirit, who'd mentally taken him deep into the mountains so he'd understand. Man and *cougar* had stood over the abandoned body of a murdered doe and heard her orphaned twins' plaintive bleating. Less than a mile away lay another slaughtered deer. This one, a buck, had had his antlers cut off. A long, bloody trail stood as proof of how far the wounded buck had stumbled before it had died. In all, five deer had lost their lives, their carcasses left to rot.

The *hunter* responsible had pitched a campsite near a creek. When Grandfather first saw him, the unshaven man had been passed out, drunk, but he'd revived and had set about cleaning his rifle. His *trophies,* the antlers, were tied to a handmade sled the man intended to haul out with him, but there was still room on it. Too many bullets, food, and other supplies remained in his tent.

"He was alone?" Mato asked, speaking for the first time since they'd begun.

His father nodded. "Cougar Spirit *told* your grandfather that this man's wife had recently left him, and he'd lost his job. He'd always hunted, but never like this. Nothing mattered to him except hunting and drinking until he stopped hurting."

In some respects, Mato felt sorry for the man, but nothing justified the slaughter. "What did Grandfather do?"

After more exchanged looks, Uncle Tal took over. Grandfather had been taken, unarmed, into the mountains by his spirit, and although a lifetime of physical labor had made him strong, he hadn't wanted to risk his life against an armed man. He also wasn't sure he could kill a killer.

But Cougar Spirit had taken matters out of Grandfather's hands by turning a human being into a predator.

Disbelief gave way to acceptance as Mato listened to what a long-dead man had told his sons about the transformation. When Grandfather had told his spirit that, as horrified as he was, he wasn't a killer, Cougar Spirit had backed Grandfather against a tree, rose up on his hind legs, and planted his massive paws on Grandfather's shoulders. The powerful mouth with its deadly teeth had opened, and those teeth had closed in on Grandfather's neck.

But instead of feeling death penetrate his flesh, Grandfather began to change. Human muscles grew larger and more powerful. His skull had thickened, spine elongated. Arms and legs had morphed into limbs made for primal strength and survival. Most telling: he'd stopped thinking like a human. As hair coated his flesh, he'd dropped onto four legs and grown a heavy tail. His senses had sharpened. His mind became simple: live or die, kill or be killed.

And the beast he'd become relived the deaths of those innocent deer.

Running down the shrieking hunter and tearing out his throat had been easy.

"Grandfather said he felt no shame or guilt when the killing was done and he became a man again," a now pale-faced Uncle Tal said. "The whole time he was returning to Storm Bay and his family, pride rode with him, and he embraced the gratitude of those dead deer. But then he stepped into his home and looked at his wife and children and knew he could never tell them what he'd done. His spirit had turned him into an animal, a killer, and might again. He became afraid of himself and even more afraid of his spirit."

His mind spinning, Mato stared at his own hands. They'd always been his tools, vital parts of him. Because of them he'd maintained his land and built a house, taken incredible photographs of nature's wildlife. And they'd held a woman's body against his equally vulnerable one.

But if Spirit wanted—

Unable to complete the thought, he lifted his head. His father was looking at him with a mix of love and pity. In contrast, Uncle Tal was staring at their surroundings. The longer he studied his uncle, the more certain he became that he knew why he stared.

"You," he barely muttered. "It was you, wasn't it?"

Still focused on something unfathomable, Uncle Tal nodded. Reaching out, Mato squeezed his uncle's hand. Uncle Tal's spirit was a wolf, another predator.

"Tell me." He forced the words. "Did your spirit do to you what Grandfather's did to him?"

"It's better if only I know. Safer for everyone."

"Maybe before, but not now." He indicated his house. "*She's* here because of that man."

"Flann Castetter." His father made the name sound like a curse.

Mato felt feathers brush his cheeks and then the sensation died, leaving him convinced his spirit had just sent him a message—or a warning. As awed as he was by the contact, he'd give everything to have Spirit leave him alone so he could bury his mind and body in the woman, the dangerous woman, inside the home he'd built. A wave of empathy for what his grandfather had lived with weakened him, but along with that came chilling awareness of how much darker his own journey might be.

Forcing raw courage into every molecule of his being, he again squeezed his uncle's hand. "I have to know."

Shutting his eyes, Uncle Tal nodded. "I was afraid I'd have to say these words, which is why it was so difficult for me to come here, but because I love you as if you were my son, I did."

"I embrace your courage."

"I'm not the one who needs courage. You are."

Incapable of speaking, he rubbed his uncle's dry fingers.

Sighing, the older man began. "Our spirits are more than givers of wisdom, more than stewards of this beloved land. Their power—their ability to force us to obey their commands . . ."

"By turning us into them," Mato finished for the slumping man he loved as much as his father.

"Tal," his father said, "I don't want you to become like our father, filled with a burden that eventually killed him."

"I have no choice." Uncle Tal opened his eyes. "Our father told us about becoming a cougar so he could prepare us for what might happen, and now I must do the same for my nephew."

Although surrounded by a sense of unreality, Mato knew what his uncle was going to say, maybe not the details, but the essence. "Is Castetter dead?" he asked.

"Yes."

"How?"

Even the breeze seemed to stop so it could listen to a tale of forces beyond most humans' comprehension. As Uncle Tal told it, he had been content to listen as Flann Castetter presented the design for NewDirections Development. Yes, he'd sensed his spirit's uneasy stirring, but because Castetter was talking about something far in the future that hadn't been approved, he hadn't seen the connection between those plans and a poacher's violent death at his father's fangs. But beginning the night of the first public meeting, he'd been beset with nightmares in which massive houses ate up acre after acre of sacred land.

Tal had heard chainsaws biting into ancient trees, seen the Spruce River's course changed and fragile banks dug up by massive earthmoving equipment. Mud and debris fouled crystalline water, while squirrels and birds dislodged from their homes in the trees threw their plaintive cries into the air. Soil enriched by centuries of pine needles was buried under concrete, fences put an end to ancient deer trails, and emissions clogged the air and compromised the lungs of what creatures still lived there.

"My wolf spirit insisted *he* be stopped before the damage could begin," Uncle Tal muttered. "It *must* not be as it had been back when too many deer lost their lives before justice was served."

Deer weren't the only example of why spirit justice was meted out, but he sensed his relatives didn't know much more than he did about which ancestor had killed a wolf poacher, the *bear* who'd stopped two rogue timber fallers, a greedy salmon fisherman whose drowned body had been found near his kill, or the careless camper whose too-large fire had started a devastating blaze more than twenty years ago. That man's remains had stood in silent testament to yet another *cougar's* strength.

Like his father had tried to do, Uncle Tal had warned his spirit that his human heart rendered him incapable of killing, but Wolf Spirit had taken matters out of his hands two nights after the last so-called informational meeting. Castetter had been on his way back to Portland to confer with his fellow investors, when he'd stopped at the rest stop just north of Wolf Bay.

Uncle Tal had been waiting for him, but not in human form. Because it was night, Castetter had had the area to himself, or so he'd believed. He'd been using his flashlight to guide him along the gravel path to the bathroom when a wolf suddenly blocked his way.

"I was thinking, and yet I wasn't," Uncle Tal explained. "I'd never felt more powerful, and my eyesight was keen. I smelled the man's fear and heard his heartbeat. The moment he screamed, nothing else mattered. I would silence him using the weapons my spirit had given me. He tried to run, but I knocked him to the ground. When he curled up, covering his head with his hands, I bit the back of his neck. Screaming, he turned over and struck with the flashlight until my jaws broke his wrist. Wanting him to know he was going to die, I straddled him, his face and my muzzle inches apart. Our breaths came together. Even with his right hand flopping, he tried to gouge out my eyes, so I sank my teeth into his throat."

Just as your father, my grandfather, had done years ago.

Uncle Tal's eyes closed, and he started shaking. "The taste of his blood made me hungry to end things, but something stopped me. Holding on to him, I let him bleed. For a long time."

Oh, god, oh, god!

"Then?" Mato prompted when silence went on too long.

"Then I killed him. And dragged him deep into the woods."

Where Castetter's body remained. "It's a public place," he finally thought to say. "No one said anything about finding blood."

"Because it started raining that night and rained all the next day. When I came back to myself, when I became a man again, I was lying under a tree with my clothing soaked, shivering."

And now you're shivering again. With that thought, Mato wrapped his arms around the frail-feeling man and held him close. But even with everything he'd heard and learned in the past few minutes, he couldn't help thinking about another body and another kind of trembling.

21

"Where are you going?"

Looking as remote as he had when he'd come in a few minutes ago, Mato sat on the side of the bed lacing up his hiking boots. Smokey had been afraid to say anything when he'd first come inside, and that fear remained with her, pushing aside her need to be in his arms.

She hadn't told him she'd spotted him talking to his relatives, concluding that he'd guessed that. Whatever the reason for his distance, it had a great deal, if not everything, to do with that conversation.

Why did things have to be so complicated between them? she wondered, though she already knew the answer. If they'd met under other, innocent circumstances, would they have immediately been drawn to each other? Maybe there wouldn't have been a spark, let alone that fire in her belly. Not being attracted to him seemed impossible, especially because the dark and dangerous nature that now kept her at arm's length was part of his appeal. Maybe his mysterious complexity was the draw—that and the understanding that he was more than just a man.

He stood, causing her to step back. What had she just called him—dark? Yes, he was that and more, as if additional layers had been added to him, maybe at birth. She'd never been drawn to moody-broody men, preferring those who were as optimistic as she believed herself to be, and yet here she was living with the ultimate in sober.

Living with? Hardly. And yet she was no longer his prisoner.

Tense, she watched him head toward the front door. He'd curled his fingers around the knob before she spoke. "I might not be here when you return. Have you thought about that?"

"I'll find you."

Of course you will. Nothing can stop you if you put your mind to it. "What if I decide to leave town?"

"You won't." He still wasn't facing her. "You have your damnable article to write."

So that's what his mood was about—at least part of the reason. Although she longed to haul him around so he had to look at her, she didn't because she didn't know what she might say. And she wasn't going to touch him, because it would undoubtedly lead to insane sex, and that would get in the way of what they needed to deal with.

He had to walk. Walk and think, but not about her.

The woods closed around him, sheltering him as they had his entire life, and even with what he'd learned about Castetter's death, a measure of peace settled around him. If he moved away he could earn a great deal more money, even become wealthy, but not only didn't he give a damn about material things beyond his home, his soul started to shrivel the moment he put distance between himself and Storm Bay. Like the rest of his family and the majority of his people, this was the only place where he belonged.

Because the spirits had spun powerful spells around them.

"I know you're watching me," he told Spirit. "And I know you heard—and already knew—what my father and uncle told me. I knew he was dead. I'd suspected someone had killed him the moment he disappeared. He deserved . . ."

Did a man deserve to lose his life because of his career? He couldn't answer that any more than he could condone what his uncle's spirit had compelled him to do.

Unwilling to draw parallels between himself and his uncle, he allowed himself to be distracted by a mouse watching from the end of a fallen tree. If a mouse was his spirit, he'd never wonder what in the way of violence might be expected of him, but neither could a mouse protect this land.

After a brief smile at the tiny gray rodent, he continued walking toward the Spirit's Overlook, where he'd gone so many times. He'd first started coming there about the time his body began changing from a boy's to a young man's, and although every step was familiar, it never ceased to rejuvenate him. Even today, knowing what he had to do, the journey felt right.

Where are you going? Smokey Powers had asked him, but his only words to her had been spoken in anger, and yet he wasn't angry at her—or at himself.

It was the world he lived in, the forces surrounding him, commitment. And yet he couldn't reject those things, because without them he'd be left with nothing except a sense of failure.

When he reached the cliff, he noted that clouds were building on the horizon, which often served to announce that a storm was coming this way. Maybe it was fitting that it started raining as it had the night he'd first seen Smokey Powers.

Smokey. It seemed as if he'd known her forever, and yet

what he felt for her was starkly new. He wanted her body with a savage intensity that deeply shook him and had a great deal to do with why he'd left her so abruptly.

She could be gone when he returned, he acknowledged, lifting his arms to the heavens. Why would she want to stay in a house where she'd been held prisoner waiting for a man like him?

Freedom. She'd want that.

Just as he did.

Not that it mattered.

Speak to me, my spirit. Don't make me beg for your wisdom. Even if I long to reject your words, I must hear what you have to say. Just as other spirits directed those who carry my blood, I have to listen—just don't command me to kill her!

His head feeling about to explode, he nevertheless stretched his arms even farther. Invisible wings again brushed his cheeks, making him wonder if Spirit was acknowledging the tears he didn't dare shed. His uncle hadn't wanted to kill, and yet he had because his spirit had given him no choice by turning him into a wolf. Living with the knowledge of what he'd become and what he'd done while in that form had nearly destroyed his grandfather.

If he jumped off the cliff—

Don't, Mato. That isn't your destiny.

"Then what is?" he demanded of the internal voice he both dreaded and craved.

To defend what's sacred.

"That's what others have done. But she—she isn't jeopardizing the mountains. She has no saws, no guns."

You know what her words are capable of.

He did, damn it. That was the hell of it. If she put everything together, and he had no doubt she was capable of it, she would be even more dangerous than a poacher or developer because her words would expose centuries-old secrets.

"Maybe it's time for the truth to be known," he said, speaking from his heart and cock. "If the world learned how truly sacred this land is, they'd leave it alone."

No, they wouldn't. They'd be drawn here.

"Not if she warned that a crush of people would destroy the link with the spirits. I can—I believe I could convince her to tell people to forget what happened in the past and keep this land as nature intended." He swallowed. "I would work with her. Instead of putting my energy into trying to block the development as I've been doing, I'd champion what is my heritage and the heritage of everyone I call family."

Stop it! Your fucking her has robbed you of your wisdom. How can you believe words from either of you will change human nature? Man is greedy.

"I'm a man, but I'm not greedy."

Aren't you? What about your need for her body?

The argument, particularly what Spirit had just said, caused his head to pulse. Concerned he might lose his balance, he stepped back from the cliff, but a force stronger than himself kept his arms outstretched. Studying his hands, he acknowledged how easy it would be for his spirit to change him in even more fundamental ways—to turn him into a raptor. A killer.

"Don't do this to me, please!" Although his pleading tone shocked him, he couldn't change it. "What my grandfather and uncle did—their spirits guided them in destroying enemies to this land. They didn't spill the blood of someone—someone they'd lain beside."

For the third time today, unseen feathers touched him, but instead of the earlier gentle caress, these were sharp pricks, the contact painful and electric. Covering his cheeks with his hands, he took another backward step.

You are my instrument, Mato. I've watched you since your infancy, looking into your heart and listening to your thoughts, feeling your strength and courage. I chose you because I be-

lieved we shared the same beliefs and you would embrace everything I stand for. But because you are human, that humanity stands between you and what must be done. That's why your grandfather and uncle and others who carried out the spirits' needs were made to change form. They became predators.

Not just predators—killers, Mato acknowledged. "There has to be another way, there *has* to be! If she promises not to write—"

What a fool you would be to believe her.

Was his spirit speaking the truth, or was Spirit influenced by the past? Just because a handful of people caused the mountains and the creatures who belonged here to bleed didn't mean all humans were bad. Smokey had taken his body into hers; surely he knew more about her than Spirit did.

"Reveal yourself to her," he said, desperation driving the words. "Send your beliefs and words to her. That way, she'll understand."

Hers is the blood of an outsider. As such, her heart can't hear mine beating; her ears are deaf to my words, her eyes blind to me.

"That isn't true. If you'd seen the way she looks at my photographs or the way she reacts to a hawk—"

Which I sent. How can she not wonder?

His thoughts raced in one direction and then the next, but no matter how hard he tried to pull them together, he couldn't think of anything to say. Besides, how dare he, a simple human, argue with an essence as powerful and all-knowing as his spirit? A small and fragile part of him continued to cling to the hope that he could change Smokey's mind, but if she agreed not to write anything, would her career be over?

If only he'd never met her! Never stripped her and slipped between her legs!

An ache across his shoulders reminded him that he was still pressing his palms to his cheeks, so he let his arms drop to his sides. It took everything in him not to slump forward or leap into space.

This place had always nourished him. He loved the smell and touch of fog, the endless sound of the sea rolling over the shoreline, the water birds, days of startlingly blue skies, and others when clouds and rain coated the world. Even with everything crushing him, he looked outward and drew a measure of peace from the horizon.

At first, he saw only a small, distant dot, but even then he knew what was coming his way. His fingers fisting, and his lungs expanding, he studied the approaching life. Longing pushed away dread at the thought of what flying surely felt like, the freedom, causing him to silently urge the hawk to speed its flight.

Smokey Powers had initially been drawn to one of his hawk photographs, an innocent interest that in essence had changed both their lives. He had no doubt she'd share his anticipation if she was with him right now, maybe wrapping an arm around him as the other shielded her eyes from the glare. She'd say little or nothing, but her body would tell him everything. He'd soak up her single-minded focus on the bird, knowing she was thinking about much more than the act of flight. Her fertile brain would contemplate what went on inside a predator's brain, whether it ever thought about its prey or wanted another life, if it knew how rare was the ability to fly or that its eyesight far exceeded creatures tied to the earth.

And after she'd absorbed her thoughts and the emotions that went with them, she'd softly speak his name and turn toward him, her breasts brushing him, the heat between her legs whispering to his cock. Eyes sparkling, and lips soft and inviting, she'd tell him she wanted them to both grow wings so they could catch the same air current.

Insane! Dangerous.

Even though he couldn't quite rid himself of the images his hot blood had conjured, he'd presented himself to his spirit countless times before and knew better than to fight the pull. Hawk, his hawk, was nearly overhead now.

Such a little thing, he noted, weighing only a few pounds. It seemed unbelievable that a hawk could kill something much larger and heavier than itself, but that was the way of predators. And although he admired the perfectly formed body and long, shapely wings, he'd never tried to trap a hawk so he could study it up close because he had no wish to be attacked by killing talons and a beak.

Once more he pushed away errant thoughts and did what he needed to—concentrate. The hawk had stopped flying and was now floating almost overhead. A breeze occasionally ruffled its feathers; otherwise, it looked as if it had been frozen in time. Awareness of a second approaching bird came slowly, but Mato finally acknowledged the newcomer. This hawk was smaller than the first, and its feathers were slightly paler, its demeanor fierce and yet somehow different—gentler maybe.

A female? The first hawk's mate?

He unsuccessfully tried to force his fingers to relax, but even as he pondered whether Spirit was sending him a message about Smokey's role in his life, he couldn't shake off his unease.

His hawk was watching the female, its neck twisting as the female circled it. He could almost laugh at what he took to be the female's attempt to seduce the male. Even from this distance, he decided that the female was a beautiful example of the species. Not only was her flight seductive, complete with coy looks and fluttering wings, but she was well formed, healthy looking and probably young. She'd produce a large number of eggs and devote herself to feeding and protecting her young; what more could a male hawk want in a partner?

Turning his attention to *his* hawk, he noted that it was pulling its wings closer to its body. The female responded with a low call and dipped her head in the male's direction with a come-hither gesture. The male pushed off, wings beating effortlessly, heading straight for the female. Calling out again, the female stopped and waited, beak open and wings widespread, her breast exposed.

His hawk struck the female in full flight, its talons slicing past feathers and flesh and tearing at vital organs. Then, screeching, the male headed into the heavens.

Bleeding, the female plummeted toward earth.

22

The oils Smokey was working with represented only a small portion of her collection, but as she'd been packing to leave Portland, she'd figured she wouldn't have much time to paint, and these had fit easily into the case she'd brought to Storm Bay. She wanted to thank Mato for bringing them to his place, but that would lead to a further conversation, specifically questions about what she was doing hunched over the coffee table in the living room instead of getting the hell out of there.

She'd have to answer with the truth, which was she didn't know why she stayed. Fortunately at the moment little mattered except transferring Mato's hawk in flight photograph onto her paper. After spending too much time pacing through his house, being able to focus on her hobby felt wonderful. Painting had always rejuvenated her, and it was no different this time, maybe even more so because of her surroundings. Thanks to the large windows, her view of the woods was almost as clear as if she'd been outside, and although clouds were now in evidence, she was content to take whatever nature handed her.

Pausing, she studied what she'd accomplished in the past hour. She still needed to fill in the feather details, and she hadn't started on the surroundings, but the hawk was perfectly formed, if she said so herself. She'd never been particularly adept at capturing the essence of muscle and flesh, yet she didn't see how she could improve on what she'd created today. The predator all but flew off the page, energy and life rippling through it. She could almost hear it cry, nearly feel the wind rushing past its body.

Peace—that's what the past hour had been about, she surmised as she added a little more white paint to the gray she'd been using to define the hawk's underbelly. Considering everything she'd been through lately, being able to relax was nothing short of a gift from the gods or nature or the spirits or whatever force had supplied said gift.

Yes, her body hummed with quiet need only Mato could first feed and then satisfy, but that hunger contributed to her overall mood. She just wished she could give him a taste of her contentment. The man was uptight, tense, worried, maybe all three and more. Maybe she should try to get him to talk about it—once she let him put back on his clothes.

Like it's that simple.

A sound snapped through her, jerking her upright and destroying her lethargy. Breath snagged, she stared at the front door.

God, but he was incredible! Shadowed by darkness and quiet but hands-down the most muscled man she'd ever seen. Granted, her reaction had something to do with the fact that he'd fucked her mindless and even more to do with their complex relationship, yet she wouldn't change anything.

What was it about him that allowed him to bring the wilderness inside with him? Even after he'd closed the door behind him, she continued to smell pine and mist. If she could bottle those heady aromas, she'd make a fortune selling it to women, especially horny ones.

You aren't horny. You can't be, she chided as he looked down at her painting. After the antics they'd been through, she should be dead from the neck down. Only, she wasn't.

Wrapping her in his silence, he leaned closer. Having people study her paintings had always made her more nervous than critiques of her writing, probably because she was hardly a professional artist, and yet she'd never more needed to hear a person's reaction. The sense of peace she'd experienced while she was alone . . . what had happened to it?

A ripple of fear forced her to her feet, but though she needed to place distance between them, she remained in place. He had to have noted her reaction, and yet he only sat in the spot where she'd been a moment ago, his fingers hovering inches over the painting. If he touched it, the wet oils would smear.

"It's alive," he said.

If she lived to be a hundred, no compliment would ever mean as much. Coming from him, a man who knew more about hawks than she could comprehend, the words had her blinking back tears. But even as she ached to touch him in gratitude, she knew she couldn't.

Wild. He was wild. Again.

"What happened out there?" she asked because her life might depend on the answer. "Who did you talk to?"

"Spirit."

Even with shock setting off an irregular heartbeat, she understood how much he'd given her. He didn't have to answer her; he could have lied, and yet he'd handed her the absolute truth— one deep down, she'd expected.

Fingers now clamped around her upper arms, she struggled not to give into emotion. No matter what form her article took, she wouldn't include her moments with Mato, because no one would believe her—and because, even if it cost her her life, she couldn't betray this man.

"What did *he* tell you?"

"It was what he showed me."

Oh, shit, he was looking at her now, probing eyes tearing through her layers and maybe revealing things about her she didn't know, setting her on fire. Suddenly and irrevocably starved for him, she breathed in rapid gasps that did nothing to cool the flames.

Was he responsible for the inner fire? Had Hawk Spirit shown him how to strip away her skin and leave her utterly exposed? Maybe that's why he seemed so wild—because for the first time in her life she was drawn to the savage. Not sure whether she'd begun to sway or if she was just imagining her tenuous self-control, she searched the room for distraction, but her painting had become a blur, and she could no longer see what was beyond the windows. The walls started closing in, trapping her and Mato in the too-small space. Freedom gone! Space shrinking. Him expanding, becoming her world! No longer human.

Fear sent her running barefoot for the door, but he caught her before she could reach it and yanked her back against him. Captured again, only not by a man this time but something dangerous and primitive, deadly!

Screaming silently, she fought an overwhelming and incomprehensible weakness. One hard spasm after another seized her; everything she'd ever believed about what her life was about shattered to leave her lost. Helpless.

Then his arms locked around her middle with her back to him, and her terror died. He was holding her, protecting her— from what? The unnerving thought that he might be defending her from himself robbed her of other thoughts.

"Don't fight me." Sealing her against him with one hand, he slid the other over her throat.

"What—what are you going to do?"

Not more silence, please, not that! But did she really want to know?

Life was precious. When it came down to it, nothing mattered more than staying alive, so why wasn't she trying to haul his fingers off her neck? Off balance and staring upward, legs splayed for balance, she acknowledged his greater strength, but that wasn't why she wasn't fighting.

Her body needed his—that and nothing else.

Shifting her weight, she ground her buttocks against him. As she did, his potent cock pressed into the small of her back. So he was wild, was he? He wasn't the only one. They had that in common. Maybe only that.

Barely aware of what she was doing, Smokey leaned into him even more and flattened his cock between them, and when he took a backward step, she kept pace. After a few more steps, he pushed her upright and spun her around. His open mouth put her in mind of a panting dog, and his eyes were filled with intensity. Beast, he was becoming a beast! Like his spirit?

Hell, hell, that's where he'd been, joining forces with Hawk Spirit, surrendering his human qualities and embracing the primal.

"Are you going to kill me now?"

Still hiding behind his damnable silence, he shook his head until she stopped its movement by clamping her hands against his cheeks. As she did, his eyes started to roll back in his head. Then he blinked and came back to her. A little. Maybe.

Ah, Mato, all that strength and sexual energy are nothing against the hold Hawk Spirit has on you. You want what your spirit has chosen for you, and yet you don't—because of me?

Her? She was the only thing standing between him and slavish dedication to an inhuman force?

Maybe.

Another time—if they had other moments together—she'd

ask if he'd been more human or primitive creature on the day he'd returned from his time with Hawk Spirit to find her working with her oils, but now was for instinct. And action.

Trying to save both of them.

He wore another of the flannel shirts that seemed to have been made for him, but much as she loved seeing him in the sturdy and practical garment, she needed nudity more. Needed to press her flesh to his.

Her low growl adding strength to her fingers; she tore at the buttons. Most slipped out of the holes, but two flew away, leaving behind torn fabric. He looked surprised, but whether because he hadn't expected that of her or wasn't fully aware of what was happening, she couldn't say. Every second he stood looking down at her was a gift; any moment he might turn against her, and if he did—

No, she wouldn't go there! She would wrap her mind around his capacity for tenderness and compassion—the man in him.

He made no attempt to strip off his clothes, so she took over the task, careful not to lose eye contact as she discarded his shirt, unzipped his jeans, knelt and unlaced his boots. After getting him to hold on to her shoulder for balance, she pulled off his boots. Still kneeling, she tugged down his jeans and shorts and helped him out of them. Looking up at the male expanse, she remembered the other time he'd been naked to her clothed state. Then she touched her tongue to his satiny tip, and nothing else mattered.

Male, all male, fully human.

Even as she closed her lips around his gift to her, she acknowledged how fleeting these moments were. So much stood between them. They lived in different worlds, and those worlds could and would collide. She'd spent so much time mapping out her future, setting goals, but now the future and goals didn't matter. There was only the gift, not just of his cock but of all of him. His impact on her heart and body. Fighting back tears she'd have to shed sometime, she stroked his flanks. Opening her mouth wide, she brought him deep into her and hung on to him, tasted.

Sucking cock. Yes, and yet expanding her throat and locking her lips around the solid, hot mass was so much more. Magical somehow. Conscious of little else, she leaned back, freeing a few precious inches of him. A hot flash that left her all but dripping in sweat made her long to strip off her clothes. Mato Hawk, lover of these rugged mountains and servant to his spirit, trusted her. She was worthy of him, she was!

But did she trust him?

No thinking! Not now.

Her mind sealed tight, she let him slide the rest of the way out so she could bring his balls into her moist cave. Sucking and bathing him at the same time made the back of her neck and shoulders twitch, but despite the discomfort, heat again licked at her. Most of it was centered around her breasts and groin and the small of her back. Her jeans were too tight, her bra size too small. And the tingling in her hands had her rubbing his flanks.

The smell of the wilderness that had come inside with him was being replaced by other scents. She couldn't recognize all of them—a mix of sweat and soap and her juices, a little oil paint. The smells rolled through her, entering her veins and sending the swirling essence to her heart.

She'd released his balls and started to replenish the moisture in her mouth when he grabbed her wrists and hauled her to her feet. Holding her arms over her head with one hand, he dispensed with her blouse buttons. Although he barely skimmed her bra, her breasts tightened, causing her to groan. He must have known what had caused the sound because, pushing aside her blouse, he ran a thumbnail over the part of her breasts the bra didn't cover. Her legs went numb.

When he released her hands, she lowered her arms and fumbled with the bra fastening. Then she stripped herself naked to the waist.

She wanted to speak, wanted to say something, anything, but silence was easier; no wonder he'd wrapped himself in silence so many times. This way, neither of them had to address what would happen after they had sex.

Fucking. Sex.

But not making love, not thinking that dangerous thought!

She was still working at stripping the two words from her mind when he freed the button at her waist. Acting in unison, they dispensed with the zipper; together they pulled off her jeans and panties.

Naked. No turning back.

Breathing in the smell of both of them, she reached for him, but he again captured her wrists and hauled her arms upward, pushing her back at the same time. The couch stopped her. Robbed of her balance, she sprawled with her legs open and breasts jiggling.

Watching her with an intensity she guessed mirrored her earlier stare, he settled himself on his knees between her legs and pushed them even farther apart. With her arms over her head, she acknowledged her hungry pussy's demands. Not long ago she'd been a civilized professional modern woman, but that female had been sacrificed to the primal. The insistent. Now, like Mato, she existed to obey needs as old as time.

Fine. Good. No hesitation or question. Only her hips lifting toward him and wet heat rolling out of her to coat her labia. Only sobbing and tearing at her hair while he lapped at that heat.

Don't stop, don't stop! Then, despite her silent command, she lowered her arms and raked his shoulders, nearly drawing blood. She told herself to stop, but his insistent tongue abusing her sensitive tissues was more than she could handle. And his teeth on her clit, oh, god! Squirming, she somehow kept herself from tunneling out from under him. Mini climax after mini climax reduced her to whimpering, pleading sounds.

Control fading, she clamped on to his shoulders and might have buried her nails in him if he hadn't jerked upright, his mouth inches from hers. A moment ago he'd been drinking from her sex, and now, surely, he wanted to kiss her. But his eyes gave out inhuman messages; she'd never seen a human so tense, so ready for what, attack?

"Mato! Mato, talk to me. Say something."

Nostrils flaring, he planted his hands on her knees and rocked forward, blanketing her body with his. His mouth remained open, and he seemed to be panting, but he gave no indication he'd heard her. The room started closing in again, pushing her against him and blocking out the world. Fire was threatening to turn them into one, to strip her down and force her to become something she couldn't possibly comprehend. Yet even with those thoughts, her cunt wept and clenched.

A hiss, a growl, something, and suddenly he yanked her off the couch and onto the floor. Then he straddled her, his legs inside hers, his arms bracketing her shoulders, his gaze locked on her throat.

Terror grabbed her with powerful teeth, but before she drowned in the sensation, he covered her mouth with his. His inhuman strength faded, flowed from him, leaving a gentleness she'd hadn't known he was capable of. How could a man's lips be so soft, the touch seeping through her layers until every part of her was involved? Not fully believing what had happened, she nevertheless fully gave herself up to the exquisite moments. Hungry for him, she ran her tongue between her lips and then against his. How sweet he tasted, still wild but infused with the warmth of a spring morning.

As a child, she'd picked wildflowers and sucked nectar from

them, letting the honeyed drops slide down her throat. She was doing the same thing now, and yet the taste was more deeply textured, filled with his messages. He was giving her everything he had, his every mood. Lightness and dark, civilized and primal all lived within the same body, sometimes at war with himself and sometimes perfectly blended.

That's what it was right now—a completeness, layered and yet simple. His gift to her.

Taking the precious gift with every fiber in her, she opened her mouth and tasted even more deeply of him, shivering as his satin lips possessed hers. Unable to see clearly into his eyes, she could believe in his tender side. He had cast off the predator that was part of him and was giving himself up fully to the act of a man alone with the only woman in his life.

It might not be true; there might be other women or at least memories of them. But he had her now just as she had him, and she was naked and willing under him, and his mouth was open, inviting her in. Fully and perhaps unwisely accepting the invitation, she ran her tongue over his teeth and pressed it against his tongue, teasing, tasting, goose bumps prickling.

Not enough.

Filled with a need no kiss could satisfy, she reached between them and drew his cock to her opening. As she did, he lowered himself, his greater weight and size closing around and over her. Then he started to lift his head, so she closed her teeth around his lower lip, holding him in place. But even as she worked to rein him in, she wanted what he was offering. Needed what they both knew was coming. Releasing him, she offered her sex to him like some animal in heat.

And like the male of all species, he accepted.

Sleek against sleek, her wetness coating him and guiding him home. He stretched her, altered her, filled her, pushed her out into space.

And because this might be the last time, she surrendered fully, coming even before he'd settled fully inside her. Then coming again when his cock powered her inner channel and his hot, quick, hard breath seared her eyes.

Behind her now-closed lids, she cried.

23

Rolling off her, Mato sat up. Then, although Smokey tried to pull him back down, he stood and walked to the front window. Once more he seemed unaware of his nudity, which struck her as a vital message about the difference between them because even though they'd just had sex, she needed back the security and protection clothing provided. Bottom line, she was human, while he—what was he? Moving quietly so not to draw attention to herself, she yanked on her pants and shirt but stopped when she'd buttoned just three buttons.

What had happened? Sex, yes, kissing, oh, yes, a little fear, but even more wonder—that damnable darkness of his interspersed with a wonderful gentleness she'd hold on to for the rest of her life. She'd been working barefoot when he came home, but now, not allowing herself to ask why, she slipped into her tennis shoes. Then, because she had to do this, she walked over to where he stood.

Instead of the sensual heat that had flowed into her a few minutes ago, cold radiated from him. Shocked, she put her hand to her throat. He didn't seem to be aware of her presence;

instead something outside had his attention. All but positive she knew what it was, she forced herself to focus.

Rain slapped against the window and made it hard to see what was out there. Having no choice, she blinked repeatedly. Yes, there the damn bird was, perched on the branch he'd been on before. Yet even as she cursed it, she acknowledged the perfect body.

She was a stranger to this land, a newcomer. In contrast, Mato's roots were deeply buried, as were those of his relatives, but none of them was as perfectly attuned to the earth as the creatures that made the forest and shore their home.

Let me know what you're thinking, please, she begged the bird. *You and Mato all but share the same mind. Can't you at least give me a small piece of yourself? When you look at me, what do you see? What do you want from me?*

Nothing.

Shocked and yet not, she forced herself to nod. At the same time she sensed that Mato was changing in indefinable and yet familiar ways, distancing himself from her even though he hadn't moved a muscle. *You want all of him, don't you?* she demanded of his spirit. *You want me gone so you can have him to yourself.*

Yes.

Why? Needing action, she rubbed the condensation from the inside of the window.

You already know the answer.

About to retort that no way could she read a *hawk's* mind, she clenched her teeth. Hawk Spirit's simple *yes* had been in response to the first part of her comment. The spirit wanted her gone—dead. And the being saw Mato as the instrument for making that happen.

"I'm leaving," she said aloud. "I have to go now."

A ripple of tension ran through the man whose cum still rested inside her. Widening her stance in case he tried to jump her, she struggled not to respond to his presence, but how could she not? "Hawk Spirit's waiting for you," she continued. "And we both know what he wants."

Another ripple, weaker this time, rolled over Mato, causing her to mourn his loss of freedom and self-determination. What would it be like to lose her will? To know that a powerful and compelling force could make her do whatever it wanted, especially to someone she loved?

No damn it, not love!

A fiery spark tore through her. To her shock she realized she'd rested her hand on Mato's shoulder. Despite the unsettling heat, she couldn't force herself to end the contact. "I want to borrow your truck, but if you won't let me, I'll walk." She indicated the door to the bedroom. "I don't care about my clothes, but I'm going to take my files with me. And my painting supplies..." Realization of how much she needed that half-finished hawk painting rocked her. "The longer I delay, the heavier it's going to rain."

Ah, hell, he was turning toward her, pulling himself free of Hawk Spirit's gaze, resting his own beautiful and yet maybe deadly gaze on her, stripping away layers of her resolve and making her ache for what they could never have.

Placing his hands on her shoulders, he drew in a long breath. "I'll drive you."

"You don't have—"

"Now. Before it's too late."

Zoos held no appeal to her because she hated seeing wild animals forced to live behind bars, but she'd never expected to feel that way about a fellow human being. Not fighting her tears, she stroked the back of his hand. "I wish it was different for you."

"So do I," he muttered. Then the pain that had overtaken him fell away, to be replaced by a creature resigned to his life. "Hurry."

* * *

The northwest storm buffeted Mato's pickup as he jockeyed it along the gravel road. Neither of them had spoken while they'd placed her belongings on the seat between them. Now, though those possessions forced her to hug the passenger's door, she was grateful that something separated her from Mato. It was still the middle of the day, but clouds the color of charcoal had stripped away most of the light. Even with the windshield wipers going full speed, she understood why Mato was leaning forward with his face close to the windshield. Making sure he stayed on the road was taking his full attention, thank goodness. Otherwise . . . otherwise what? They might talk?

Things were ending between them. As soon as he'd taken her to the cabin where her car was, hopefully he'd turn around and drive back to his world. Wiser than she'd ever thought she'd need to be, she'd throw her belongings into her trunk and plow north through the downpour until she'd put Storm Bay—and Mato—behind her.

And then? What was she going to do with her life?

"I have to write something," she said around the mass in her throat.

"I know."

"If I don't . . . My readers are expecting . . . my editor . . . I've never been able to turn my back on a story. If it's within my ability to explore the truth, I'll do it."

"I know."

He wasn't looking at her; even with her gaze resolute on the smeared window, she knew that. Sanity, to say nothing of self-preservation, warned her to shut the hell up so she wouldn't risk pushing him over the edge, and yet she couldn't let everything end like this. Telling herself she wasn't crying—not yet, by hell—she sucked in damp air. "He really is dead, isn't he? Castetter."

"Yes."

Another breath. "I know I asked this before, but I'm doing it again. Did you do it?"

Silence. Long seconds of it. Her heart hurting.

"No."

Thank you, thank you. "But you know who did, don't you?"

"Yes." He flicked her a look filled with warning and regret. "No more questions because I'm not going to answer them."

"I didn't think you would." Trapped by her heavy heart, she pulled silence over herself until she realized she couldn't end things like this. "I have to say the same thing you just did. Don't ask me if I'm going to quote what you just told me, because I don't know."

"If you do, I'm not the only one who'll wind up between bars."

Him, in prison for refusing to cooperate with authorities, and someone precious to him in that same prison because that person wouldn't allow him or herself to hide behind Mato's silence. She'd never hated her job more, and yet no story had ever excited her like this. "I wish it didn't have to come to this. You do understand that, don't you?"

"Yes."

"Castetter isn't the only mystery," she continued. "The deaths I've uncovered—and maybe more—the spirits and their, what, their human hosts are responsible, aren't they? How far does it go back?"

Before he could respond, if he was going to, he hit a pothole, causing her to grab the dashboard to keep from being thrown about. The jarring distracted her from her inner turmoil, but then she heard the tires' muffled crunch, and her turmoil all came back.

This man would live inside her for the rest of her life, but not just because of his passionate commitment and the heat of his body. Her world had changed because of the incredible and too-short time they'd spent together. She'd thought that diving headfirst into whatever story she was working on, only to put it behind her so she could embrace the next one, was the way she wanted to live her life, but she'd been wrong, so incredibly wrong.

How could she have turned her back on people and situations as if they were yesterday's newspaper? Pieces about a child in need of a transplant; a couple who'd turned their home into a haven for abandoned dogs; a man who'd finally found his birth mother only to have her beg him to forget her; a cancer survivor embracing life by spearheading construction of a nature trail in the foothills around her own—they'd brought her into their lives and hearts only to have her walk away when she'd mined them for what she needed to fulfill her job requirements.

It would be different this time. There'd be no turning her back on Mato Hawk.

Sex, that's what she wanted. Only sex and no thinking—heat and cries of release and bodies churning, maybe a little laughter.

What did Mato's laughter sound like?

"What's going to happen?" she asked because the question demanded life. "To you and the other Storm Bay residents?"

"You have to ask?"

"Yeah, I do." But maybe she already knew.

His knuckles turning white, he shrugged. "Castetter's absence won't change anything. The spirits believed it would, but they don't understand man's complexity. Man's greed. Before . . ."

"Before NewDirections's people discovered this area and made their plans, all the spirits had to deal with were solitary poachers, a handful of rogue timber fallers, some idiot with a match."

"Yeah." Mato drew out the word, and if she hadn't been concentrating on him, the rain might have swallowed the powerful word. "The world's becoming more complex." His sigh held a ragged edge. "Maybe the only thing to do is give up."

"You or the spirits?" *Don't cry, not yet! Not so he can see.*

"Both."

Arguments backed up inside her, but when she tried to open her mouth, her jaw remained locked. She lived in a city complete with modern conveniences and ways and endless distractions while Storm Bay stayed true to something primitive and simple and precious. And this man, this incredibly complex man's heart, had been woven into the land.

Seeing the highway just ahead took her by surprise. Although the only other vehicle in sight was a school bus, it served as inescapable proof that she and Mato had reentered the world beyond his home. After letting the bus pass, he pressed on the gas, and though she wanted to beg him to turn around, she didn't, because sooner or later they'd have to go their separate ways. Besides, hadn't he warned her that he didn't trust his ability to remain civilized?

Hawk Spirit was with them; she felt the spirit's presence and its hold on Mato. Nothing she said or did, even offering her body to him again, would change that.

"The spirits don't understand something like the Northwest Fisheries Council," Mato said as the city-limit sign came into view. "They have no comprehension of how such things work."

"But you do."

"Yes." He claimed her with another glance. "My spirit has given me one set of weapons—talons—but that isn't enough."

Talons. Becoming a predator. "No," she had to admit, "it isn't. Laws, regulations—"

"The council will rule in favor of NewDirections." Mato's somber tone caused her eyes to burn. "Castetter's fate won't make a difference in their decision. If anything, it might tip the voting toward NewDirections. The *poor* bastard, losing his life to his cause."

Will his body ever be found?

"Do you really think the council members are that simple?"

"No, of course not. But NewDirections has the goddamn law on their side. Zoning regulations—believe me, I've studied it every way there is for something to be studied. Interpretation of those regulations is supposed to be objective, or at least it could be, but you heard that man, Jacobs."

"He cut you off."

"He made it clear that his mind's made up."

It really was that simple, wasn't it? A man who knew nothing about this land and had never heard its heart beating had the final say on its future. True, Jacobs had to report to the other members of the Northwest Fisheries Council, but they'd be swayed by his advice. His conclusions and recommendations would become theirs.

And nothing Hawk Spirit commanded Mato Hawk to do would change that.

Clenching her fingers, Smokey stared at the sign identifying the small motel Mato had kidnapped her from a few hours ago. He had to return to his world; she had to drive back into hers.

And when she took her next shower, his scent and semen would flow away from her.

24

It wasn't raining, so at least she didn't have to listen to a storm's song when she got out of her car and walked up the steps of the schoolhouse where she'd first seen Mato Hawk. She'd been gone for four nights and days, barely sleeping, crying when she couldn't stop the tears, putting off her editor, and silencing the inner investigative reporter's insistence that she write the story of her career.

Expecting animated voices, she was taken aback by the silence that reached out to envelope her as she stepped inside. She'd been on her way back to Storm Bay today before she'd tried to get in touch with Mato, but he hadn't answered his phone, and she hadn't left a message. Taking the coward's way out, she'd called the place where she'd seen Mato's hawk photography and talked to Halona, who'd told her that a number of local residents would be at the school for an urgent meeting.

Mato would be there.

Under her raincoat, her skin came alive, and although she should have been thinking about what she was going to do with what she had in her briefcase, she remembered Mato's smell and the sound of his voice and the way his cock had filled her. Her crotch burning, she stopped and filled her lungs. Then, fighting the urge to press her hand between her legs, she headed toward the auditorium.

The closed door stood as proof that whatever was being said in there wasn't for outsiders to hear. Why had she allowed instinct and need to bring her here? She should have waited until she was certain she'd have Mato to herself before letting him read the article that would appear in tomorrow's newspaper.

But he wasn't the only one who needed to know, and what if Hawk Spirit prevented Mato from hearing her out—or worse?

Damn last night's dream and the identical one she'd had night before. The scenes hadn't faded as she'd woken up. Instead they'd become more and more vivid until she'd smelled her own blood and heard her own screams as the predator Mato tore her apart. His talons had done most of the damage, ripping her skin open and laying bare her internal organs, clawing relentlessly until her heart stopped beating.

After waiting out a now familiar tremor, she turned the knob with clammy fingers and tugged on the door, which squeaked loudly as she pulled it toward her. Then she was standing in the opening she'd made, and some twenty pairs of eyes stared at her.

Those seated around a large rectangular table were all men, ranging from teenagers to a white-haired gentleman in a wheelchair, but even as she worked on learning all she could about those she'd have to face, she easily spotted Mato. True to his position as spokesman, he was standing, his hands resting on the table and leaning forward. From this distance she couldn't read his expression, but, then, maybe he'd keep his secrets even if she were in his arms.

Not in his arms. Not now, and maybe never again.

One of the older men got to his feet, pushed back his chair, and started toward her. As he did, she recognized him as Mato's uncle. "You don't belong here," he said by way of greeting.

"Hear me out first, please."

Mato was watching, his body still.

"Why? So you can try to convince us to let you exploit us?"

"No. I'm sorry you feel that way, but that's far from my intention. Look, if I wanted to make things easy on myself, I'd still be in Portland."

Frowning, Mato's uncle indicated her briefcase. "What have you brought?"

How she'd love to tell Mato how much she admired his uncle. Despite his unassuming appearance, he was direct. At the same time there was something vulnerable about him, as if he were carrying secrets he prayed he could carry to his grave. What secrets? she pondered. Then, though she didn't dare allow herself to be distracted from why she'd returned to Storm Bay or from the hostility directed at her, she settled her gaze on the older man's eyes.

Like Mato, he wasn't fully human, as witnessed by an instinctive wariness. Like Mato, essential elements of his spirit lived inside him. And, she realized as she continued to study him, that spirit demanded a great deal of its host. Maybe even killing.

Time seemed to stop, and her awareness tunneled down until only she and Mato's uncle existed. She was no longer standing inside a building but on a gravel path leading from a parking lot to a small, tree-surrounded public restroom. It was night; the only illumination came from muted lights spaced along the path. In the distance the ocean churned endlessly, and up close the wind wrestled with the trees. A man ill-clothed for the wilderness was on the trail, his shiny black shoes squeaking, suit jacket pulled up around his neck, tie constricting his loose flesh.

Suddenly the man's head came up, and he stared wide-eyed

into the underbrush. Seconds later he jumped back, screaming. Something dark and fierce charged the man and knocked him to the ground, lowered the doglike head. Another scream.

No, not a dog.

Maybe more shaken than she'd been in her entire life, Smokey clamped a hand over her mouth. Too late she realized how much she'd given away with her gesture. Mato's uncle was still staring at her, thankfully not coming closer, looking even more vulnerable than he had before, and yet proud.

And she understood.

"Say it," Mato ordered from his place across the room. "What just happened?"

"I saw—something."

"What was it, Smokey?"

With his voice like velvet and sandpaper scraping at her nerve endings, she tore her attention off the older man and faced her former lover, her captor, her everything, her nothing. "What I needed to," she admitted because she couldn't lie, not just to Mato, but to the others. "About a violent death."

How is that possible? Mato's stance said, and if he voiced his question, she'd have to tell him she didn't understand what had just passed between her and his uncle. Just the same, she questioned nothing about the vision.

Everyone except for the man in the wheelchair was standing now, not closing in on her like a pack of wolves but telling her they wouldn't let her leave the room. Any other time, she would have been terrified, but she'd entered the surreal. The spirits were responsible for her new world, but so, too, were the humans—Mato most of all.

"What are you going to do with your knowledge?" Mato asked. "Write about it?"

Was that sarcasm or a question? Either way, she couldn't ignore what he'd thrown at her. "No one would believe me if I did, but even if that wasn't a concern, the answer is no. I won't go there."

His expression said he didn't expect that response, giving rise to painful thoughts about how little he trusted her. But, then, could she blame him? After all, how many times had outsiders betrayed those who made this land their home?

"Maybe I'm being tested," she offered. "Your uncle's spirit revealing something to see if I'm worth of its trust."

A sharp shake of his head said Mato didn't believe that, but then he frowned, and she wondered if he couldn't explain what she'd been privy to any more than she had. Despite wondering if he wanted them to be alone as much as she could, she forced her mind off him.

Aware that—like the man in her vision—she might not survive the night, she approached the table. She could have chosen any spot but somehow wound up standing near Mato. Not breathing, she placed her briefcase on the table and unlocked it. The lid popped up, revealing not just what had brought her to Storm Bay in the first place but also what had consumed her since her return to Portland. Before she could start to sort through the papers, Mato did it for her. Holding up a copy of an old newspaper clipping, he scanned its contents.

"Prospector found with his skull crushed," he read.

The others had been stirring, clothes and shoes and even old bones and muscles making sounds, but now the room went quiet again. Dividing his attention between her and the article, he continued. The clipping dated back to the early 1900s and had been in a now defunct newspaper in a town several hundred miles northeast of Storm Bay. According to the article, a trio of gold miners trying their luck at one of this area's streams had discovered the body of another miner. The dead man's skull had been shattered, and wild animals had torn most of the flesh from his bones. Although no one recalled the man's name, and he'd had no identification on him, those who'd found him remembered that he'd boasted about his determination to utilize hydraulic methods to force the ground to give up its wealth.

Hydraulic mining, Smokey knew, called for hitting hillsides with powerful jets of water capable of uprooting boulders, stripping layers of dirt, and exposing extensive root systems. Back then few people had objected to that earth-destructive method, but eventually it had been outlawed because nothing grew on those wounded hillsides and rain too often caused mud slides.

She didn't need to look at Mato to know they shared the same thought. The spirits had exacted their own brand of justice.

"It keeps piling up, doesn't it?" Anger and something else weighed Mato's words. "You're going to have to write a goddamn book."

"Maybe I will," she shot at him because otherwise she'd drop to her knees, wrap her arms around his legs, and press her cheek against the bulge she didn't dare look at. Then, deeply sorry she'd said what she had, she yanked the paper out of his hand. "That's not what my being here is about, all right? It isn't!"

"Then what is?"

The room was shifting again, shadow and fog dimming her sight. She thought maybe the vision at the rest stop might return, and she looked for Mato's uncle, but the others had closed in around her, and she couldn't see him.

Mato then. Mato was responsible.

Sensing this might be the most important moment in her life, she laced her fingers through his and stared into his eyes. She felt surrounded by him with invisible and yet powerful ropes wrapped around her. They were back in his bedroom, and she was stretched out on his bed, helpless. Bound. Whimpering under her breath, she fought the wild energy tearing through her body and soaking her panties. Her nipples ached, and her hips were heavy. The insides of her thighs burned, as did the back of her throat.

More fog, night clouds pressing around her.

Still holding on to Mato, she found the courage to step into the clouds.

Now she was in a place without form but that weighed with the smell of evergreens and earth, birds softly singing and the wind gentle while warning of strength and fury. Her clothes were gone, the bottoms of her feet shredded. Feeling sweat on every inch of her body and her lungs sharp with pain, she surmised that she'd been running.

From what or from who?

To where?

Gathering courage from cupping her hot breasts, she scanned her surroundings, but whatever living things were watching her kept their secrets. *Hawk,* she thought. *Hawk.* But whether she meant the small bird or the otherworldly being she couldn't say.

It was going to be night soon, night and cold and dark and being alone with her thoughts and needs and the fear that had caused her to run. Even when she stared at her hands and breasts and tried to make them her everything, she knew she didn't belong here. Wasn't wanted here.

Aching and lonely, she lifted her head and sniffed the air. Another scent was coming, cutting through the others so it could circle her and paint her skin. More fog now—and heavy clouds. Pressing against her and trying to drive her to the ground.

No!

The fog and clouds were cold and wet, without life, but

what briefly brushed her in the wake of her silent cry carried heat. Although she tried to pull the heat into her lungs, it floated just beyond her reach, teasing and maybe promising.

That's what she needed: a promise. And Mato—his touch, his body, his hands strong on her and turning her weak. Even though that weakness might be her undoing, she remembered what they'd been and done to each other, and as she did, the cold, damp air began to heat.

By mentally attacking the fog and clouds, she managed to push them away, but though she could now see more of her surroundings, she mourned the loss of the building warmth. She was also having trouble breathing.

Shapes began forming around her. Fascinated and fearful, she ordered herself to be patient. As she waited, she concentrated on filling and emptying her lungs. Shouldn't Mato be here with her? After all, he'd been an integral part of her world and life since she'd met him—and maybe before. But she was alone except for the shapes.

Clarity came slowly, a growing certainty that dropped her arms to her sides and made holding her head up difficult. She was standing in a small clearing surrounded by massive old trees, but that wasn't what held her attention, because what had been misty movement had solidified into something that had her heart trying to fight its way out of her chest.

A wolf. And a massive bear. And there, a cougar. Perched on a branch, an eagle. And closest to her, a hawk the size of a man.

They were taking up the space, pushing against her without moving, stealing the air, demanding she accept them for what they were.

Spirits.

"Mato!" she screamed. Her voice, laden with fear and awe, startled her. "Mato!"

The great hawk spread its wings and opened its beak. Talons

made for ripping and killing reached for her. And its eyes—a mix of man and predator.

Something squeezed her hand. Afraid that one of the creatures had reached her, she tried to jerk free only to feel her fingers being pressed together. She wasn't going to panic, she wasn't! And she was going to face who or whatever had hold of her.

"Smokey, what's happening?"

Mato's voice settled over her, and as it did, the fog and clouds floated away. So, too, did the creatures, all except for the hawk, which continued to regard her with eyes that belonged to both a human and a bird of prey. If she'd been able to make the move, she could have easily touched it.

"Smokey, talk to me!"

Jerked free of the mesmerizing image by Mato's sharp tone, she pulled herself out of whatever had taken over her existence. Mato was holding her hand, or maybe the truth was that she was clinging to him. She was back in her slacks and turtleneck, thank goodness, surrounded by men instead of animals and birds.

So shaken she had to press her hip against the table to keep her balance, she breathed her way back into the here and now. She wanted to smile, to laugh, to say and do something stupid so the others wouldn't guess what she'd been through, but maybe they knew.

"I'm not going to talk about it," she told Mato because only he mattered. "A little—too much . . . I've been through a great deal lately. That's it. Everything that's been happening has—"

"I thought you weren't going to say anything," he said and released her hand.

Being free of him, if that's what she could call it, made things both easier and harder. She'd come here to accomplish a vital piece of business. Once she had, she'd go back home, away

from this mystical place with its dangers and the man who'd—
what, turned her inside out and upside down?

Not trying to come up with an explanation for him, she
forced her attention back on her briefcase. Mato had dropped
the article about the miner on top of the contents, but because
what she wanted was in a side pocket, she easily retrieved it.
She'd finished composing the article on her laptop a little after
noon today. After e-mailing it as an attachment to her editor,
she'd packed an overnight bag, grabbed her briefcase, and headed
out of town. Her editor had called just as she'd reached the city
limits to tell her that her piece wasn't at all what he'd expected.

"But it'll work, won't it?" she'd asked.

"Hell, yes."

Shaking off the memory, she held up the two pages she believed would change a great deal. After scanning the room to
make sure she'd connected with everyone, she swallowed. "I'm
obsessive-compulsive," she started. "That's part of why I've
succeeded in my career. I go after the stories behind the stories,
ones other reporters don't think to explore."

Realizing she was talking about herself when that didn't
matter, she looked over at Mato. Did he have any idea how incredibly sexy he was, sexy and dangerous, at least to her? Maybe
that was his appeal—the dark and rugged man who played by
his own rules and never backed down, who championed his causes
no matter what the personal consequences. Only, did he defend
this land because he believed in the task or because Hawk Spirit
worked through him?

Maybe, if he were inside her and he couldn't see anything
except her, smell anything except her, he'd break free of his
spirit.

But if he did, what would be left of him, and would she want
what remained?

Dizzy from the question and his closeness, she forced herself to concentrate. "While I was here before, the editor-in-chief

of the newspaper I work for published an editorial promising readers that I was preparing something spectacular. He did so because I'd told him I was researching those mysterious deaths; that's what brought me here in the first place."

She could have detailed the trail of violence and primitive justice she'd been compiling, but not only didn't everyone here already know more about that trail than she ever could, that wasn't what she'd written after all.

"I had my reputation to uphold," she continued, "but even before I left Storm Bay the other day I knew I couldn't expose the truth about this place."

What was that, a collective sigh? But much as she wanted to believe that, how could she expect these unique men to blindly believe what she'd just said? Mato had pivoted toward her, and his arms were now crossed over his chest, his head tilted as he took his measure of her.

You changed me. Even if you care nothing about me, please understand how grateful I am.

"All the way home, I kept thinking about what happened during the public hearing." That had hardly been the only thing going through her mind, but focusing on anything except Mato had helped keep her sane. "I know it won't come as a surprise to any of you that I had questions about Mr. Jacobs's behavior. Some of the things he said about—"

"Were far from objective."

Wondering if Mato were reading her mind, she nodded. "It's his job to gather facts, nothing except facts. That's what the council is designed for. Instead he was biased."

"What are you getting at?"

If she ever had the chance, if they ever spoke privately again, she'd let Mato know how much she admired his intellect. "I think the best way to answer that is by letting everyone know what's going to appear in tomorrow's newspaper," she said. Then, though she knew the words almost by heart, she started reading.

"Something's rotten in Denmark. No, not the real Denmark, but a place much closer to home. The stink overwhelms me, and once I'm done explaining, I believe you will agree. And demand action."

Done with the grabber introduction, she launched into the meat of her article. "The Northwest Fisheries Council is a state agency charged with safeguarding this part of the country's fish population while at the same time acknowledging the inevitability of growth. Established twenty years ago, it was designed to function independent of political and private influences. Neither commercial or environmental, at the core was a commitment to ensure viable fish populations now and in the future, a worthy and perhaps idealistic premise. Unfortunately human beings are council members, and as such they are fallible and corruptible."

She'd deliberately ended the paragraph with the word *corruptible,* so she let it hang. No one spoke; she couldn't even hear anyone breathing.

"That's what bothered me in the wake of having attended a recent so-called public hearing monitored by council employee Beale Jacobs and held in a small and isolated community that was selected as the site of an ambitious upscale development by NewDirections."

She'd gone on to describe NewDirections's background and goals, naming the principal backers and their financial resources but saying nothing about her sources. One of the benefits of having lived and worked in Portland as long as she had was that she'd developed a number of reliable contacts. By keeping their identities to herself, she'd ensured that they'd continue to supply her with the information she needed.

"Red flags started flying while I was researching the New-Directions backers, specifically the principal one. Andrew Stephens, who, although he'll probably deny it, is what passes as NewDirections's president. He married into money with his first marriage to Maggie Thetford, only child of Kip Thetford. Yes, that's Kip Electronics, the region's largest electrical firm, perhaps most well known for its successful bids on many city construction contracts."

She paused, wondering if anyone would ask how she'd uncovered that information, but the movers and shakers of the state's urban areas meant little to these people.

"Andrew divorced Maggie three years ago and promptly married a woman twenty years his junior, an exquisite creature. One might call her Andrew's trophy wife. Oh, her name? Jennifer Jacobs."

A collective gasp followed her last words. Mato's eyes first widened and then darkened, and in their depths she saw the silhouette of a hawk.

"I have no doubt readers are ahead of me now," she continued reading once she'd pulled herself together. "Yes, Jennifer Jacobs is related to the Northwest Fisheries Council fact finder. They're siblings. In other words, guess who is guarding the henhouse?"

Another gasp, along with a number of curses, let her know she'd hit her mark. Excitement born of a reporter's instincts filled her as she went on. Although there was a lot more to the story than had made its way into her article, she believed her summation had hit all the high spots. She'd taken everything she'd uncovered to the governor's office. Instead of allowing herself to be shuffled off to some obscure aide, she'd held firm until she was granted a meeting with no less than the lieutenant governor. The state's highest office could do what it wanted with her facts, she'd told the somber and intense man yesterday. But she'd made it clear she intended to air the council's dirty laundry in public, trusting that the public would insist on a thorough investigation into an illegal financial connection between NewDirections Development and the Northwest Fisheries Council.

"I received a call from the governor's legal team this morning," she concluded. "In two days I'll be meeting with them. I have no crystal ball, but I wouldn't be surprised if NewDirections withdraws its application for this resort development. I'm also convinced Mr. Jacobs will soon be resigning from the council. There might be more rocks to turn over, but I believe the largest boulder's underbelly has now been exposed to the light of day and accountability."

Suddenly exhausted, she let go of the pages she'd sweated over, and they drifted back into her briefcase. Did these men understand how much effort had gone into not just her article but her demands to be heard?

Did Mato?

Sensing someone approaching, she looked up to see Mato's uncle closing in on her. She started to backstep and then stopped as he reached for what she'd been holding. "Can I have this?" he asked.

"Of course. Like I said, it's going to be in tomorrow's paper."

Muttering something she couldn't understand, he began silently reading. Tension seemed to be flowing out of him, giving rise to a desire in her to get to know the older man, to understand what he'd been through in life and what, if anything, he still wanted to accomplish.

Then Mato grabbed her arm, and nothing else mattered. "We need to talk. Alone."

Somehow they were outside before she'd decided to accompany him. The night, though cool, was probably warmer than it would be in Portland, thanks to the coastal influence. If she lived in Storm Bay, she could open her window when she went to bed and—live in Storm Bay, what was she thinking?

Half leading and half pulling, Mato backed her against the side of his pickup. He didn't have to touch her for her to know she wasn't supposed to move, not that she wanted to. In the dark she couldn't tell whether a hawk silhouette still lived in his eyes, but it didn't matter, because she sensed the predator's presence. Surrounded by its energy, she only just managed to keep her reaction to Mato at bay.

"That's all you're going to write?" he asked, his breath sliding over her forehead and along her temples. "Nothing about what brought you here in the first place?"

"I said—"

"I heard you, but now you're talking to me, not a room full of men who might turn on you if they believe their safety and freedom's at stake."

She didn't care about those other men—just him. "You don't believe me, do you?" Her heart ached, and yet could she blame him?

"I don't dare."

"Yes!" she snapped. "You do dare! Damn it, Mato, why would I lie to you?"

Looming over her, he exhaled. "Because it would be the biggest story of any reporter's career."

He was so much more than she'd ever expected, energy and strength and the sexiest man she'd ever know. And elusive, like his spirit, capable of flight. If he turned from her now, she'd never see him again. A hawk in every way that counted, he'd let the wind carry him away.

Not long ago she'd been his prisoner and desperate to regain her freedom. Now everything had turned around and she was the one holding the ropes and chains—unless he disappeared into the wilderness.

Or believed her.

"Go back inside," she whispered, feeling as if she were losing form and substance herself. "Bring out my briefcase. We'll tear everything up together. Or, if you want, take it to your place and throw it into your fireplace. My laptop's in my trunk. Do you want it as well?"

"Your laptop?"

"And my backup files. All yours."

Placing his knuckles under her chin, he lifted her head. Connecting with him kept her from drifting off like fog, but it would take so little to lose herself.

"Your career is wrapped up in your laptop?" he said.

"And in the backups. Every article I've ever written, names and phone numbers of my sources, future story ideas—do you know what I'm saying?"

"Why?"

"Why what?"

"Are you willing to do this?"

Don't you understand? You're worth more than—suddenly

trembling, she tried shaking her head to clear it, but he cupped her chin, stopping her.

Impossible! another voice insisted. No man was worth her career, her means of supporting herself, her sense of self-worth.

But without at least Mato's trust, did anything else matter?

"There's nothing about you I'd change," she told him. "Not even the things I don't understand. You stormed into my world and . . ."

Dizzier than she'd been a moment ago, she steadied herself by holding on to his hips. The contact was all it took for her to remember the liquid moments not just in his arms but pressed against his body. Him inside her.

Walking into his home, shedding their clothes as they hurried into the bedroom, reaching out at the same time and tumbling onto the bed that smelled and even tasted of him and sex. Guiding his hand to her core and crying out as he stroked her so she became wet and soft for him. Reaching between her legs and gathering some of the liquid heat and depositing it first on his lips and then her own.

Letting him flip her onto her belly and lifting herself as he placed a pillow under her hips. Opening her stance as far as she could and gripping the bedspread and looking back over her shoulder at him as he positioned himself and then speared her.

Lifting her head and sobbing in delight, following his journey deep inside her and then—then becoming lost in fireworks and a screaming climax. Trembling from trying to keep him in her and the hot flood of his cum shooting deep and spreading throughout her, closing down her senses until only inner sight remained.

Above them a hawk clutched a poster. Watched. Judged.

"Are you all right?"

"I don't know." *Do you approve, Spirit? Because without that, Mato and I have no chance.* "Being around you does crazy things to me."

"I'd never want that."

Wouldn't most men embrace the sense of power that came from knowing they could turn a woman into butter? But, then, Mato wasn't most men, as witnessed by the images that had her silently begging for him. "What *do* you want?" she recklessly asked.

Releasing her chin, he slid his hand behind her neck and began massaging her. A few minutes ago she'd thought she'd been turning into fog or mist, but that was nothing compared to the sensations wrapping around her now. Portland was a world away, her job and rent and utilities payments the concern of some person she barely recognized. Where once Mato had kept her in place with ropes, now all it took were his fingers for her to feel complete.

Mato the man, not the hawk.

"I want sanity," he whispered. "When you left, I told myself I could put myself back together. Again become what my spirit needs me to be. But I was wrong."

Even with his heat slipping through every inch of her being, she understood what he was saying. Hawk Spirit exerted an ancient power over Mato, but she'd made her own impact on him.

Just as he had on her.

"Why are we fighting?" she asked.

"I didn't know we were."

"All right, maybe not fighting." *Think. Find words that make sense.* "We're like animals sniffing around each other, not allowing ourselves to trust or show vulnerability."

On the tail of a long sigh, he asked, "Why do you believe that is?"

Don't put it all on me! Don't you understand, I can't think with you this close. But maybe he felt the same way. "Maybe—maybe because what we're feeling is too much."

"I don't want it that way."

"Neither do I."

Their admissions seemed to float between them not as something to be afraid of but to be embraced and built on. Believing he felt the same way, she wrapped her arms around his neck. She was lifting herself onto her toes when he met her mouth-to-mouth.

On her back now, legs uplifted and resting against his chest, nails digging into him as her release crashed into her. She rode on his cock, more part of him than a separate being, sweating and loud, absorbing his harsh grunts and fierce pummeling of her.

His explosion freed her, took her over the top again, had her laughing and crying at the same time.

"Do—do you need to stay here?" she asked.

"No. Do you?"

"Not if you aren't going to."

Silence. Familiar. Hunger pressing at her from all sides, and his hold on her making it difficult to breathe. Finally: "Wait here. I'll get your material."

She wanted to tell him that her briefcase could wait because she trusted those men, but he was already walking away from her, his strong legs taking him up the stairs and inside, leaving her alone—briefly.

He needs you.

"No more than I do him," she told Mato's spirit. "What about you? You aren't done with him; you might never be."

As long as threats to this land exist, he must stand strong against them.

"Yes, he does. But, Hawk Spirit, there's more than one kind of weapon, more than violence. Laws and the written word can be just as powerful."

Together.

Yes, together, she agreed. Just like her and Mato Hawk.

Turn the page and
ESCAPE TO ECSTASY
with Jodi Lynn Copeland!

On sale now!

1

"Treah?"

The lone word drifted from the speaker of Treah Baldwin's office phone, slipping around him like an old favorite love song. Warm and inviting, soothing yet smoky. Hers was a voice he could never forget.

Unlike breathing.

Hearing Dana Lancer's voice now, after eight years of no contact, had the air stilled in his throat and his body stone stiff in the desk chair. This call shouldn't come as such a surprise. They hadn't spoken personally, but she'd contacted the female-targeted, sensual healing resort last month to book an appointment for her twin sister, Deanne.

Apparently, knowing that she'd called and hearing her voice were two very different things.

Letting his breath out, Treah grabbed the cordless phone off the receiver. He would be damned if she hung up because he was too dumbstruck to say hello. He also didn't want Sonya Grigg—his recently hired, incredibly reserved personal assistant, who was stationed in the receptionist area outside his closed door—overhearing the conversation. The young blonde came highly recommended, but something about her timidity rubbed him the wrong way. Honestly, though, it could be nothing more than losing Gwen, his previous PA and one-time lover, to her greed, that made him leery of anyone handling resort information outside of himself and Chris, the resort manager and a long-time friend.

With Gwen's deception still so fresh, frustration added to his surprise, making his response sound near breathless. "Hello, Dana."

Soft laughter pealed from the other end of the phone line. "Sorry to disappoint you but this isn't Dana."

Of course it was. Had to be. Or had endless thoughts of her, piqued by Gwen's accusation that he was still in love with his ex, made him so eager to hear from Dana that he made another woman become her?

Regardless of the answer, he needed to regain control of his emotions.

Relaxing in the chair, Treah looked across the office to the patio door. He kept the storm door in place for when hurricane warnings went up. On days like this, when the temperature was nearing eighty and the sun blistered down on the private island's white-sand beach, the screen door was more than enough protection against the elements.

The warm salt breeze drifted in off the ocean, slowing the rapid beat of his heart as it almost always managed to do. "No need to be sorry. I was just expecting a call from someone else. What can I do for you?"

The woman's laughter sounded again, lighter and with a teasing edge that called him a liar despite his relaxed tone. "Someone else, huh? Someone who happens to sound exactly like my sister?"

"Deanne." Not Dana but close enough to his ex to bring a smile of familiarity to his lips. "How are you?"

"Good. Just not good enough for Dana's liking." The amusement vanished from her voice. "She signed me up for a trip to your resort."

Dana knew that he owned Ecstasy Island? How did she feel about it?

Hell, he shouldn't care and, yet, he had to know more. "How did she find out I own this place?"

"She didn't. We read about it in the *Herald* last month. There was no owner name listed, but you know how Dana and I tend to think alike?"

"Yeah." Most of the time they did. Deanne had never agreed with Dana's leaving him.

"We obviously both thought the resort worth trying out, because I called to schedule her an appointment and found out she'd already booked one for me. I don't need to come there. Dana does. I asked your manager to arrange a swap, but he said I would have to speak with you. There aren't too many Treah's out there. Probably only one Treah Baldwin."

Their self-assurance was another way in which they differed. Deanne he could see potentially needing help with getting over a fear. Dana, not unless she'd changed drastically. The woman he knew had confidence in spades. Not to mention obstinacy and passion. She took life on full speed ahead, with no thought to fearing the outcome. "Why do you want her to come here?"

"You're there."

"You didn't know that when you called."

"No. But I do now. You're exactly what she needs."

Why? Because this was the first time Deanne had managed to track him down in eight years and she was still anxious to see them end up together?

In Dana's mind, they hadn't had enough in common to make their relationship worthwhile, once she'd finished her master's degree and gotten herself situated in a pretentious career he didn't have. It was crazy to think they would have a chance now. Crazy enough that he'd lost sleep more than one night while he turned over Gwen's words: If there was a chance that he still loved Dana, he should do whatever it took to give them another try.

Even if he wanted that, the odds were next to nil that Dana would. "What about you, Deanne? What does Dana think this resort has to offer you?"

"A lesson in self-esteem," she admitted grudgingly. In a more upbeat tone, she added, "She's wrong. I'm not. She needs you, Treah."

Damn, it wasn't right how much he wanted to believe those words and have Dana believe them as well.

Needing more than a tranquil view of the ocean from afar, Treah pushed back the chair from his desk. He moved through the patio door and sat at one of several picnic tables, his back to the table and front to the quartet of boats that bobbed along twin docks a hundred feet away. "I'll admit it's a tempting offer, but I don't do the healing."

"I don't need you to cure her of any fears. I just need you to show her that her fiancé doesn't have what it takes to make her happy."

The lightened beat of his heart falling by the wayside, he pulled the phone from his ear to glare at the receiver. Dana was engaged? Like this call, the news shouldn't be surprising. At one point, he'd written her off as married with children. But she wasn't. She was just engaged. Engaged but not happy, at least to her sister's way of thinking.

Treah brought the phone back to his ear. "What makes you think he doesn't?"

"Professionally, they're perfect. As lovers, she's always left wanting."

No matter what his feelings for her were these days, he didn't want to think of her sleeping with another man. Even so, hearing she wasn't pleased by that man's sexual prowess brought a measure of both comfort and conceit. Personally, he'd never left her wanting. Of course, maybe if he'd pleased her a little less and acted like he understood her work a little more, she wouldn't have walked away.

Old frustrations rising up to taunt him, he pointed out, "Dana's career is her life. At least, the Dana I remember. If he's a perfect career match, then she's happy."

"You don't believe that. I know you better."

"You knew me eight years ago, Deanne. Time changes most everything."

"Are you still single?"

He winced with the soreness of the subject. "At the moment."

"Then what's your price?"

Time did change most everything, but not Treah's lack of love for money. It was at the root of far too much evil in his life, including the primary reason behind Gwen's deception. "You can't pay me enough to seduce your sister into breaking things off with her fiancé."

"You *have* changed." She sounded disappointed. "There was a time when you would have done anything for Dana's happiness."

He didn't like to disappoint people, least of all a woman who'd gone against her own twin to take his side. Like his feelings on money, those on Dana's happiness hadn't changed. They still mattered, as did finding out if he loved her before it was too late. "I never said I wouldn't help you. I just won't take money for it and I won't play the seduction game."

"How else are you going to show her what she's missing out on?"

"I'll think of something." Something that didn't involve greeting her in his bed and proceeding to make her wish that she'd never left it.

When Treah got his hands on Chris, he was going to wish he was dead. Per Treah's approval, Chris had arranged the swapping of the two sisters and then promised to personally see a sedated Dana delivered to Treah's spare bedroom. But she wasn't in Treah's *spare* bedroom. She was in *his* bedroom. In his bed. Her face was buried in his pillow and, somehow, she still managed to snore loudly enough to wake the dead, just the way he'd remembered her doing.

He'd been exhausted when he'd mounted the stairs from the administration offices and meeting area that made up the first floor of his house. He'd considered coming up earlier but he hadn't been tired, what with thoughts of Dana's arrival thick in his mind. Then he'd gotten into work and the hours had slipped away until it was after three in the morning.

Now it was close to three thirty, and he wasn't feeling exhausted any longer. He was feeling like his heart might slam through his chest for its fierce pounding.

Drawing in calming breaths, he moved to the side of the bed and allowed himself to do what he hadn't been able to for so long. Watched her sleep. Her hair was longer and the once dark brown shade was streaked with golden highlights. He curled his fingers at his sides to keep from reaching out and sliding them into the silky waves.

Pulling back the top sheet and a thin blue cover brought an immediate smile. She still slept semicontortionist style, with her knees tucked up under her belly and her ass in the air. Such a nice ass it was, too. A little rounder than it used to be, in white cotton pajama shorts. Now, it would be all the better for gripping while he stroked his cock into her and met her thrust for eager thrust.

Not the thoughts he should be having, Treah acknowledged. They had his shaft rousing against the fly of his trouser shorts as he bent and scooped her off the bed. She'd always been a heavy sleeper. Between that and the natural sedative she'd been given for her trip to the island, moving her into the spare bedroom and, in turn, himself away from temptation, should be a cinch.

It should have been. But it wasn't.

With a soft sigh, Dana curled her arms around his neck and nuzzled her face against his shoulder. "Missed you."

His heart stuttered a beat. If only she really had. But she was asleep, probably dreaming of her fiancé. Lucky bastard. At least, the guy was lucky for now. Maybe before her time at the resort was through . . .

It wasn't a maybe he should contemplate now any more than he should consider her lusciously curvy butt. "It's time for—"

Her head lifted to reveal her copper-laced brown eyes partway open and her smile so bright it stopped his words on a dime. Her lips parted. He thought she would say something until her mouth contacted soft and warm against his own.

Her tongue pushed inside with his surprised breath. The damp, lusty sweep of it against his own took one hell of a potshot at his good intentions. Her fingers kneaded at the back of his neck in such a familiar way that Treah sank into the kiss without thought, without care. Just sank his tongue against hers and let his head spin with how incredible she still tasted. Warm and sweet with a generous coating of brazen.

Dana's mouth pulled from his. Eyes once again closed, she snuggled back against his chest and murmured a low, throaty, "Yummy."

God, yeah, it was.

He'd vowed not to seduce her. He wouldn't let her seduce him, either. Not while she was out of her rational mind. Her eyes had opened for a second or two, but he didn't buy that she knew what was happening.

Tipping his head back so that she couldn't get her mouth on his again, he started for the bedroom door. "Time to go to your own bed, sleepy girl."

"Want you."

He groaned with the toll her breathy disclosure took on his body. "Trust me, you don't want me."

Or maybe she did.

Her hand moved between their bodies to cup his crotch. Through his shorts, her fingers closed around what was quickly becoming a full-blown erection, and she let out another throaty murmur. "Do."

Before his judgment could be swayed by his dick, Treah hurried down the hallway to the spare bedroom. Not bothering to turn on the light, he crossed to the bed, whipped back the covers, and lay her down.

At least, he tried to lay her down. She still had ahold of his cock with no apparent plans to release it.

Moving them onto the bed as a unit, he laid her back while he hovered over her, the weight of his thighs around hers pinning her in place and a hand on either side of her head. Far too intimate of a position. Particularly now, when he could see all of her.

The bedroom light wasn't on, but the light from the hallway bled in to throw shadows across her face. Dana had always thought her nose too straight and uppity to match the softness of her mouth and eyes. Personally, he thought it fit her well, particularly considering her tendency for snobbery that had emerged toward the end of their relationship. Only, in the shadows, her nose didn't look uppity and not an inch of her came off as snobby.

Her body was hot beneath his. The contrast of her smooth, bare upper thighs as they contacted against the crisp hair of his legs was more intimacy than Treah had known for months. Too much intimacy when coupled with a woman who was his ultimate temptation.

As if she knew his thoughts and was granting leniency, her grip on his shaft released. He breathed a sigh of relief for the second it took her to wrap her legs around his ass and wrench him forward. Caught off guard, he went down fast and hard, losing his handhold on the bed and then quickly replanting his palms before his face pummeled into her breasts. His mouth still brushed against a hard nipple through her thin pajama top, but the fall could have ended much worse for his peace of mind.

She made it much worse on his mind then, by tightening the hold of her legs around his butt and pressing her groin flush to his.

The heat of her sex warmed into his despite the layers. On a needy whimper, she wrapped her arms around his back, trapping him entirely while she wriggled her pussy against his solid cock.

Fuck, he'd always loved how passionate she was. If her fiancé was missing out on this part of her personality, then Deanne might just be right. Dana might not be happy. She couldn't be happy with a guy who catered to her professionally only. Just as she hadn't been happy with Treah for catering to her physically while professionally he was a clear miss to her way of thinking.

That cold slap of reality had him risking the full press of his face against her breasts so that he could use his hands to get her arms unlocked from his back. Focusing on anything but the nipple pressed against his mouth, he grappled for her hands. He found her fingers interlocked and damned impossible to get unhooked.

Moaning, she segued her pelvis into a circling grind. His

264 / Jodi Lynn Copeland

cock gave a savage throb and he muffled against her breast, "Stop, Dana."

"Nah uh. Want you, Treah."

Oh, hell. Not his name in that sexy, smoky voice. She still had to be sleeping, dreaming, just not of her fiancé, the way Treah had presumed. But of him.

She was going to kill his good intentions yet.